A Week of Criminal Happiness

Michael Giorgio

Published by Rogue Phoenix Press, LLP
Copyright © 2020

ISBN: 978-1-62420-501-9

Editor: Sherry Derr-Wille

Dedication

To Kathie and Olivia, always and forever.

Thursday

Mandy Heinemann, no, Mandy Masamoli, she had to remind herself, had less than three hours as a married woman under her garter belt when she and her husband committed their first robbery. It, the robbery, was Stuart's idea—everything was always Stuart's idea—to pay for their honeymoon and a start to their new life together better than he could realistically provide. She tried one last time, for almost three minutes, to talk him out of it, to convince him all she cared about was spending some legitimate quiet time with him rather than doing it in the back of his dad's half-rusted out Chevy pickup or behind the loading dock of Bortmann Produce. But then she saw how eager he was, how much like the little boy she met in Sister Mary Dymphna's first grade room, the boy who chucked an eraser at the nun and lived to tell about it, and Mandy gave in. He had to know she would. She always did, from the first game of I'll-show-you-mine-if-you-show-me-yours that same first grade afternoon fourteen years earlier to a little while ago, when he put the pistol in her hand and any chance at backing out was gone.

Now here she was, pistol pointed up at the quivering bank guard's neck. Her right hand held the gun surprisingly steady. Her left she held out in front of her, admiring the small, shiny near-gold band on her third finger. She barely paid attention to what Stuart was doing. It looked like the teller was handing over the cash, so he had things under control. Mandy just wanted to look at her ring. It showed he loved her. Stuart Masamoli loved her. No one else did.

She was too short, too chunky, and way too pale, and that's why her sister, Linda, was Daddy's girl and Mandy got nothing from him. She was too stupid, too awkward, and way too sassy, and that's why her brother, Craig, was Mama's boy and Mandy got nothing from her. But Stuart called her his angel and treated her that way and that's all that mattered. Mandy had Stuart and Stuart wanted Mandy and she'd do anything for his love, even hold a gun to an old bank guard's head.

The guard started crying, drawing attention away from Mandy's admiration of her ring. The words, "Shut up, old fartface," were out of her mouth before she realized she said them, and his sobs abruptly stopped in a snot-clogged snort. Disgusting, but it made her giggle a little. It reminded her of the time Stuart kept making farting noises in Mr. Boscolovski's English 10 class and got sent down to Old Man Penobscot's office. Stuart always called him Old Poppin'-Snot, the bastard who pushed them out of the class of '52 a couple of years early and for no good reason. They weren't the first couple to fake being sick so they could do it in the health room while the elderly school nurse was snoozing and they wouldn't be the last. As always, Poppin' Snot overreacted and their school days were over two weeks into their junior year.

Still, she almost said sorry to the guard, but she stopped herself just in time. Stuart would be so proud of her for putting an Old Poppin'-Snot kind of guy in his place. She pushed the barrel of the gun further into the guard's gray bristles and turned her attention back to the ring.

She was so focused on it that she missed seeing Stuart until he was right in front of her. He grabbed her left hand, blocking her view of the ring, and yanked her toward the door.

"We got to skedaddle, Angel," he said when he pulled her off-balance, making her start her run in a stumble. "Just run," he commanded. "Don't look back."

She didn't. Stuart knew best. Mandy hopped in the passenger side of the Chevy while Stuart hotfooted around to his side. He took off so fast the tires squealed, laying a great patch of burnt rubber, she was sure, and startled a couple of elderly woman looking in a shop window.

"We did it, Angel," Stuart said. "There's got to be four thousand smackers here at least. We're gonna have one hell of a honeymoon. Treat you with style."

Two minutes later, they were outside of the small town of Cloverdale. Stuart slowed at a fork in the road just beyond the last houses. "Which way, Angel? Left or right?"

Mandy saw a squirrel crossing the road on her side of the truck and pointed away from the little creature. It seemed the right thing to do, saving a life after robbing a bank. Keep things even with God.

Stuart veered left and put his hand on Mandy's knee. "We'll stop at the first restaurant—" He glanced at the money bag at Mandy's feet. "The first decent restaurant we come across once we're far enough away from that last town, and get some food. Our first meal as Mr. and Mrs. Stuart Masamoli." He grinned the same grin he did on that private show-and-tell day fourteen years earlier.

"You sure nobody's gonna know what we did?"

"Not a chance, Angel. Not a chance. We're just a couple in love. People will think we're adorable. And we are. Now, keep an eye on your side for an isolated house."

"An isolated house?"

"What I said."

"Why?"

"Just do it."

Stuart's tone indicated the topic was closed, so Mandy turned her attention to the window. Her husband wanted to find an isolated house, so she'd find one for him. Maybe he planned to find a place for them to start their married life. No, that didn't make sense this close to home. They were only fifty or sixty miles outside of Bascombe at the most. She wanted to press him for details, but after fourteen years growing up with Stuart, Mandy knew when, to use his words, to shut her yap.

As the scenery flew by, Mandy marveled at the way their week was turning out. A week ago, Stuart was as low as she ever saw him. He arrived at her house in a very quiet mood, which was unusual for him, and said he needed to talk to her and he didn't want to do it at the Heinemanns', even though no one was home but her. She didn't question. She never wanted to be at her family's house either. Instead, she did as he wanted, climbed in his boss' truck, and waited for him to tell her where they were going.

Only he didn't. They just drove, straight out of Bascombe to Hanover City, the next town over. Stuart was silent the entire time, and it scared Mandy just a little bit. Stuart was never quiet. He said quiet was overrated and words needed to fill the air since he went through the trouble to learn them. But on this day, there was nothing. Mandy studied him as they drove along. His expression was somewhere between extreme anger and extreme sadness, with some hatred thrown in. Though she'd never seen him like this before, she knew the best action to take was to go with his flow. He'd spill in time.

Hanover City was fairly quiet when they arrived. Stuart parked at the edge of the town square, but made no move to get out of the truck. "Stuey?" she said softly.

"Sorry, Angel," he said. "Just thinking for a sec. Hop on out."

He got out and she followed suit. When he reached her side, Stuart took her hand in his and led her to a bench in the middle of the square. "Angel, we really got to talk."

Mandy never had a boyfriend other that Stuart, but she knew from other girls when a guy said that, it wasn't a good thing. Her insides churned as she asked, "What about, Stuey?"

"Me and you."

Damn. What had she done? "What about us?"

Stuart took a deep breath, let it out slowly, and said nothing. He took a second breath before speaking. "Angel, I got to get away from Bascombe. I can't take it there no more."

This was a little better, maybe. Maybe it wasn't her, wasn't them. "Stuey, what's wrong?"

"My father." Stuart's voice was flat when he answered. "My goddamn father."

This was a too-familiar story. Stuart's dad was horrible and Stuart and his brother Ralph had the scars to prove it. But Stuart never reacted like this. He got angry or he acted like nothing was wrong. He never went to this too-quiet mood.

"What did he do?" she asked, afraid of the answer.

Stuart stood up and moved a few paces away.

Mandy thought about going after him, but decided better of it. He needed to say whatever he was going to say his way and in his time. She watched him pace for a moment. The silence was overwhelming and Mandy desperately wanted to say something, but she didn't know what to say.

Eventually, Stuart sat beside her. "He shot at me," he said simply, no emotion, as if he was talking about something that didn't matter.

It was Mandy's turn for quiet. She knew Mr. Masamoli was a worthless drunk who beat the crap out of his sons, but she didn't realize he was bat shit crazier than Stuart ever let on. When she could finally form words, she asked, "What happened? Tell me everything, Stuey."

Stuart addressed the ground rather than look at her. "Real quick, then we never talk about him again. Deal?"

"Deal."

Stuart breathed in deeply before starting. "I come home from work that day and he's sitting in the backyard, drunk off his ass. I know he's supposed to be at the factory so I asked him if they let out early. He says no, that his foreman fired him because he was better than the foreman. That's when I see his gun by his side and think, oh shit, what's he doing? He starts rambling about how if a guy's a good worker, and he's a damn good worker, he says, there's nothing wrong with having a bottle in his locker."

Stuart paused and Mandy noticed a hitch in his breath. She didn't look at him in case he looked up at her. If he had tears, he wouldn't want Mandy to see them.

"He had a bottle in his locker?"

"Stupid ass always has a bottle everywhere," Stuart said. "Anyways, he keeps on rambling about bosses and that switches over to bitches who leave a perfect good man to go off with other guys and leave the good ones with kids they didn't want and have to take care of. Then he lifts the gun and takes a potshot at me. Doesn't come close, but I don't stick around to give him another chance."

This time, Mandy did turn to Stuart, taking her hands in his. "You can't go back there, Stuey. He's snapped. It ain't safe."

Stuart shook his head. "I'm going back one time to get my shit. I'll do it when he's at Newberry's. He closes the place pretty much every night."

"Where you gonna go? With Ralph?"

"With my brother and his wife and brat? No thanks. I'm gonna hide out at work. Old Man Bortmann will let me for a few days. Long enough

5

for you and me to get blood tests and a license. Then we get hitched and get the hell out of here."

Hitched? Was this a proposal? Out of Bascombe? With Stuey? Her, Mrs. Masamoli? She didn't know what to say.

"Angel, are you with me, or am I going alone?"

Mandy had a ton of questions, but she said, "I'm with you, Stuey. I'm always with you."

And she was. Just a few hours earlier, Mandy Heinemann was sitting on her front step, waiting for her boyfriend, her fiancé, to pick her up so they could start their new life. She put two sets of everything; blouse, bra, dungarees, panties, socks, in a paper sack and started to roll it up. On a whim, she added a nightgown and her small makeup kit. They had the blood tests, they had the license, but there was no way they could afford a honeymoon. They hadn't even discussed what they would do after they were married.

As promised, Stuart was at her door at eight sharp. "Man of my word, Angel," he said. "I said eight o'clock and eight o'clock it is. Right on the button."

Stuart took her clothing bag and put it in a suitcase in the truck bed. She looked at him for an explanation, but he offered none. Instead, he told her to climb in the passenger seat, even opening the door for her. After she was settled, he said, "Just be ready for anything, and for the best day ever."

Mandy scooted to his side and didn't object when his hand fell high on her thigh. "So, what do you have planned today?" she asked.

His hand crept a little further up, his pinky making contact with the top of her inseam. "You know what I always wanna do, Angel." Stuart waggled his finger. "Always."

She didn't push his hand away. "Where can we go? It's broad daylight."

"Oh, I got a plan in mind. Don't you worry about that."

Stuart shifted the truck and peeled rubber, letting out a loud whoop that echoed in the cab of the ancient Bortmann Produce Chevy. Mandy loved when Stuart was excited and loved it even more when he had a surprise in mind for her. Last time he planned for them to be together, they ended up on the bank of Kellnor Creek. That one didn't work out so good between the mosquitoes and the ants and the unexpected appearance of the Boy Scouts Summer Explorers literally at their feet. Those little monsters had quite the visual exploration that afternoon, that was for sure. Stuart's heart was in the right place and the view, other than the Scouts, was very pretty.

When Stuart pulled up at a mostly tumbled down barn just beyond the city limits, Mandy started to protest, but Stuart shushed her. "We ain't staying here, Angel. There's just something I left out here the other day and I need to get it. Stay here and I'll be right back." He kissed her and hopped out of the truck.

She watched him bound into the barn, clearly pleased with whatever he had up his sleeve. When he came out a minute later, he carried a small box. His grin was infectious.

Stuart opened the door, placed the box under the driver's side of the bench seat, and resumed his place behind the wheel. "This," he announced, "was step one."

"Step one of what?" Mandy's curiosity was bursting.

"Our day. And our future."

"Our future? What are you jawing about, Stuey?"

His lopsided grin kicked up a notch and Mandy knew she'd get nothing out of him. "Patience, Angel, patience, and trust your Stuey to look out for you." He turned on the radio before she could answer, filling the cab with Joan Weber singing "Let Me Go, Lover."

Stuart listened to music constantly to, as he said, drown out his boredom at work and to drown out his father at home, and he sang along to pretty much every song. When Weber was done pleading, he said, "Just a song, Angel. No way I want my lover to let me go." His hand went from the gearshift to her thigh.

The DJ played a couple more songs before Stuart said, "Step two, coming up."

Mandy looked around and saw nothing but trees. "Where?"

"You'll see."

Stuart shut off the radio and turned down a path Mandy barely saw. The produce truck wasn't the smoothest ride on the best of roads and this weed-choked forest path hardly qualified as a road at all. By the time they pulled to a stop, Mandy's head was swimming. Still, she was eager to see what Stuart had planned, so she shoved her discomfort aside and followed his instruction to hop out.

"Where are we?" Mandy asked.

"Middle of nowhere," Stuart answered, grabbing the box from beneath the seat and slamming his door.

He took her hand and led her down a much narrower overgrown path that, in places, they had to traverse single file. It wasn't long, though, before they came upon a clearing, and the unmistakable sounds of rushing water—and insects. "Stuey..."

"No, no, Angel. Not that, much as I want to. Not yet. Look," He pointed to a place behind Mandy. "There's a bench over there. Great view of the water. No creek this time. That's the Wolf River right there. Let's go sit." Again, Stuart took her hand and led her the few steps to the stone bench.

"Why would there be a bench here?" Mandy asked.

Stuart shrugged. "Way I understand it, all this used to be somebody or other's land and this is where Mrs. Somebody or Other used to sit while Mr. Somebody or Other did whatever he did to be able to afford it all. When the Somebody or Others died, nobody gave a shit and everything they had disappeared, but the bench is still here and the flowers are growing wild and pretty, just like you."

Mandy felt herself blush. Stuart was full of compliments today and she knew he was leading up to something big. He directed her to sit on the bench. He then put the box underneath it and fished in his pants pocket.

"Keep playing pocket pool and you ain't gonna need me," Mandy said, regretting it instantly when she realized he was trying so hard to be serious and romantic.

"Always gonna need you, Angel, and I ain't playing anything." Stuart pulled whatever he was after from his pocket and sank to one knee in front of her. "Amanda Heinemann, will you marry me?" Stuart opened a little box and showed her a matching set of gold bands. "I couldn't afford an engagement ring too, but I'll get you one someday soon, I promise. I know we already got the tests and license, but a girl deserves a proposal. Amanda Joan Heinemann, will you marry me?"

"Yes," she said with a squeal. "Of course." A dark cloud crossed her happiest of thoughts. "But we can't till we can afford to. Our parents'll kick us out for sure."

Stuart picked up the bigger box and sat beside her. "We can afford to. Today."

"How?"

He held up the box. "The answer's right here, Angel." He stood. "Let's go back to the truck and I'll show you."

As they walked back along the path, Mandy said, "So what do you have in there? A cash making machine?"

"In a way, yep. You'll see, Angel. Don't worry. You'll see real soon."

A sudden jolt and Mandy's attention was back to the road, the proposal by the river several hours in the past. She realized Stuart had slammed the truck's brakes, causing the jarring that nearly threw her on the floor. "Did you find the house you were looking for?" she asked.

Stuart guided the truck to the side of the road. "Might be the perfect one. You just wait right here, Angel. I'll be right back. Don't you worry none. I'll only be a minute."

Mandy watched Stuart go around to the rear of the house, a small place with just a gravel driveway leading to the back. There didn't look to be any movement inside, thank God. She didn't want Stuart to get caught and get in trouble. She couldn't drive the truck home herself. She didn't even know where the heck they were. She smiled when Stuart emerged from behind the house, gave her an okay sign with his thumb and forefinger and went back to whatever he was doing. Since Stuart said he'd only be a minute, Mandy decided to close her eyes and just relax until he came back. Getting married at the Bascombe County Courthouse just after breakfast, robbing the bank and anticipating the night to come had taken a lot out of Mandy. A few seconds of unmoving calm wouldn't hurt.

She barely started to relax when Stuart was back. He shoved something in the space behind the seat and jumped in, starting up the Chevy with a roar. "Success, Angel," he said. "We're one step closer to our honeymoon." He laughed and peeled out. "Our honeymoon in the nicest hotel we can find."

Stuart had that eager little boy face, and this time, Mandy immediately knew why. He was ready to have their first married game of I'll-Show-You-Mine-if-You-Show-Me-Yours, and it was going to happen in a nice hotel room instead of the truck or an alley or in her bedroom on a grounded Saturday night. She dreamed of this day for so long and now it was going to happen, after a good meal and finding the right hotel. And they had money to do it right. Stuart was so smart.

"Angel, we're going to have to make one more stop before we hit another town."

"How come?"

He hooked a thumb toward the back. "New license plates for the truck. Boosted them off a Pontiac at that house. Got to change ours for those. Cops will be looking for ours if anyone caught sight of the number when we pulled outta that bank. Only way they're ever gonna find out who we are is tracing the truck."

Cops. What her and Stuart did. Mandy really hadn't thought about the fact they committed a real crime. A Federal crime. Like in a Bogart movie. Holy crud. They were outlaws, like Al Capone or Adolph Hitler. They robbed a bank and, so far, got away with it. Holy moly.

"Stuart, we're going to be okay, right?"

"Of course, we are." He patted the seat next to him. "Scoot over here, Angel. You'll feel safer with my arm around you."

So, she did. And she did. Stuart always knew what was best for her. He had the radio on and was happily singing as the never changing scenery; trees, farm, barn, cows, fields, trees, repeated itself over and over, broken occasionally by a small town or a gas station. Beneath her seat, the cardboard box bounced, its purpose served.

She was sitting in this same place a few hours earlier when Stuart showed her what was inside. Guns. Two of them. One large and ugly and the other small, shiny, and kind of cute. "What are these for?" she'd asked him.

"Money," her new fiancée answered.

"We gonna sell them?"

"Nope. We're gonna use them."

Stuart explained how, a few weeks earlier, he made a delivery to a new customer in Cloverdale. The market was next door to a bank, so he stopped in to see if he could use their bathroom to take a quick whizz. "Stupid Jasper at the store told me their toilet was for employees only," he told her. "Never mind that I'd been driving for two hours and had a couple Cokes in me and had to take a leak so bad the snake was spitting. So I tried the bank. Guy there looked at me like I wasn't good enough to piss in his pot and said no. So I said screw you and went around back and pissed on the bank's back door."

Mandy laughed at that. People were always treating her and Stuart like crap, so any chance for revenge was a good thing.

"Anyways, I just put it away and zipped when this woman comes out for a smoke. I bummed one from her so it looked like I had reason to be there and talked to her."

"Was she pretty?"

"Angel, she was about eight hundred years old and looked like a tomato that sat rotting in the sun for a week. Anyways, like I was saying, we got to talking and I asked her if she was having a busy day like I was. She said yeah, cause Thursday afternoons was the day companies always come for their payroll money. That got me thinking. If they come on Thursday afternoons for their dough to give out on Friday morning, then the bank's got to have lots of moola on hand Thursday morning to be ready for them."

"Makes sense."

"That's when I got the idea," Stuart said.

Mandy wasn't so sure she wanted to ask the obvious question. She looked at the guns in her lap. "What idea?"

"To make what's theirs ours. Angel, think about it. A nice honeymoon and money to live on after."

She shook her head. "Stuey, people would ask questions. A produce guy and a grocery checker don't pull down big bucks."

He kissed her on the forehead. "And that's the clincher for you to say yes. We do this, we don't go back to Bascombe. Ever." His smile faded for a moment "No more family for neither of us. Never again. We'll be our own family."

"What about the woman you talked to? Won't she recognize you?"

"That's the best part. Like I told you, this broad was ancient. She told me she was counting down the weeks. She retired two weeks ago, so she won't be there. Nobody else saw me."

"What about the guy who said you couldn't use the bathroom?"

Stuart thought about that for a moment. "Yeah, okay, he saw me, but he don't know who I am. All he'd know is a guy in a blue work shirt and pants asked to use the toilet once, a month or so ago. Old man Bortmann's too cheap to have names put on our shirts. Even the truck don't have his name on it."

The silence in the truck cab was deafening. Stuart had clearly thought all of this through. No more Bascombe. No more family. Money and a new life with Stuart. Maybe it was a long shot, but what else did they have? Bascombe was never going to be any better for them. "How will we do it?"

Those five words set everything in motion. Stuart started the truck and they headed back toward Bascombe. The plan was to drive back to Bascombe and get married at the county courthouse, then off to Cloverdale and the bank. The way Stuart had it figured; they would be at the courthouse by nine-thirty, back on the road by ten, and in Cloverdale by noon. "Dinosaur woman said the factory people started coming for money around two, so there's plenty of cushion."

As it turned out, they didn't need it. The clerk and the judge were very efficient and within twenty minutes of arriving, Mandy and Stuart sported their matching gold-colored bands and were back in the truck. As they drove, he told Mandy all about the inside of the bank and what her role would be in his plan. As he talked, his enthusiasm and her fear were on a collision course and only one could win out in the end. She was sure, at first, he wasn't serious and that if he was, she wouldn't go through with it. But when they pulled up right in front of the bank and Stuart pressed the gun into her hand, she knew she wasn't backing out. She tried to talk him out of it one last time because she figured she should, but she was all in. She and Stuart were in it together, no matter what.

Thinking back now, she was still amazed they actually did it. Now here they were, two hours out of Cloverdale and about four from Bascombe. Stuart pulled into a Standard station for gas and told Mandy to hit the vending machines outside the garage. They needed a snack and some soda, he told her, in case they didn't find a place to eat soon. He headed off to the men's room while the attendant filled the tank.

Mandy locked the truck doors when she got out, drawing a puzzled look from the skinny string bean working the pump, but with guns and cash stashed on the floor, Mandy wasn't taking any chances. She'd wait for Stuart to return before taking her turn in the ladies' room. Her husband wasn't the only one on this trip who could make logical plans.

A few minutes later, the tank was filled, their bladders were empty, soda bottles and Hershey bars were on the seat between them, and the Masamolis took off again. Except for the courthouse wedding and the bank robbery, this felt just like an ordinary ride in the country. Mandy relished it, especially the wedding.

Another few hours of driving brought them to a town deemed suitable by Stuart for stopping for the night. Mandy didn't see it as any different than the other towns they passed through, but Stuart was the planner and he knew what he was doing. After all, he picked the bank, he picked the house for the license plates and the place to switch them, and he picked her when he could have had Dottie Anne Bortmann and been in good with his boss at the produce company. Instead, he chose to marry Mandy, daughter of a line worker at Mother Meatworthy's Canned Sausages. So Mandy knew when Stuart made a decision, it was the right one.

"Where are we?" she asked.

"Sign outside of town said Mishawaskum."

"Mishawhoskum?"

Stuart laughed. "Don't be an idiot. Mishawaskum; named after Chief Mishawaskum, who won the Battle of Lickmelightly for his people and took over all of the land in the Belchinbelly Valley. Don't you remember from Mrs. Fulbright's history class?"

"When did we go over tha—you're making it up. Belchinbelly Valley! Stuey, you're a hoot! You really are."

Stuart was always so funny that way. He could get her every time with his puns.

"Yep. Mr. Humor, that's me." He squeaked the truck to a halt at a stop-and-go light. "Angel, it's your wedding day, so you're the boss. What's it going to be first? Food or hotel?"

Mandy thought about the question. She really wanted to get to a hotel. She was tired and a nap sounded so good. So did time to enjoy fully becoming husband and wife with Stuart, but she knew if she chose that, they wouldn't get food anytime soon and a nap was an unrealistic pipedream. Stuart's manly appetites could be tremendous at times, after all. And she was hungry. They didn't take time out for lunch; the Hershey bars their only food all day. And really good meals didn't happen often in her life and now they had the money for something really good at a fancier restaurant, one with tablecloths and waiters and everything. Private time with Stuart could wait another hour or so. "Restaurant," she said.

Stuart hit the gas right as the light turned green. "Let me know when you see one you like."

About two blocks into town, Mandy spotted a restaurant with a neon sign advertising steaks, chops, and seafood. "There," she said. "That one looks great."

Stuart obediently pulled into the lot and parked right outside the door. "You got fancy tastes, Angel. I like it. I bet we can get a three-course meal in here. Grab some money out of the bag." He jumped out of the truck and headed for the door.

Mandy opened the money bag. How much should she take? A good meal at Grossinger's Drive-Inn back home was around a dollar and a half, so if she brought a twenty, that should be plenty, she figured. She grabbed one, looked at the portrait of Andrew Jackson for a moment because she hadn't seen it too often in her twenty years, and, after hiding the money bag under the seat, she pushed the lock on her door, went around and did the same thing on Stuart's and headed inside.

This place put any restaurant back home in Bascombe to shame. Dark, solid woods decorated the whole thing, with sharp white linen on each table and silver polished to a high shine. She wanted to eat here more than anything in the world, she realized, but she didn't think they'd fit in. They were dressed in dungarees, with a blouse for her and a white tee for Stuart. Plus, they were road grimy and tired-looking and she knew it. "Stuart, maybe I picked wrong," she said softly. "We don't fit here."

"Hell, no, Angel. This is perfect for a wedding night feast. We're not going to eat supper tonight. We're going to dine on a full, fine dinner in style."

A man who bore more than a passing resemblance to President Eisenhower approached them. "Two for dinner?" he asked in a voice as rich as the wood beams around them.

"Yes, my good man," said Stuart. "Your finest table for my new bride."

The man smiled at him, but it didn't look genuine to Mandy. "We have a special place for newlyweds," he said.

He led the Masamolis past a few diners dressed in clothing that matched the cars outside and to a secluded cove on the far side of the room, where he pulled out a chair. Stuart sat and motioned for Mandy to sit across from him. She did, and the man said, "Byron will be your waiter this evening. He'll be with you shortly. Enjoy your dinner."

Mandy waited for the man to be out of earshot before whispering to Stuart, "If that guy's not our waiter, what is he?"

"That's...that's what you call the table show-er, Angel. Get used to it. This is how we'll be living regular soon enough."

A white-haired man with a bushy moustache and a suit matching the table guy's appeared at their side. "Welcome to The Calder House. My name is Byron and it will be my pleasure to serve you this evening." He handed each of them a massive leather menu. "This evening, the chef is featuring garlic roasted veal with new potatoes and baby carrots. We also have a nice rack of lamb with miniature peas and a baby corn and cherry tomato medley you might enjoy. Of course, all meals come with a choice of soup or salad and dessert."

After taking drink orders, Coke for Stuart, iced tea for Mandy, the waiter left them to ponder the bill of fare. Stuart leaned in at Mandy. "Do you think they serve anything grown up here? Baby cow, baby sheep, baby potatoes, carrots, peas, corn, tomatoes. They're baby killers." He laughed at his own humor, so Mandy chuckled too, even though the other patrons in the room looked disdainfully at Stuart's loudness.

Mandy opened the menu and was relieved to see that the twenty would be enough for two meals, though these prices were far higher than anything she ever saw before. "I'm not sure what some of this stuff is," she confided to Stuart.

"Then either order what you know or be daring and pick something you don't."

"Not sure I'm all that daring."

Stuart chuckled. "Really? Remember the bleachers at the football field during the homecoming game? The health room? Your parents' bedroom when—"

"Stuey, stop. I don't mean that way."

"Well, you were pretty damn daring this morning at that bank—"

"Stuey, not so loud."

He looked annoyed at being shushed. "All I was gonna say was you were brave back at...our last stop, so you could keep being brave and order something you don't know."

She returned her attention to the menu. There was no way she was going to take a chance on some unknown food when she finally had the chance at a decent fancy meal. She settled on a pork chop because it promised to be a decent cut rather than the gristly scraps Daddy brought home from the sausage factory. Stuart, not surprisingly, went for the largest steak on the menu, telling her that a huge slab of red meat in his tummy would fuel his lower regions for a long, good wedding night. His wink assured her he was thinking of her. Byron the waiter didn't seem impressed with Stuart's humor or his request for the meat to be extra well-done and served with plenty of ketchup.

While they waited for their soup—vegetable, on the waiter's recommendation, though Mandy and Stuart both gagged at the alternate, shrimp bisque, since neither had ever eaten shrimp and didn't know if a bisque was animal, vegetable, or mineral—the newlyweds watched as more patrons entered the dining room. "Man, this is a fossil collection," Stuart said. "There ain't nobody here under thirty-five. Maybe that's why they stuck us in this dark hole in the wall, so they wouldn't have to look at us. We probably remind them of the youth they've lost. Ain't no other reason for the way they're looking at us."

Mandy saw red creeping up Stuart's face and knew she had to make it go away. "Don't worry about them, Stuey. They're probably just looking at us cause we're not from around here." Not because their description was on the news or anything, she hoped, her stomach churning. Mandy made a mental note to turn the radio on in the Chevy and not let Stuart change the station when the news came on, just in case.

He snorted and took a large swallow of Coke. "Yeah, they're just jealous. At least there's no way none of the crones in here can compete with you for prettiest girl in the room." He reached across the table and took her hand. "And I could whip any of these old farts with my arm in a cast and my legs tied together."

The waiter brought their soup and quickly retreated. "Damn," Stuart said. "I was hoping for another Coke, but Zippy the Penguin got away too fast." He took a loud slurp of his soup. "I'll get him to stop next time if I have to trip him."

They talked about how they'd break the news of their wedding to their families and decided that a telegram would be their best course of action. "No use getting on the horn and listening to them tell how we gave them the royal shaft after all they done for us. Not like they ever done anything for us anyways, so it ain't worth the bother. We split, we ain't seeing them ever again, it's over. Hell, ain't none of them even worth the telegram," Stuart explained.

The waiter returned with their main meals while each still had half a bowl of soup to go. Luckily, Stuart caught the waiter's arm before he could take off and ordered his second Coke.

Mandy knew Stuart was especially glad to be away from Mr. Masamoli, who was about six inches taller and fifty pounds wider than his son. Stuart's dad was a top-notch jerk who hated Mandy and expected nothing but trouble from Stuart. Stuart had scars from disappointing his father in the past and she didn't want him hurt again.

Her own family would be a different matter. They wouldn't care. She knew her parents would tell Stuart she was his problem now, good luck, and good riddance to them both. Mandy was never sure if they hated her or just didn't care enough about her to bother to hate her. Either way, Stuart represented freedom and happiness and a chance in life she wouldn't otherwise have.

As she thought about all of the good things life with Stuart would mean, Mandy ate the best pork chop she ever had. Stuart tore into his steak with wild abandon. She never saw him look happier than he did during their first married meal. The marriage, the money, the future, all of it came together to create this moment, the best and brightest of their lives. Mandy hoped it would never end, and she knew it was up to her to see that it didn't. It was a wife's duty, after all, to keep the family happy, and she wanted to be the best wife ever. Stuart deserved that.

Stuart's fourth Coke and their dessert, a treat the restaurant called the Honeymooners' Delight showed up. It was a round chocolate cake with whipped cream and cherries in the middle, and it arrived long before they finished their main meals. They moved the cake to the side and kept working on their steak and chop and talked about their future together. When they were ready for dessert, Stuart stood. "Before I start this," he indicated the Coke, "I need to lose the other three. Be right back." He headed off to find the restroom.

He was back fast, even for him, and Mandy didn't like the look on his face. "Is something wrong, Stuey?"

"The penguin," he said. "The damn penguin and the table show-er. Heard them talking. Waiter said he was pushing our food out as fast as he could to get us out of here. Like we ain't good enough for their fancy-schmancy joint." He took a knife to the cake and served up two very slim slices. "Angel, we're gonna eat this cake nice and slow, one little slice at a time, and we're gonna laugh and have a good time and really piss them off."

After spending more time on the cake than they did on the meal and laughing louder whenever Byron or the table guy glared at them, Stuart finally served himself the last little slice. While Mandy watched him slowly and deliberately polish it off, she got an idea. After he ate the last forkful, she said, "Stuey, honey, while you pay the bill, I'm going to make a quick stop in the little girls' room. Will that be okay?"

He laughed. "There ain't no such thing as a quick stop in the little girls' room, but of course it's okay, Angel. I'll settle up and meet you at the truck."

Mandy stood, grabbed her pocketbook, and headed to the ladies' room. She did her business, went to the sink, applied and blotted fresh lipstick, gave herself a squirt of Evening in Paris, and ran a brush through her hair. She took as much time as she could to check her look because she wanted to be perfect. Needed to be perfect. But she couldn't dawdle too long. She was too keyed up for what she had in mind.

She peeked out of the bathroom door and saw Stuart exit the restaurant. Taking a deep breath, Mandy reached into her pocketbook and pulled out the little gun Stuart gave her that morning. The gun was so cute, she thought, before she learned it was real and what Stuart was planning to have her use it for. Now, while it was still cute, it was oh-so-practical. And Mandy Masamoli was about to prove that she, too, was practical.

She approached the counter where the cash register was discreetly hidden behind a dark wood panel, went around, and jabbed the table show-er in the side. "This here is a gun in your side," she said, trying to sound as serious as she could. "You and the waiter didn't want us here, and that's bad service, so I want our money back. And whatever else you got in there too, as a penalty." She snickered a little at that, thinking that was something Stuart would have said to be funny while showing he was in charge.

The old guy looked down his nose, discreetly, of course, and Mandy pulled the gun back a little so he could see it plain. That got him moving. Without comment, he emptied the bills from the cash register into a little paper bag with the restaurant's name on it. Good thing he had something to put it in, she realized. She didn't think to get anything to carry the money out like Stuart did before they went into the bank. He was so smart that way. She had a lot to learn.

But that was a minor mistake and, if she had to, she could have used her pocketbook in a pinch. The table show-er was shoveling cash into the bag as fast as his old shaky hands could move, so she was doing something right. Lucky for her, no customers came in during the couple of minutes it took and nobody came out. She was to the side of the counter and the guy was behind it, so even if someone came through, it would be pretty close to looking normal anyway. But she couldn't stand there forever. "Get a move on, old fartface." As at the bank, calling somebody older than her parents fartface made her want to giggle despite the seriousness of what she was doing.

The guy handed over the bag and Mandy grabbed it, took a couple of picture postcards from a rack by the register, and flew out of the restaurant. The parking lot was clear of snoot-faces, so she ran straight for the truck and jumped in.

"Way you was running, you looked like you got something biting your—" Stuart stopped short when he saw the bag. "What did you do, Angel?" he asked. "Get some takeout for an energy boost later tonight?" He gave her a dirty leer, which Mandy enjoyed. "I, for one, won't need it, but you already know that, don'tcha?"

She giggled and held the bag open for his inspection. "I suggested they should give us some money back for being so snooty. They agreed."

"Shi—you…"

Stuart threw the truck into gear and zipped out of the parking lot so fast, Mandy could smell burnt rubber. She started to think she did something wrong, but then he let out a full-bellied laugh. "Oh, Angel, you are something else. What the hell? We'll just have to drive a little further to clear this town, find us an even better hotel to consummate this marriage proper."

He laughed again, this time with Mandy joining in, and led them out of Mishawaskum into the dark Wisconsin night.

As they drove along, they talked about their day, the wedding at the courthouse, and everything else they'd done. Mandy relaxed during the conversation, thanks to Stuart's reassurances. Sure, they might have broken the law, but they'd been careful. They'd been smart. Stuart had been smart. Nobody back at the bank or the restaurant knew them. They had money to start a new life on their own, no matter what their families thought. Their marriage was starting off on the right course, with smooth sailing into the future.

"Angel, we got one problem to deal with," Stuart said, one hand on the wheel and the other high up on her thigh.

His words crashed her back to earth in a hurry. "What's that?"

"The truck. Plenty of folks have seen it and, let's face it, this bucket of bolts and rust is pretty damn easy to spot. Especially with the most beautiful woman in the world riding shotgun."

Stuart's hand moved all the way up her thigh and she closed her eyes to enjoy the ride, her reverie interrupted only when he pulled his hand away to shift gears, which was far, far too often.

When she opened her eyes again, Mandy had no idea where they were. Stuart had them parked on the side of what appeared to be a motel. "Where are we?" she asked, rubbing sleep sand from her eyes.

"This here is the Patriot Arms Motor Lodge. According to the sign, it's all new and the finest accommodation in Devlin's Crossing, Wisconsin."

She yawned. "Devlin's Crossing. We've come pretty far, haven't we?"

"Not as far as we're gonna go, that's for sure."

"You get us a room?"

"Hell, no, Angel. We ain't staying in this here place."

Mandy wasn't sure what was more muddled, her still sleeping brain or Stuart's words. "You're not making sense, Stuey. Why are we here if we ain't staying?"

He snorted a quick laugh, just a hair too loud for the surrounding darkness of the truck cab. "Part of my plan. We'll leave the truck here, then walk up the street to where there's a nicer hotel. I already scoped it out. We stick to the side street and ain't nobody gonna see us."

"Why don't we just park at the other hotel?"

"Because," Stuart said slowly, his tone indicating he was getting irritated by her questions, "that ain't the plan. We leave the truck here and go down to this joint called the Grand Devlin. Looks pretty snazzy fancy. Perfect for our honeymoon night. Then, in the morning—late in the morning—I'll slip back to this house I spotted with a beautiful Buick sitting and gathering rust. I'll hotwire the car while you're checking out of the Grand Devlin and we'll leave the police looking for one of the guests from this here dump." He hooked a thumb at the Patriot Arms. "Meantime, we'll be on our way to our future."

Mandy liked the way he said "our future" and the thoroughness of his planning. She could feel the look of awe and admiration on her face. "That's brilliant," she said. "You're brilliant. I'm so lucky you picked me to be your bride."

"You were the only one smart enough to want me, Angel. Now you, you got an important job to do."

"I do?"

"Yep. I'm gonna carry our suitcase. I'll throw the guns in it too so they won't be seen. You'll have to carry the money. Now, make sure you don't slam the truck door getting out. We don't need to kick up a lot of noise and draw attention to ourselves. It's near eleven o'clock."

They slipped out of the truck and Stuart led Mandy down a quiet residential street. All of the houses were dark and she relaxed into him as they strolled along. They didn't talk during the short walk, and Mandy was thankful for that. She knew Stuart's mind was on consummation, and so was hers, but probably not for the same reason. Men focused on the act, women on the atmosphere, and this would be her first time someplace classy. It would be like her first time all over again.

Mandy and Stuart had sex before, as many times as they could. This was different. This would be making love, like they talked about and didn't show in the romance books and magazines she devoured. This would be legitimate, that was the word. Not rushed in the truck or listening for her parents or his dad to come home. This would be fully naked, not slacks around ankles or dress hiked up, with the lights on and without rush. This would be how it should be and, though she'd been with Stuart before, she couldn't help but be nervous about being with him tonight. She wanted everything to be so right and so grownup for him.

She snuck a glance at her new husband. From the expression on his face, he seemed as jittery as she was. Or was he just antsy to get inside and have at it? No, she decided. She knew Stuart's overeager look and this wasn't it. He was nervous too. Though she felt bad about it, Mandy took some comfort in this. He wanted things perfect for them too.

They arrived at the Hotel Grand Devlin sooner than Mandy hoped and Stuart stopped and spun her into a hug. "Angel," he whispered, "welcome to your new life as Mrs. Stuart Masamoli."

Mandy smiled. Despite her jitters, there was no better thought than spending the rest of her life as Amanda Joan Masamoli, Mrs. Stuart Masamoli. She took a deep breath to steady herself. "Are you ready to go inside?"

Stuart reached in the bag, pulled out several bills and stuck them in his wallet. "I'm ready now. While I get us checked in, you sit pretty in the lobby and give the joint some class." Arms around each other, they entered the hotel.

"Fan-cy," Mandy said in a soft voice.

"Fancy schmancy," Stuart answered. "This is a shack compared to what you deserve." He pointed to a red velvet davenport in the middle of the lobby. "You go ahead and sit and I'll get us checked in." He gave her a kiss on the cheek. "I love you, Mrs. Masamoli."

Mandy watched Stuart strut across the lobby to the registration desk. He was always so confident, no matter what life threw at him. She was the opposite. Until today. The bank holdup. The restaurant. The Masamoli name was helping her become bolder, more like her new husband. Stuart had always been bold. On the day old Poppin'-Snot told them they were expelled from Bascombe High, he asked if they had any questions. With both of their fathers sitting right there, Stuart asked the principal if he was jealous because Stuart was getting some and he wasn't. Later on, Stuart told Mandy the punishment at home wasn't too bad— Stuart's father wasn't big on education or any authority that wasn't his anyway—and it was well worth it. When they went back to the school the next day to moon Poppin'-Snot's office, Mandy noticed fresh welts on Stuart's rear. He never said a word to her about it.

That endurance is what she thought about as she studied Stuart's back while he talked to the clerk. His strength was obvious. Hers was emerging. Stuey, she thought, tonight, you are going to learn just how bold your new bride can be.

As if he somehow gleaned her intentions, Stuart turned from the desk, key in hand, and grinned before walking her way. "We're all set, Angel," he said. "Room 210." He helped her stand. "Our honeymoon suite."

Butterflies the size of bald eagles suddenly took flight in Mandy's stomach. Honeymoon suite. She really was a married woman. This was all very, very real and she was nowhere near as bold as she convinced herself she was just a moment before. Her newfound confidence watered down to thoughts of whether or not she'd ever be woman enough to be Stuart Gaylord Masamoli's wife. Wordlessly, Mandy took Stuart's hand and let him lead her to the elevator. His hand was clammy and she felt him tremble slightly.

Dang it, how excited was he? She wondered. She took a deep breath and tried to calm herself. She didn't want to disappoint her new husband on their first true night together.

All too fast, they arrived at Room 210. Stuart pulled the room key from his pocket and brandished it with a flourish. He inserted the key in the lock, turned it, and the bolt slid with a loud click. He opened the door and waved his hand into the room as if he were a magician at the climax of his best trick. "Our suite of love awaits, Angel."

Mandy looked down at the floor. "Stuey, honey," she said, his voice barely a whisper to keep him from hearing her nerves. "A new groom is supposed to carry his bride over the threshold."

"Threshold? Huh...Oh, oh, yeah, like in the movies." He turned toward Mandy and took her face in his hand, kissing her softly. "Of course, Angel, of course." Stuart took a step back and looked at her as if he were still unclear on what she expected, then hoisted her over his shoulder so her rear end faced the room.

"Stuey, I don't think this is how it's done."

"Sorry. Fireman's carry is the only way I know to carry bulk stuff, like the potato sacks down at work." He brought her into the room that way and deposited her, a little roughly, onto the bed.

"Stuey, put the suitcase on that little bench so I can get a few things," Mandy said.

Now he had his overeager face on. "All you'll need is your pretty little self." He moved to the bed and began to lower himself toward her.

She pushed him away. "Stuey, a girl wants to be all special for her husband on her honeymoon. It won't take me too long. I promise."

He looked disappointed, but he said, "Of course, Angel. How many honeymoons does a girl get in her life?"

Mandy grabbed her nightgown and her cosmetics bag and retreated to the bathroom. She reminded herself that she was ready for this new life; she wanted it, longed for it. And Stuart was so good to her. He deserved it. And he deserved her to be as close to perfect as she could make herself. Her makeup might not be the finest brands, but it was the best she could afford from Woolworth's and the Rexall and would have to do. She'd make herself beautiful with what she had, and Stuart would be pleased with the result.

She put on her face; not too heavy on the makeup, not too light, as quickly as she could and turned her attention to her nightgown. Did she wear anything beneath it? At home, she did. Her parents considered nudity beneath nightclothes whorish for girls, though her brother Craig exchanged pajamas for boxer shorts as sleepwear, when he turned twelve three years ago, and that was okay. Her mother said boys were different and she might as well just accept that, so she did. There was nothing else she could do.

She held up her panties and sighed. They were baggier than Craig's boxer shorts and in no way attractive, and these were the best she had. She looked at her nightgown; pale yellow, not sheer but not flannel, and thought she'd look good with just that. If she went back out with nothing underneath her nightgown, Stuart would be more than pleased. If her parents thought that was whorish behavior from a wife, it was their loss, not his and not hers. She slipped the nightie on over her naked body and reached for the doorknob.

When she emerged, she found Stuart in his baggy shorts, off-white, striped and in no way flattering to his masculine body. Still, this was as close to being fully naked in front of her that he had ever been and she was appreciative of what she saw. No jeans puddled around ankles and no t-shirt barely rolled up. And his excitement at what the night held in store was obvious, and this pleased her too.

Together, they unmade the bed and, once the covers were down, Stuart pushed off his underwear and tried to lower her to the bed, but she held firm. "Stuey, slow, okay? Romantic. For me." She pulled her nightgown over her head and presented herself to her new husband, whose eyes showed his approval as much as his body did. He, gently this time, lowered her to the bed, and they snuggled in together to start their new life.

Friday

The jangling alarm clock woke Mandy from a sound sleep and she reached for the side table to shut it off before Daddy heard it in his room and came roaring in. She didn't need him angry first thing in the morning. Her hand fished around, but no clock. Panic filled her, then she felt an arm draped over her. Stuart. Honeymoon. No Daddy, no alarm clock. Then the sound registered. Telephone. Somewhere in the room, a telephone was ringing.

Next to her, Stuart stirred. "Shut that thing up," he mumbled.

Mandy forced her eyes open. "Stuey, it's on your side."

Grumbling, Stuart turned over and fumbled for the receiver. When he did, the blanket twisted with him and Mandy saw a side of him she never had such a casual view of before.

This is what being husband and wife is, she thought. No secrets. Then she realized she was stark naked as well and shivered. She wanted the blanket back.

Stuart finished muttering into the phone and looked over his shoulder at Mandy. "Nine thirty, Angel. We have to be out of here by eleven and—hey, you inspecting the back view, are ya?"

Mandy felt herself flush at this. "That's okay, Angel. It's all yours to look at, or to touch. Call it a perk of being Mrs. Stuart Masamoli." He reached behind himself and put her hand on his bare rear end. "You like?"

"Not a bad perk," Mandy answered, figuring he'd like hearing that.

Stuart quickly rolled over and Mandy's hand landed on his erection. "There's another perk for you, and I know you like that one."

That wasn't a bad perk either. Not overwhelming, but not bad. "We still got an hour and a half before we got to give up the room." Stuart kissed her lightly and gave her his most hopeful look.

Since her hand was already there, she started with that while slowly kissing her way down his smooth, bared skin. Stuart leaned back, folded his hands behind his head, closed his eyes, and clearly enjoyed her work. When she reached her goal, she glanced up his torso. He looked so good to her and she so wanted to please him. Then she stiffened a little. She thought about how she must look, all hunched up between Stuart's legs, butt in the air and boobs bobbling between his thighs. She snuck a peek at Stuart's face. His eyes were still closed and he wore an expression of pure bliss. If she kept him in this state, he'd not open his eyes until she was finished and wouldn't see her bottom reflected in the dresser mirror beyond the foot of the bed. After kissing him gently in the most intimate way, she set about her duty with vigor.

As she planned, Mandy was up and snuggled beside Stuart before he opened his eyes again. Undignified sight averted, a little of her confidence returned. She trailed her fingers on his chest and said, "Good morning, Mr. Masamoli."

He made a pleased, guttural sound and opened his brown eyes. "A very good morning, Mrs. Masamoli." Stuart kissed her and glanced at the wall clock. "We still have about eighty-seven minutes. Why don't you go ahead and take your shower? Then while I take mine, you can get us all packed up and ready to roll. We need to get that Buick and get some miles behind us."

"Of course, Stuey."

She slid out of bed and headed for the bathroom. Behind her, Stuart let out a low wolf whistle. "The perks ain't so bad to look at from this side, that's for sure."

Bare-assed and embarrassed, Mandy scooted into the bathroom, quickly brushed her teeth, and got into the shower. The luxury of a hot shower with no one banging on the door to hurry her up while she finished the job Stuart didn't do in bed appealed mightily, and she intended to savor it.

She made the water as hot as she could stand, feeling the nervousness of the day before melt away as she focused all of her thoughts and energy on Stuart and their new life together. Late, loving nights and long good mornings. Two becoming one, with their whole lives ahead of them. The warmth and her thoughts combined for the best shower ever in her twenty years of life.

But they had to get moving and the shower had to come to an end. She reluctantly turned off the water and pulled back the curtain. To her surprise, there stood Stuart, stark naked and unashamedly peeing in front of her. And whistling. "No secrets between married folks, Angel," he said, not bothering to turn away or stop the stream.

Mandy turned away instead. "Stuey, there's some things that just should be...you know, private."

"Apologies, Angel," he answered, finishing nature's call. "I promise I won't never walk in on you when you're using the can." He wiped his brow with the back of his arm. "Damn, it's almost as hot in here as you are. Ought to make shaving easier, at least."

She wondered why he would bother to shave since his face was whisker-free, but decided it was a man thing she wouldn't understand so she kept her yap shut. Instead, she moved to the side so Stuart could get into the tub and quickly toweled herself dry. Her husband was right. It was way too warm and uncomfortable in the bathroom.

Mandy dressed fast and set about picking up the room, laying out Stuart's clothes and packing their things. There wasn't much work to do, so it was a task done in no time. When she was finished, she sat at the vanity to deal with her makeup while she waited for Stuart to get out of the shower. He said it would be a traveling day, so she wanted to be extra pretty, for his eyes only, except when they stopped for food or gas, of course.

Once Stuart was out and dressed, he pulled a chair to where Mandy was applying her lipstick. "Angel, today's plan is simple. Give me ten minutes, then you take the suitcase and bag of cash and go downstairs and check out. Don't let the jasper at the front desk see the money in the bag. Put some in your pocketbook and the rest in the suitcase before you head down. Meanwhile, I'll boost that Buick I showed you and pull up out front. You hop in and we're outta this berg and off to...well, wherever we decide to go."

"What are we gonna do today?" she asked.

"What do you wanna do? We got the whole day ahead of us. No

place in particular to be and nobody to tell us what to do."

Mandy thought about it for a minute. "Stuey, how far are we from Illinois?"

"I don't know exactly. Maybe seventy, eighty miles. Why?"

"I never been out of Wisconsin before in my whole life. Not even for a day. If I'm gonna be a worldly married woman, I got to stretch my wings a little, don'tcha think?"

Stuart smacked his knees and stood. "Then it's settled. We'll blow this joint and head...um...south, I guess. Who knows? Maybe we'll see all forty-eight states before we settle down." He headed toward the door. "Remember, give me ten minutes, then head on downstairs and check out."

Mandy looked at the clock to make sure she'd know when ten minutes passed. She didn't want to disappoint Stuart on their second day of married life.

A long, contented sigh escaped her freshly blotted lips. She was actually going to leave Wisconsin. Finally. Maybe she could even talk Stuart into making it permanent. If they never returned to Bascombe, they could completely reinvent their lives. No families to put them down or keep them down. No Poppin-Snots with their silly rules. No idiots they grew up with doing the same stupid stuff and telling the same stupid stories and pulling the same stupid pranks. A change would do a world of good for them both. They could be what they both wanted to be all along, respected and respectable.

Though only eight minutes went by while Mandy let her thoughts of a Wisconsin-free life consume her, she gathered their things—and the money—and headed for the elevator. She didn't know if Stuart allowed time for her to check out in his plan, but it was better for her to wait outside for him rather than the other way around.

The elevator operator greeted Mandy with a cheery "Good morning, miss," and helped her with the large suitcase. She saw him lift an eyebrow at the well-worn piece of luggage and thought briefly of the snooty table show-er back at the restaurant in Mishawaskum. She restrained herself from commenting, though. The guy was old enough to be her father and was working as an elevator operator, a nothing job. His family probably didn't even own a suitcase, battered or otherwise. Besides, she couldn't pull a gun on everyone who looked at her wrong. She had to learn to be smart like Stuart and pick her spots.

Pick her spots? What the hell was she thinking? The bank robbery, she could justify, and the restaurant happened because those snobs hurt her Stuart. Amanda Joan Masamoli was a respectable married woman now, and respectable people didn't solve their problems with anger and violence. They were nice about it and worked them out. That was why nice and respectable went together so good. Mandy and Stuart were going to have to work on remembering this. Maybe she would start by convincing Stuey to get rid of the guns. They had served their purpose and wouldn't be needed anymore.

When she reached the lobby, she kept her luggage on the floor behind the counter, out of sight of the bespectacled man at the front desk. The checkout process went very smoothly. She gave the man enough cash for the room, a few postcards from a carousel on the counter, and a tip for "the dear elevator boy who helped me with my things." Mandy figured that was a classy touch.

No one helped her to the exit, so she lugged the not-too-heavy suitcase through the revolving door and out to the sidewalk just as Stuart pulled up in their new Buick. He drummed an unrecognizable rhythm on the steering wheel while she stowed the suitcase in the backseat and then slid into the passenger side up front, pocketbook in hand.

"Stuey, this is a really nice car," Mandy said at a stoplight.

Stuart revved the engine into a purr. "Nothing but the best for my Angel. Dumb clucks left the keys right in the ignition for me." He smiled, but it faded quickly. "Gonna miss the truck though. Been borrowing her from old man Bortmann for four years."

His tone held a tinge of regret and Mandy came up with an idea to make it go away. "Stuey, nobody's looking for this car. Why don't we go by that other hotel so you can take one last look at the truck?"

It worked. Stuart's face showed it. "Angel, you truly are an angel. We'll do that very thing and then head on out of this burg and find ourselves some lunch chow on the road to Illinois."

When the light turned green, Stuart drove the Buick nice and steady toward the Colonial Arms. "Most guys do stupid shit and that's what trips them up," he explained. "Speeding or getting into a bar fight or mixing it up with a bad female or things like that and that's how they get busted by the cops. We're smarter than that." He patted the steering wheel. "I'm gonna drive this baby as carefully as a new mama pushes a baby buggy down the sidewalk."

Stuart signaled his intention to make a left turn and waited for a break in the midday traffic. When the chance came, he moved the car as gently as he promised and pulled up on the side street. "We'll have to say our goodbyes from here, Angel."

He pointed to where a tall, red-headed policeman and an older man in a suit were looking over the rusted Chevy. Mandy noticed the older man was writing on a pad and figured he must have been a detective. It was impressive that Stuart's old truck drew the attention of someone so important. She felt a momentary surge of pride in her husband, and then turned practical. "Maybe we should get out of here, Stuey." She hated the quaver in her voice.

"Don't you worry none. Ain't nobody here knows anything about us. All those cops'll see if they even look over our way is a good-looking young couple in love."

Even though the detective and the policeman were facing the truck, Mandy still felt too exposed right across the street from their getaway vehicle. She wanted to tell Stuart that sitting in plain sight was one of those stupid things he wanted to avoid, but Stuart could get riled easy sometimes and she didn't want to spoil their day.

She decided instead on a different tactic, sliding over and snuggling into him. "Stuey, I'd really like to get to Illinois soon. You promised, after all."

He glanced at the truck one more time. "Angel, when you're right, you're right. The Chevy wasn't mine. Mr. Boortman will get her back."

Mandy thought she detected a bit of sadness in his voice.

"This baby is a doozy, sleek and powerful, just like me, and beautiful, just like you."

About five miles outside of Devlin's Crossing, Mandy remembered she wanted to check the radio for news. She turned it on and left it on the station it was already tuned to. "Earth angel, earth angel. Won't you be mine?" Stuart sang with the radio. "My darling dear, love you all the time."

"You sing good, Stuey. I'll never understand why Miss Radkill kicked you out of choir."

Stuart mumbled something about "lying bitches" and Mandy worried he'd slip into a mood, but he quickly shook it and brightened. "Heard an old lady at the company tell one of the secretaries that the first song she heard with her new husband would be their song. Couldn't have picked a better one for us if I tried." He resumed his singing. "I'm just a fool. A fool in love, with you." He touched his index finger to the tip of Mandy's nose.

Soon their song ended and, after a brief fanfare, a voice came through the speaker. "Noon and time for the WDCW News with Hamilton Philo."

"Hamilton Philo. What a name!" Stuart hooted.

"Our lead story is the ongoing search for the robbers of the First National Bank in Cloverdale. The criminals are described as young, late teens to early twenties, driving an old rusted Chevrolet truck. The male is dark haired, pale, thin, with a boyish, pockmarked, nondescript face. The young lady is blonde and, in the words of bank guard William Blaisdell, 'rather pretty in a low-class way.' It is believed the same woman held up The Calder House Restaurant in Mishawaskum before spending the night at the Colonial Arms Motor Lodge right here in the Crossing."

"Stuey..."

Stuart shushed her and pointed to the radio.

"Police Chief Morgan says there are several couples who fit the descriptions who were guests at the motel," the newscaster continued. "I fully expect the chief will make an arrest before nightfall." The announcer paused. "How do youngsters such as these two hoodlums turn bad? One known influence is rock and roll. Tonight on *The Philo File*—"

Stuart snapped the radio off. "I'm not so pale."

"They don't know for sure. They called you nondescript. Means they don't know what you look like. Nonsense means not sensible, so nondescript would mean not described."

"You sure?"

"Who did both your homework and mine in English 10?"

"Yeah, I guess you're right." He turned the radio on again and fiddled with the dial until he found a station playing music and was happily singing again. Mandy wished she could be as easily distracted as Stuey was.

As they passed by small farms and endless trees, Mandy's mind wandered to the words of the radio announcer. Criminals. Hoodlums. Bad. Were they these things? Yeah, okay, they broke a couple of laws, but not for bad reasons. They didn't do what they did because they wanted to make anybody's lives miserable or for power over anybody. They just wanted a good start in their married life, and that wasn't a bad thing at all. Someday, when they were established real good, maybe they could even give everything back and make it all even and square. Still, being called bad was something she heard all her life, and it stung, hearing it again. And just what did that old Poppin'-Snot bank guard mean by "pretty in a low-class way." Yeah, she didn't have diamonds or gold, but she was still pretty, dammit. Stuart said so. That low-class crack wasn't necessary.

"Angel," Stuart said, interrupting her thoughts. "Didn't we get D's in English 10?"

"Isn't a D a passing grade?"

"Oh. Oh, yeah. Guess so." Stuart resumed his singing, this time letting his voice go high enough to reasonably pass for a girl wondering "How Much is That Doggie in the Window?" He added a growl to every one of the dog's barks and let his hand bite loosely at Mandy's dungaree-covered thigh.

Around one o'clock, Mandy's stomach rumbled loudly enough for Stuart to hear over the radio. "Little hungry there, Angel?"

"Well, we never did have breakfast..."

"Next town we hit, we stop." He looked at the car's gauges. "We're going to need gas soon anyways."

As if on command, a town appeared as the Buick rounded a bend. A sign in cheery blues and greens greeted them. *Welcome to Borderville. Gateway to Wisconsin. Gateway to the World.* "Looks like we're awful close to Illinois," Stuart said. "You wanna wait until we cross the border or stop here?"

Mandy was torn between desire to be out of Wisconsin and needing desperately to eat. She was about to say Illinois when she spotted a sign in front of a drive-in. *Leon's Root Beer. We proudly serve Ordell Sausage products exclusively.* Her father was always complaining about Ordell's, the main competitor for the company he worked for. She pointed at Leon's orange painted building. "Let's eat there."

"You sure?" Stuart asked, though he obediently slowed and pulled into the lot. "We can afford better."

"It's such a nice day, Stuey. I want to sit at one of the picnic tables with my new husband, push up my dungarees and just soak up the sun."

"That does sound perfect, Angel. We ain't in no particular rush anywho." He pulled the Buick into a parking spot on the side of the building and cut the motor. "You pick a table you like and I'll go get the chow, 'kay?" He was gone before she could answer.

That was okay with her. Mandy thought it romantic when the man ordered for both himself and his spouse in the movies. Besides, she wanted a moment just to enjoy the sun's rays on her bared legs. She picked a table half in sun and half-shaded by a nearby tree. Stuart, she knew, hated the heat and, though she would never tell him, when he got overheated, he sweated quite a bit and the resulting smell wasn't necessarily pleasant. It reminded her of the time she was dared to 'accidentally' go into the boys' locker room after a football team practice. The odor was the one part of the experience she wouldn't want to repeat.

Mandy kicked off her shoes, pushed up her pants legs and stretched out on the bench. The Buick was a beautiful car, alright, but it felt so good to be out of it for a little bit. She closed her eyes and inhaled deeply. The scents of fresh air and French fry grease mingled in her nostrils and she felt what she needed all her life. Freedom. For the first time in her life, Amanda Joan Heinemann Masamoli was truly free, no parents, no teachers, nothing. It was truly paradise.

A hand on her knee interrupted her. "Penny for...nah, we can go better than that. Buck for your thoughts, Angel." He put a tray of hot dogs, fries, and frosty mugs of root beer on the table.

"Thinking about us, mostly."

"Good subject." He sat in the shade across from her and took a huge bite of mustard-smothered hot dog. "What about us?"

She dipped a fry in a puddle of ketchup. "I've been thinking that, outside Bascombe, nobody knows us. Maybe once we do get to Illinois, we should just stay out of Wisconsin altogether. Settle someplace we find that says this here is the home of Stuart and Mandy Masamoli." Someplace not Bascombe, Wisconsin, she added in her head. "Once you hit it big," she added, "we can go back to Bascombe and show all the people who said we'd be nothing just how good we turned out. We'd show all the Poppin-Snots and parents and everybody we weren't what they thought at all."

Stuart rubbed his chin thoughtfully, leaving a mustard smear in his wake. "You know what? That's not a half-bad idea. Lots of people need a damn wake-up call about the quality of Stuart G. Masamoli, and his lovely missus, of course." He chugged half of his root beer in one gulp and let out a mighty belch. Even across the table, Mandy could smell the pungent mix of mashed meat parts, mustard, and soda. "Damn good root beer," he said, adding another, smaller belch as an exclamation point before devouring most of his remaining hot dog.

Mandy took a sip of her drink. She thought Leon's special secret recipe root beer tasted like cough syrup mixed with tree sap, but since Stuart liked it, she kept that opinion to herself. She dunked another French fry, popped it in her mouth, and glanced toward the Buick. "Stuart!" she whispered.

"What's wrong?"

She pointed toward the parking area. "There's a C-O-P looking over our C-A-R."

Stuart thought for a minute then muttered, "Shit. Just stay calm, okay? He asks, we ain't nothing more than a young couple stopped for lunch. Stay calm and let me do all the talking. And stop S-P-E-L-I-N-G stuff."

Neither of them ate as they watched the policeman examine the Buick. After a long minute or two, the officer strode right up to their table. "That your car, young fella?"

"Yes, sir...uh, no, sir...well, sorta, sir."

"Which is it, son? Yes or no?"

Stuart looked befuddled by the question, so Mandy stepped in. "Both," she said. "You see, Officer, it's my daddy's car. He loaned it to us for this trip because we weren't too keen on using my husband's old car for such a long distance."

"Where you two lovebirds headed?"

"Downstate," she answered, figuring that was non-committal enough to be forgotten. "We just ain't—haven't—had a break since the baby and all, so Mama and Daddy are keeping her for the week and we're going away for a little break." Mandy shut up before she started to let the story get too out of hand.

The policeman took off his cap and ran his fingers through his short, dark hair. "I wish me and my wife had done that. She got so miserable, being home all day with Jimmy Junior. He was a colicky little guy. Better now that he's older, of course."

"Of course," Mandy said.

She wondered why the cop was talking about any of this.

Stuart swallowed the last of his cough medicine root beer. "And that's why we're getting away," he said, making too showy a show of checking his watch.

Mandy started cleaning up the remains of their lunch. "Aunt Minerva and Uncle Teddy are expecting us today. She has the guest room all ready for us." She looked at the policeman with what she hoped was a sad, pleading expression. "I haven't seen them since I was in high school."

"Oh, right, right. I'm sorry. Didn't mean to hold you folks up. I'm something of a car lover. I saw your beauty when I pulled in for lunch and had to look it over. It's a beautiful machine. Your dad's a lucky man, little lady." He tipped his hat. "You folks have a good rest of your trip." The policeman walked into Leon's without a glance back at them.

"Angel, clean this crap up. We got to get out of here and ditch the heap pronto."

Mandy's mind raced. "I thought the story I made up was pretty good."

"It was, Angel, it was. You done great. But like I was saying before, it just don't pay to take chances. Now, let's get out of here." She barely had the last of their trash on the tray when he grabbed her by the arm and led her away.

Once they were safely on the road again, Mandy relaxed into the front seat. "Why don't we just switch license plates again, like we did with the truck?"

"Because that cop was looking too close. He'd remember little details. They're trained to do that."

That made sense. "So what are we gonna do?"

"I've been doing some thinking on that very thing and you know what I think?"

"What?"

"Well, we got a few thousand dollars in that bag, right?"

"Right."

"So we'll stash this heap someplace it won't get found too soon and we'll go and buy ourselves a car. Legitimate."

"Won't that take a lot of our money?"

"Not so much and, with a car of our own, we won't leave a trail that's easy to follow."

Again, Stuart was making a lot of sense and Mandy felt a surge of pride in her husband. She spotted a used car lot up ahead and said quickly, "Stuart, honey, I think we should wait till we cross the border before buying the car. We don't got no way of knowing who the cop's friends are in this town."

Stuart reached his right hand over and patted Mandy's thigh. "This is why I married you, Angel. You and me make one smart, unstoppable couple." He drove past the car lot and into a gas station on the edge of Borderville's business district. "We'll get some gas; make sure we don't run out before we get to the first town in Illinois."

"Stuey, honey, while you're having the car taken care of, I'm going to go over by that little drugstore across the street and see if they have any picture postcards."

"More?"

"Why not? Every place we stop. Put them all together in a scrapbook to show Stuey Junior someday."

Stuart gave her an indulgent smile. "Aw, how can I say no to Stuey Junior? You go on over. But don't take too long. Illinois isn't too far away."

Mandy scooted across the street and into the store. Out of Wisconsin was practically in sight, so she wouldn't have dawdled even without Stuart's admonition. She spotted a small rack of postcards and thumbed through them. Most were generic Wisconsin cards with pictures of farms or cows or cheese or beer. Finally, she chose pictures of the town's high school and some church, neither of which she'd actually laid eyes on. At the last minute, she added a couple of Hershey bars to her purchase, since she barely had a chance to touch her lunch, and some Lifesavers for Stuart in case he gave out with another hot dog belch, and brought everything to the counter.

"Afternoon, little lady," the too-smiley clerk with a too-bald head said. "New in town or just passing through?"

"Passing," Mandy answered without making eye contact.

"You headed north, south, east, or west?" The ding of the cash register punctuated the man's question.

"Ill...laine. Elaine. Heading up to visit my cousin Elaine. At school. In Madison." Mandy breathed a sigh of relief at catching herself before giving their true destination.

"Who's we?" he asked.

"Me and Stu—my brother." Mandy gave a shy giggle. "Me and my brother, Artie. He's over by the gas station across the street. We had a little tiff about the best route to take and I almost called him Stupidhead. But you wouldn't know his nickname, right?"

The clerk laughed along with her. "I wouldn't know his real name either, but I'm sure you've got the better plan. You seem like a bright little lady." Mandy wondered if "little lady" was the town's nickname for any visiting woman. "Would you like a couple of two-cent stamps to mail them cards home to Mama and Papa?"

Mail them? To her parents? "Uh...no. I've got some," she said.

"Good enough." He looked at the register. "That'll be thirty-seven cents then."

A loud crash from somewhere in the store made them jump. "Those little Shill twins. Monsters need a whipping, the both of them." The man raced around the counter and started toward the aisles, then stopped. "Just leave the money on the counter. I'll trust you so you can get on your way. I have to go see what them little hooligans have done this time." He ran off.

Mandy dutifully left a quarter, dime and two pennies on the counter.

On impulse, she grabbed a few magazines and a newspaper, and walked out of the store. Stuart had the car pulled next to the station and was leaning against it and drinking a bottle of 7-Up. He let out a loud belch after draining the bottle and gave her a smile. Mandy was glad she thought to buy the Lifesavers. "What'd you get, Angel?"

"Bought you some wintergreen Lifesavers…"

"My favs."

"And a couple of Hersheys and my postcards, and I picked up a paper and some magazines in case we get bored or something." The truth was Mandy never shoplifted before and she decided on the spot to find out what it was like. It wasn't, she concluded, the same thrill as holding a gun on the old Poppin'-Snots at the bank and the restaurant.

Stuart kissed her as a thank you for the mints and they got back in the car. "In just a minute, Mrs. Masamoli," he said, "you'll have your first look at Illinois."

Sure enough, when Mandy glanced right, there was the sign. *Welcome to Illinois, the Land of Lincoln.* Mandy let out a whoop. "Goodbye, Wisconsin! Forever." She practically screamed the last word in her excitement.

Stuart whooped right along with her and squeezed her left hand. "Forever works for me," he said, peppering his words with another large belch.

Mandy handed him the Lifesavers and was relieved when he immediately popped two in his mouth. "How far away from Wisconsin you thinking you want to get?" he asked.

That, Mandy realized, was something she hadn't thought about. She focused so long on getting out of Wisconsin that she didn't really consider that an out needed an in. "If we keep driving like we're going, what state would we get to next?"

Stuart thought about it for a moment. "Missouri, maybe, or Mississippi or something. Someplace southern."

"Oh. Southern. You remember Mary Ellen Bellmore, that girl from Alabama?"

"You mean the one with the huge ju—uh, yeah, I remember her alright."

"I never knew a thing she was ever saying with that accent of hers," Mandy said.

"Guys didn't hang around Mary Ellen Bouncemore for the conversation," Stuart said.

"I know the reason they boys all hung around her. Both reasons. Her and her tight sweaters." Mandy looked over at Stuart. "Stuey, did you ever do any...talking...with Mary Ellen Bellmore?"

"Me? Oh, hell, no, Angel. My first time was with you. My last time will be with you unless you croak before me. And all my times between will be with you." He patted her leg. "Don't never doubt I love you, Angel. Never."

Mandy felt foolish for even asking the question. She always knew how Stuart felt about her, maybe even before he did. Boys were slower that way, after all. She decided to get back to the subject at hand. "Well, if the south is full of funny-talking Mary Ellen Bellmores, then it's out. What happens if we turn right?"

"We hit those trees and die."

Mandy rolled her eyes. "You know what I mean, silly."

"Iowa. That's where my cousin Elbert lives."

"Is Elbert the one with the big blotch on his face?"

"That's Albert and it's a birthmark, not a blotch. Anyways, he lives up north someplace. Elbert's the one who started to grow a bald spot in twelfth grade."

The one who felt up her boob at the Masamolis' Christmas party last year and rubbed his erection against her thigh, Mandy remembered. "Small, bald farmers ain't my style," she said.

"Elbert's over six foot," Stuart said.

I didn't say he was short, Mandy thought. "Oh. What's after Iowa?"

Stuart slowed the Buick as they approached their first Illinois town. "Buncha square states. More cows than people."

"No to them. I'm leaving cows behind me for good." She looked out the window. A rundown grocery store, a small post office, and three bars made up the entire business district. "Not much of a town, is it?"

"Nah. Definitely not Masamoli style. We'll just breeze right on through. At a steady twenty miles per, of course."

Once they were back on the open road, Mandy's attention went from the view outside to working on their future. "If straight is out and turning right is out, where would we be if we went left?"

"In about a half-hour, we'd be at the bottom of Lake Michigan."

Lake Michigan! Though she lived in Wisconsin all her life, Mandy only ever saw the Great Lake once when she went there on a trip with a friend's family. They weren't allowed to touch the water that day, but she'd still been entranced by the lake. She felt its power and its permanence and knew that day she'd come back to it somehow.

"Stuart! The lake! Can we head that way?"

"You wanna get drowned?"

"No, Stuey. It's just I ain't seen the lake since I was a kid." She put a purr in her voice when she added, "It would be really romantic."

That clearly got Stuart's attention. "Never let it be said Stuart Masamoli is anything less than pure romantic. You say lake, then we'll head that way, get to the lake, and follow it till we find a place we like for the night. In the morning, we'll find a place to buy a car. How's that sound?"

"Like heaven."

She took the Hershey bars from her bag, gave Stuart his, and turned the radio on. They were far enough away from where they heard the news about the truck that she had to fiddle with the dial to find a station. She hit on one just as the DJ announced he'd be playing "'Earth Angel' for all the swooning lovers out there."

As before, Stuart sang along and, this time, Mandy snuggled into his shoulder and joined in. She definitely felt like Stuart's angel and there was no place she wanted to be more than at his side. They were a team, as it should be.

They rode this way through "Shh-Boom," "Rags to Riches," "This Ol' House," and "Young at Heart"—Stuart knew the lyrics, mostly, to all of them—before the three o'clock news came on. Stuart's hand paused midway to the dial when the announcer said, "In today's news, an update on yesterday's bank robbery in Cloverdale, Wisconsin."

"Stuart..." Mandy hated the fear that crept into her voice.

"Shhh...Let's not worry yet." He unnecessarily turned up the radio volume.

"The robbers have been positively identified as Stuart Gaylord Masamoli and Amanda Joan Heinemann, both twenty, of Bascombe, Wisconsin."

"Stuey, they know it was us."

"Shut your yap and listen." The fright in his voice matched hers. Mandy didn't like that.

The newscaster went on to talk about how the truck was found and temporarily threw investigators off the trail, but now officials were certain the pair was heading due south out of Devlin's Crossing. After promising more information as it developed, he moved on to news from Madison.

Stuart snapped the radio off. "Angel, we got to change our thinking." His hand was shaking when he pulled it away from the dial. "We're on the right track with buying a car legitimate. We just got to keep thinking like that."

"How do they know we're going this way?"

"They guessed right is all. Anyways, we got to get off this road and do some planning." He put his arm around Mandy's shoulders. "Don't sweat it, Angel. Your Stuart is always gonna protect you."

She tried to relax, but her nerves were too tight. The police knew their names. They knew what they looked like, at least, what she looked like. They knew where they were headed. There was no way any of this could be good for the two of them. Mandy didn't want to tell Stuart, but this all scared the crud out of her. Home in Bascombe may have been horrible, but this wasn't any better.

Mandy was startled when Stuart suddenly signaled a left turn. "What are we doing?" she asked.

"Angel, I promised you the lake, so that's where we're going. Besides, getting away from the main highway seems like a pretty darn smart idea just about now."

Mandy snuggled into Stuart's one-armed embrace and made herself relax. She didn't allow for Stuart's smarts when she started to panic. Smart and romantic, he had it all, and it was all for her. Despite her fears, Mandy Masamoli knew she was loved, and that mattered more than anything.

She was just drifting into a nap when her husband's voice intruded.

"Coming up on a town in a couple miles. Waterport, sign said. You're gonna get your lake in just a few minutes."

Mandy yawned. "First thing I want to see is a bathroom," she said.

"Why? You'll have a whole lake real soon." Stuart laughed at his own joke.

When buildings appeared in the distance, Stuart slowed the Buick to an in-town crawl. "Waterport. Sounds nice," Mandy said.

"It will be. I promise." Stuart's easy grin slid into a tight, thin line. "But we need to do some figuring once we find a place to stay. Cover our tracks."

Mandy sat up. "I got an idea," she said, surprised at herself for coming up with something so fast.

"Let's hear it."

"You know your brother, Peter, right?"

Stuart looked confused. "Peter? My brother's name is Ral—oh, I see what you're getting at. Fake ID's." He started laughing and took a bit to get himself under control. "Peter Ballsac. Worst fake name ever." He launched into the too-familiar story of how Arthur Dellagreto, the baddest badass of Bascombe County, charged Stuart's brother Ralph thirty-five dollars for proof he was old enough to drink and said he knew the perfect name to describe him. "Dellagreto was damn right too," Stuart concluded with a laugh.

"Do you know how he found somebody to make it?" she asked, hoping to keep Stuart focused on the problem at hand.

No soap. "Ralph was so pissed at Dellagreto. He was with Kelly Krakovich—"

"That tramp."

Stuart looked annoyed at the interruption. "She said she'd go out with Ralph only if they could go to Skipper's Hideaway Rec Room, out by Highway L. Idiot Ralph never looked at the name on the ID he bought until when they go to the bar. Bouncer looked at the ID, looked at Ralph, and said, 'Yeah, you look like a Ballsac.' Rest of the night, every time they got beer or anything, the bartender called out 'Hey, Ballsac,' as loud as he could. Killed the mood." Stuart burst out in a laughing fit. "Ralph never got to first base with Kelly Ann that night and never got another chance."

"He was probably the only guy in school who didn't." Mandy didn't want to sound catty like that, but Kelly Ann Krakovich was one of the easiest girls at Bascombe High, and that was saying something.

"I never did, Angel. It was always you for me and nobody else." Stuart actually sounded hurt.

"I didn't mean you, Stuey. Of course not you," Mandy said quickly. "Hey, look," she said, pointing out the windshield. "It looks like some kind of festival is going on."

"Excellent," Stuart said. "We can just blend into the crowd here, get some good food, ride some rides, figure out what's next later." He turned into a makeshift parking lot and cut the engine. "It's our honeymoon, Angel. Let's have some fun."

"Stuey, we can't. We got to do something about the car. They got our description—"

"Your description," Stuart corrected. "Remember, they said I'm nondescript."

"Fine. They have my description. Plus, I don't know how much I want to walk around a carnival with a bag of money. We don't dare leave it in the car, after all."

Stuart sat, staring straight out the window, hands tight on the steering wheel. "I want a corndog."

Mandy could be stubborn too. "You just had hotdogs."

"And now I want a corndog."

"We can't haul all this money around a carnival and we can't leave it in the car."

"I want a corndog."

"Go get one. I'll wait."

"I want to get one with my wife."

From the too-even tone of Stuart's words, Mandy knew the battle was lost. "Okay, I'll put the money in my pocketbook, at least as much as I can, and you'll have to stuff your pockets full. The rest we'll keep in the bag with the guns and stuff and carry it with us. But promise me, no rides that turn us upside down or shake us around or anything."

Stuart smiled. "Thanks, Angel. Nothing but gentle rides, I swear it. Nothing scarier than the merry-go-round and the kiddie train. Let's go." He opened his door.

Mandy didn't move a muscle. "Two more things, Mr. Masamoli."

He sighed and slammed the door. "What?"

"First, we are not leaving this town without me seeing the lake."

"Fine. Fair's fair."

"Second, when we leave this festival tonight, we work on figuring out how to get our hands on new ID's."

Stuart nodded. "Yeah, we def got to do that. But first, I've got a hankering for a corndog and nothing else happens till I get a few."

She patted his knee. "You'll get your corndogs. I can't say no to you."

"You'll get your chance to prove that tonight." He leered at her and gave her a Groucho Marx eyebrow waggle. "Many times. If you're lucky."

Mandy made a face, but she enjoyed the attention and his intentions and she knew he knew it. This was part of what made them such a good couple. She followed Stuart's lead, locking the Buick's door and heading to the trunk. There, she stuffed her pocketbook with a good amount of the cash they had, helped Stuart put what he could in his pockets, and put the guns and the rest of the cash in the bag from the drug store. The brown paper bulged, but held together, and that made Mandy feel a little better. When they were ready, she accepted his outstretched hand to guide her to the festival gates.

"Welcome to Waterport Days," said the woman at the ticket window. She peered at them through cat-eye glasses. "You two from around here?"

"No, we're from downstate. On our way to visit relatives," Stuart said. "Decided to stop and have a little fun."

"How nice. It'll be two dollars apiece for the two of you. Four each including the fish boil."

Stuart pulled a five from his wallet, which he held low, outside of Cat Eyes' prying peer. "Just the admissions," he said.

Cat Eyes looked both suspicious and disappointed. "You sure? The Waterport Days Fish Boil is an institu—"

"No," Stuart said.

"My boyfriend has fish allergies," Mandy said quickly. "So we'll have to pass."

The woman pushed two admission tickets at Stuart along with his dollar change and pointed to the furthest gate. "That's the no-fish boil entrance." Her voice dripped with tortured sarcasm and Mandy wanted to be away from her.

They went to the gate and entered the festival grounds. "Ditzy dame," Stuart said. "This gate goes to the same place as all the others. I ought to go back and tell her a thing or three..."

She put her hand firmly on his wrist. "No, Stuey. We don't need to be remembered by her or nobody else around here. No use taking any chances. Like you said." Mandy added the last three words to placate him.

It worked. Stuart's scowl melted into his usual lopsided grin. "You're getting awful quick thinking, Angel. I must be rubbing off on you." He kissed her forehead. "Let's go find those corndogs."

Stuart's mind was made up, so Mandy obediently was at his side in the search for a corndog stand. She hoped the LifeSavers she bought would last a second hotdog belch attack, because she knew her husband loved to loudly show his appreciation for a good wiener, or pretty much anything he ate. She decided stocking up on mints at the first opportunity wouldn't be a bad idea.

"Hey, Angel, get your prettiest smile on."

"Huh?"

He pointed ahead to a beer vendor, a young guy maybe two or three years older than them. "You flirt, get him all hot and distracted, then I'll come along and order us a couple of brews. You play it right and he won't bother none with checking my ID."

Mandy took a closer look at the guy. Reddish-brown flattop haircut, loafers, Northwestern University sweater. Everything about him screamed total nerd. The question was, was he the type to be overwhelmed by a pretty girl's attention or would he be suspicious and standoffish?

"Ain't nothing better on a warm night than an ice-cold beer," Stuart said, his voice as persuasive and smooth as a radio announcer's. "Go give the guy the thrill of his life. Go talk to him."

Why not? Mandy did pride herself on her flirting skills, after all, and maybe seeing her in action would be a memory for Stuart to pull out if he ever thought of taking her for granted. "Give me a couple minutes with him," she said.

"I'll be watching," Stuart answered, a bit of warning hovering behind the lighthearted tone of his words.

Mandy undid a button on her blouse, just as she did whenever she needed to ask her boss for a day off. Her boobs, she knew, were a good enough size for men to appreciate without being too much to handle. A little rearranging of blouse and brassiere and the college boy wouldn't waste a split-second looking at Stuart.

Clothes artfully arranged, Mandy approached the college jasper at the beer stand. She added some extra wiggle to her walk and stopped before him with an exaggerated hip thrust. "Kinda quiet over here by you. You got bad beer or something?"

"The beer's good," he said, his voice deeper than she expected. "But it's flat compared to the newly-arrived company." He smiled, revealing perfect teeth.

She matched his smile with one of her own, using a slight overbite that she knew guys thought sexy. "You're sweet. Thank you."

"No, thank you for stopping by. Added class and beauty to my stand."

She giggled and trailed a finger up his arm. "Do you go to Northwestern?"

"Oh, yeah. Law school. Third year."

"A lawyer? Wow, I'm impressed." She kept her hand on his arm and gave a slight squeeze.

"Continuing the grand family tradition. I'm a fourth generation Strattlemeyer at Northwestern Law."

"Strattlemeyer?"

It was his turn to laugh. "My last name," he said. "Nothing interesting." He stuck out his hand, the awkward gesture looking like a well-bred afterthought. "Bryce Strattlemeyer. From right here in Waterport. And you are...?"

Mandy took his hand, delicately sliding her fingers into his. "Kelly Ann Krakovich," she said with what she hoped was a slight southern lilt in her voice. If she had to play trampy, she may as well use a tramp's name.

She thrust her breasts out some to direct his gaze south.

For a moment, it worked. "Well, Kelly Ann," he said, "are you enjoying the festival?" His eyes came back up to meet hers.

"I am now," Mandy purred. "I'm new here, so I don't know nobody."

"Well, now you know me."

"Couple beers, please." Stuart's voice made them both jump.

Bryce's eyes never strayed from Mandy's. "You got proof you're twenty-one?"

"I...uh...left my wallet—"

"No soap. Bye."

"What the—"

"Got to have proof of age, friend. Soda stand is just down the midway...Boy. Bye."

Stuart glared at Mandy and stomped a few paces away before turning back toward her. Mandy stiffened and pulled away from Bryce. "I should probably get going," she said. "My family will be looking for me."

Bryce looked dejected, but Mandy could tell it was for show. "You want a bottle of beer? My treat."

Though it would have pleased Stuart if she accepted, Mandy shook her head. "I'm not twenty-one. Wouldn't want you to get in trouble."

"Eighteen for gals in Illinois. Twenty-one for guys." Bryce handed her a bottle. "State law. You don't know that, you're not from Illinois."

"Really? That don't make sense."

Bryce shrugged. "I don't make the laws. I just follow them. Sometimes. Well, when I've got nothing better to do. Anyway, I promise I'm telling the truth about this one." He pointed to a sign tacked up on the back wall of the stand that told visitors the state's strange law.

It didn't make sense, but since it was okay with the law, Mandy took the beer. "Thanks."

"My pleasure." Bryce Strattlemeyer flashed that perfect smile again. "Enjoy. And I'll be sure to look for you later." He turned his attention to an old guy and his equally old wife.

Mandy took advantage of the distraction to slip away and return to Stuart. She handed him the bottle. "How did you score this?" he asked, twisting off the cap and taking a huge swig.

"Legal age is eighteen here for girls."

"How the hell is that fair? Sorry ass kind of state is this?" He spat on the midway. "Guys handle alcohol way better than girls. Scientific fact." He took another swig. "Hey! Corndogs ahead at ten o'clock."

Mandy was never so glad to see corndogs in her life. Stuart's mood visibly brightened as he drained the bottle, pitched it into a nearby trash barrel, and practically ran to a wagon emblazoned *Sal's Sausage Shack*. Maybe once he had his corndogs, she could get him focused on their two problems, ID's and a place to stay the night.

She caught up with her husband just as he ordered four corndogs, fries, and a Coke. "What you want, Angel?"

Mandy took a quick look at the chalked menu on the side of the order window. "Sausage pizza. Oooh, and a funnel cake." She loved funnel cake and only got it at the county fair when she wasn't in sight of her parents and their reminders of her 'fat ass', which she knew wasn't fat, but wasn't worth arguing with them over. Stuart liked her ass. Shaking those memories, she promised herself that, if they spent any length of time at this carnival, she'd have a second funnel cake before they left.

The last time she had the sweet treats was at the Bascombe County Fair with her parents when she was sixteen. The Heinemann family had just eaten supper—at the Mother Meatworthy's Canned Meats stand, of course, where her father got free food for the five of them—and were headed off to the science exhibits, where Craig had a poster on flowers or planets or something. Her little brother spotted the funnel cake wagon and whined for one. Their father clapped the boy on the back and said sure. When Mandy headed over with them, her mother pulled her back. "Amanda Joan, you barely fit in your older sister's jeans. You do not need that sugar and fat added to your thighs."

"Mom, I'm not—"

"Amanda Joan! No arguing. I said no and that's it."

Later that night, when she told Stuart the story, he convinced her to sneak out of the house the next day. He led her through a hole in the fairgrounds fence and each of them had two funnel cakes and shared a lively make-out session behind the bovine barn.

Now here they were again, at a different carnival in a different state, and nobody was stopping Mandy from having funnel cake ever again.

The man behind the window, Mandy was pretty sure it was a man, pushed the food out to Stuart after collecting his money and she and Stuart found a reasonably isolated table nearby. Stuart straddled the bench and Mandy sat between his legs, hers stretched out in front of her, and leaned against his chest. He picked up one of the corndogs. "Damn, I love me some good carnival food." He took a bite and moaned like he was in heaven.

Mandy sampled her pizza and decided it was pretty good. "Stuey," she said, once she chewed enough to speak, "what are we gonna do about a new car?"

He paused, corndog in the air, to ponder the question. "Well, we got to hang on to the Buick for a little while longer. We got no choice unless we want to stay in this burg forever, cause we ain't getting out without a car. Once we get closer to Chicago, finding an Arthur Dellagreto type to help us should be a heck of a lot easier. *Capice?*" He bit the rest of the corndog off the stick.

"*Capice*," she answered. "How hard can that be?"

"Not very. Every town's got at least one wise guy who can do it."

They sat that way for a little while, Stuart enjoying his corndogs and Mandy polishing off her pizza in order to get to her funnel cake. The summer twilight couldn't be more beautiful and, despite her worries, Mandy found herself surprisingly relaxed. "Stuey, do you think there's gonna be fireworks?" she asked.

"Absolutely," answered a male voice that definitely wasn't Stuart's. "They shoot them off every year on Friday and Saturday night."

Mandy looked up and saw six feet of Bryce Strattlemeyer hovering over them. The Northwestern University sweater was gone, replaced with a Waterport Warriors football t-shirt, which looked ready to burst from the effort of containing the young man. Bryce Strattlemeyer may have been a law school nerd, but he was a well-built, solid law school nerd.

"Good to know," Stuart muttered.

Uninvited, Bryce sat across the table from the Masamolis. "So tell me, Sport, you still hankering for an ice-cold beer?"

"Had one."

"I figured. Want another? I can help you with that."

Stuart said nothing, so Mandy piped up. "What are you talking about? You're not even working the beer stand."

Bryce laughed. "That's penny ante shit I have to do to keep my old man happy. If Sport here would quit being a wet rag and make eye contact and talk to me like a grownup, he could get a beer whenever he wanted."

Stuart pushed away from Mandy and swung his leg around to sit facing Bryce. "What're you getting at...Clyde?"

"Bryce. Bryce Strattlemeyer."

"What are you getting at?"

"And you are...?"

"Huh?"

"I've already met Kelly Ann here. If I'm going to do business with somebody, I like to know his name."

Stuart looked bored, but Mandy could tell he was masking his confusion. "Ralphie, hear the man out. For your Kelly Ann." She squeezed his thigh beneath the table.

"Why not?" Stuart said.

Bryce extended his hand. "Pleasure to meet you, friend Ralph."

Stuart shook Bryce's hand and Mandy's nerves subsided a little. "So what is this business you think you have with me?"

Somewhere in the distance, Mandy heard a police siren and she felt herself tense right back up. "Well, Ralph," Bryce said, "earlier, you said you left your wallet home, but when you walked away, I could see it outlined in your back pocket." Mandy marveled at his ability to see such a detail while talking to her.

"So, I forgot I had it. So what?"

"So, you aren't twenty-one. Tell me the truth, Ralph."

Stuart spat. "I'm a few months shy. Again, so what?"

"Don't flip out on me, Sport. I can put you right with John Law and make you twenty-one right now. Tonight." Bryce leaned in at Stuart. "For the right price."

The two young men stared at each other, neither speaking for a moment. Stuart dipped a corndog in twin blobs of ketchup and mustard and took a large bite, his loud chewing accentuating the carnival sounds around them. After he finally swallowed, he took a deep breath then spoke. "What are you? Some sort of magician?" There was a sneer in his voice.

"Look, if you're not interested, just say so." The contempt in Bryce's voice more than matched Stuart's. "Just thought I'd try to be friendly, help a guy out."

"No, no," Stuart said quickly. "Just that money's kinda tight and well, you know how it is."

Mandy wondered how Stuart could say this with a straight face.

"Sure. I get it. We all have to watch our finances."

Stuart took another bite of corndog and followed it with a long swallow of Coke. "What do you mean, you can make us twenty-one?"

"You need ID that identifies you as twenty-one. I got ID's that will identify you as twenty-one. It's that simple."

Mandy's breath caught. Was it really possible she and Stuart would be able to scratch this off their list and completely begin their new lives tonight? Before she could speak, Stuart said, "Why would a rich guy like you be in the fake ID business anyways?"

"It's not a scam, Ralphie Boy," Bryce said. "And I'm not a shuckster. Truth is; I wasn't such a good boy in high school. Pater disapproved of some of my activities, but got me out of trouble anyway to preserve the family name. Now he makes me pay part of my college experiences as a way to return his alleged generosity. Selling beer at carnivals isn't nearly enough. This is much more lucrative. It's a hell of a lot more fun, too, for me and a few other hepcats who like to say go to hell to the overlords." He took one of Stuart's fries and Mandy was surprised her husband didn't react at all. "So, you interested in a new ID or not, man? I've got other customers to deal with yet tonight."

Mandy bit her lower lip. "Do...do you think you'll be able to get one for each of us?"

Bryce's eyebrows contorted into a question. "Why? You're of age in Illinois."

"We need to have ID's with the same last name." Mandy heard the pride in her voice at being able to say that out loud.

A smile crept up the law student's face. "Oh, so that's what this is about. Easier to indulge in hanky-panky as a married couple, eh? Nothing wrong with that, not in my eyes." He looked at Stuart. "Didn't think you had it in you, Sport."

"Hey—"

Bryce put his hands up in a calming gesture. "Pull it back, pal. Don't have a cow. I'm just joshing you. I'll be able to help you two out. Give me, oh, an hour and then meet me by the Ferris wheel with cash and the ID's are yours." He smiled at Mandy. "With matching last names."

"No goofy names," Stuart warned.

"Of course not. I deal in quality. You have a preference for what you do want to be called?"

This wasn't something they'd discussed. "They should be easy names to remember," Mandy said. "But not our own names, just in case."

"Okay," Bryce said. "Both of you say the first name that comes into your head."

"Joan."

"Uh...Stuart."

Bryce produced a notebook and pen. Mandy watched him write their names in surprisingly neat handwriting. "Stuart—time to get used to being called that now—stand up and come over here." Stuart complied without complaint.

Bryce took some time looking him over. "Let's see. Five foot eight, one fifty or so, brown hair and eyes. Joan, come stand next to your...husband."

Mandy didn't like the way he mocked their marriage, but didn't want to push the matter. Instead, she moved next to Stuart and linked her arm in his; just like they stood back at the courthouse when the judge pronounced them husband and wife. Was it really only yesterday morning?

For a brief moment no one spoke as Bryce glanced at Mandy. "Five-four, one-thirty, blonde, blue eyes," Stuart said, a growl in his voice.

She kissed him on the cheek. "I love you, but don't ever tell anybody I weigh one-thirty. It has never been more than one-twenty."

"Alrighty, then, one-fifteen it is," Bryce said with a wink. He returned his attention to Stuart for a moment, consulting his notes. "Twenty-five bucks now, twenty-five on delivery," he said. "In an hour or so, you'll be Stuart and Joan and will be able to fulfill whatever carnal needs you've got."

Stuart looked at Mandy with a whattya-think expression. She nodded slightly and Stuart pulled out his wallet and handed Bryce Strattlemeyer a twenty and a five. The college student took the money with amazing speed, and then looked at his watch. "It's six forty-five. So meet me at, let's call it eight, and I'll have brand new driver's licenses for you. Later." He stood, shook their hands, and left.

Once Bryce was gone, Stuart swung back around so they could sit in their original position. "I hope like hell it wasn't a mistake giving that guy twenty-five smackers upfront," Stuart said. "He don't come through, I'd want to find him and kick his ass back to that fancy school of his. Let him find out what a Masamoli knuckle sandwich tastes like."

Mandy ripped off a piece of her funnel cake and popped it in her mouth. Though no longer hot, it was still plenty warm, and the sweet, greasy goodness flooded her mouth. "Would you? Kick his ass, I mean."

"Ordinarily, Angel," Stuart said quickly, "but remember what I said about guys doing stupid crap and getting busted? That there would be a prime example. That character's family could probably buy off a thousand judges, but somebody like me would have his ass rot in jail 'til he was too old to do anything but die." Stuart broke his corndog stick and threw it on the ground. "At least until we make it big."

Somewhere in the distance, a band started playing a jumping dance number. Stuart bounced up and took Mandy's hand. "Dance with me, Angel. Our dance of freedom." He let go of Mandy's hand and leapt up on the bench, waving his arms in the air and gyrating in somewhat of an approximation of the song's rhythm.

"Juvenile filth." a gray Poppin-Snot in a suit said, loud enough for them to hear. In response, Stuart turned around and shook his rear end at the old fart, making Mandy laugh and drawing approving shouts from a group of passing high schoolers. The Poppin-Snot managed to sneer in two directions at once.

"Stuart," Mandy whispered. "Get down. People are staring and we probably shouldn't draw attention to ourselves."

He jumped down from the bench in mid-gyration, landing directly in front of Mandy. "Smart thinking, Angel. Why we make such a good team." He put his arm around Mandy's shoulder and led her to the pathway.

They strolled without talking for a bit, taking in the flashing lights of the amusements and the fragrant aroma of deep-fried treats and the odor of summer-soaked bodies. Overwhelming this was the smell of fish and the voices of excited people. Mothers deciding the best time to shepherd their kids to the fish boil. Those same kids racing from ride to ride as fast as their ticket supply would allow. Bored men were seeking out the beer garden and the camaraderie of their peers. Vendors hawking their wares, carnies hawking the rides and game runners hawking prizes. Voices everywhere.

In the middle of it all, Mandy relished her silent stroll with her husband. To passersby, they had to look like just what they were, two young people totally in love. There was no greater feeling than this. After twenty years of misery living in her family's house, never home, just house, this was what she deserved. She earned it. She was going to savor it forever.

She felt more than saw Stuart point at a game booth to their right. "Look, Angel, it's the dart throw." He tugged at imaginary lapels. "I am a grand master champion at this game. You see that little orange bear on the end. That's the one I'm gonna get for you."

"Hey, young man," came a gravelly female voice. "Heard ya tell the little lady you're gonna win the orange bear for her. Only cost ya a dime to try."

Mandy looked over to the source of the voice. An older woman with straggly gray-streaked hair topped by, of all things, a rhinestone princess tiara, held three darts out toward them. The game runner, wearing a perhaps-blue blouse with stains layered on stains, managed to look more slovenly than Mandy's mother, something Mandy never thought possible.

"Hear you're a grand master," she said to Stuart, her tone more mocking than encouraging. "Ten cents, just ten measly cents, to make the little lady happy. Won't find a better bargain anywhere on the midway, especially for a grand master champion like you."

Not unexpectedly, Stuart rose to the bait. "Here's a quarter," he told the woman. "And I'll expect fifteen cents change when you give me the bear."

Stuart snatched the darts and assumed an exaggerated thrower's pose. He waggled his rear, a sight Mandy appreciated, brought his arm back, and let the first dart fly. His aim was true and the tip of the dart struck dead center of a bobbling red balloon—and bounced off, falling harmlessly to the grass below.

"What the—"

"You got to put some oomph in your throw, Champ." The woman smiled, revealing severely tobacco-stained uneven teeth even worse than Mandy's father's, something else Mandy never thought possible.

Stuart smiled back. "I still got two, and that's all it takes." He took aim at a blue balloon next to the original red, with the same result. "Goddammit."

"You still got one," the woman said. "You can win a shiny plastic ring for the pretty lady. And, of course, you still got fifteen cents coming to ya." She held up an ugly trinket ring that wouldn't pass muster in the five and dime's bargain bin.

"Bitch," Stuart muttered.

Mandy couldn't tell if the woman heard him or not.

"Stand back," he instructed.

Since Mandy had no interest in the ring, she started looking at the balloons. The balloons in the center of the board, she noticed, looked much firmer than those around the edges.

"Goddammit," Stuart said again. "Damn balloons are rigged."

Mandy grabbed Stuart by the shoulder so she could whisper what she realized in his ear. A slow smile spread on his face and he leveled his glare at the old woman. "Have my nickel and her orange bear ready. Three balloons are about to die."

"I got all night, Champ. How many dimes you got?"

"Won't need more than the one you already got. Gimme the darts." Stuart stuck out his hand.

Darts were in his hand in a flash and Stuart assumed his throwing position again, this time with even more theatrics. In rapid succession, three balloons in the bottom row, a blue, a green, and a yellow, fell to stringy remains after popping.

"Bear, please," Mandy said with as much sweet innocence as she could.

The woman turned, coughed a rattling growl into a wad of

something that mercifully landed out of sight, and grabbed the bear. She didn't hand it over right away. "You know, you do that just three more times and you can get a bigger prize for your girl. Whattya say, Champ?"

"No," Mandy said firmly before Stuart could speak. "I want this one."

Stuart cocked his head. "You heard her." He reached over the rail and plucked the toy from the woman's hand. "Thank you, Princess," he said. "Keep the nickel." Mandy couldn't make out the woman's mumbled reply.

They moved quickly away from the balloon pop stall and, once a decent distance away, slowed back to their earlier pace, Mandy hugging the little orange bear. "Thank you, Stuey," she said softly.

"A pleasure, Angel. What're you gonna call it?"

"Blue," she answered without hesitation.

"Uh...Angel, you gone colorblind? That bear ain't near blue."

"Long story. Not now."

After a few minutes, they melted into comfortable conversation, mocking those who passed them and remembering festivals and carnivals in their shared past. Mandy was incredibly happy. She had Stuart and now she had Blue and their adulthood was off to a fine start.

Stuart suddenly stopped in his tracks. "I could be cuckoo crazy, but I swear I just heard somebody walking by talking about somebody driving a stolen Buick. Just in case, we should get those ID's and get the hell out of here."

The Ferris wheel, though small, towered above the other rides, so it was easy to locate. At eight-ten, there was still no sign of Bryce Strattlemeyer. "Where is he?" Stuart fumed.

"I'm sure he'll be here, Stuey."

"That bastard best not have stiffed us."

"He didn't," came a voice from behind them.

Mandy and Stuart turned around to face the law student. "You've got the other twenty-five, I assume."

Stuart pulled the cash from his shirt pocket. "Right here. You got the ID's."

Strattlemeyer held two cards up for Stuart's inspection. "Right here."

The two quickly traded money for identities and shook hands. With a "See ya around, young lovers," Bryce Strattlemeyer was gone.

"We should get out of here," Stuart said, stuffing their new lives in his pocket.

Mandy wanted to find out what their new last name was, but Stuart was walking too fast to try to convince him to stop. They made a beeline through the front gate and out to the parking area, where they stopped so abruptly Mandy could have sworn she heard a cartoon skid sound. "Shit," Stuart said.

Halfway across the small sea of cars, the Buick was surrounded by uniformed police officers. "Stuey, what are we gonna do?" Mandy asked. "They got our car. And our suitcase."

"I'm thinking, I'm thinking," he answered, his hands at his temples.

Around them, people were pointing toward the police and car and speculating on what was going on. More than once, Mandy heard mention that the couple being sought had to be somewhere on the fairgrounds. The pizza and funnel cake threatened to bubble up from her stomach and Mandy forced them back down. She looked at the crowd watching the police and got an idea. "Play along," she whispered.

"Huh?"

"Just go along with what I say. I think I got a way to get us out of here, even though they got my description."

"Angel—"

"Trust me, Stuey. This worked all the time in school. It'll work here."

Stuart grimaced. "Don't got a hell of a lot of choice, do we?"

"No," she whispered, then cleared her throat and spoke up. "You know, I bet they're looking for those criminals from up in Wisconsin," Mandy said just loud enough for a teenage girl near them to hear. "But I heard on the news a little bit ago they decided they were wrong and those two are headed toward Madison, not here." She pulled Stuart down so she could whisper in his ear. "Watch."

Sure enough, the girl next to them whispered to the boy next to her, who said something to another guy, leading to more bent heads and whispering in young ears, then to older ones.

"Well, then, I guess there's nothing to see here," Stuart said with a chuckle in his voice. "Let's head on home."

Together, they scooted around the perimeter of the parking lot to the street they originally drove in on. "Angel, that was genius."

"Just like the halls at school. Remember when prissy Priscilla Kendrick did it with Bertram Glouster?"

Stuart laughed. "I seen Glouster in the locker room. I ain't so sure doing it with him counts. Not much to do there, if you know what I mean."

"Yeah, well, Leslie Vorhees asked her about it at down near old Poppin'-Snot's office and the word yes was barely out of Priscilla's mouth before it traveled all the way down the main hall faster than she did. She ran into her older brother who was ready to kill both Bertram and her." Mandy turned serious. "But that's ancient history. What are we gonna do about now?"

"We got to get the hell out of this place," Stuart answered, his laughter stopped.

"How? By walking?" She didn't want to do it, but the tears came.

Stuart pulled her behind a parked car and held her in a tight embrace. "Angel, this is a one-time setback. We still have our money and we're out of Wisconsin and we're together. Tonight might be a little rocky, but I promise you we're going to be better than alright by tomorrow night."

The sincerity in his voice wrapped around her as tightly as his hug. "You sure?"

"Positive." He snapped his fingers. "You know what? We were heading for the lake, right?"

Mandy sniffled. "Right."

"And we're in a place called Waterport, right?"

"Right."

"So, if there's water and a port, there must be the lake near here. Let's go find it."

"But—"

He brought his finger to her lips. "We'll find a place to sleep right out by the lake. It'll be an adventure." He softened his voice. "It'll be a story we'll be able to tell Stuart Junior someday."

That did it. The tears stopped. The thought of there being a Stuart Junior one day made everything worthwhile again. "Adventure," she repeated. "Stuart Junior will enjoy hearing about it." She held Blue the orange bear close.

A short walk brought them to the few blocks comprising the Lakeport business district and, beyond it, Lake Michigan. Unfortunately, there was no way to get down to the lakeshore, thanks to poorly placed foundry buildings that ran at least three blocks. Mandy needed to touch that water, something denied to her all her life. To feel its cool touch on her warm skin, its muddy floor rise between her toes as she walked. Something she only heard about, but never experienced.

"There's a hotel up the block," Stuart said, intruding on her private thoughts. "Wanna give it a try?"

"I thought we were going to stay outside."

Stuart shrugged. "Just thought I'd offer. But yeah, we should get away from this town. Which way you wanna go, left or right?"

"Whichever way isn't Wisconsin."

They turned south and followed the main street until, about fifteen minutes later, they were clear of the last of Waterport's neighborhoods. Just beyond the last house, the area become heavily wooded and, despite the darkness of the night, they decided together to move a little way off the road to lessen their chances of being seen.

Just out of town, they found a small break in the endless trees and decided to see if it would lead to Lake Michigan. It did. "Not much of a moon tonight, Angel, but there's your lake, just like I promised."

Mandy looked out at the water, which she could barely even see. She wanted the lake to be large and sparkling and inviting, and all she got was a sliver, a cold, lifeless sliver. Less than her share, like always. She sank to the ground and sat, arms on her knees, and glanced at the water again. Blackness with a little ripple of moonlight was all there was. Mandy put her head down and started to cry.

Stuart was beside her in a flash, but when he tried to embrace her, she shook him off. "Don't."

"Angel—"

She stared over at him. "Just go away. Please? Just go."

He started to say something, then stood and walked away without a word. She didn't watch him go, didn't care where he went. This was all so wrong, so very wrong. They never should have gotten married, never should have robbed the bank, never run away. What did it all bring them? Money that wasn't theirs, police on their trail, and a dead sliver of a cold lake. Back in Bascombe, she didn't have much—a room with a broken window, a family who thought of her as a two-bit whore, and a job that would never be anything more than just a job—but now, she didn't even have that much. Not even a place to sleep for the night. A broken window in summer wasn't so bad to live with compared to sitting outside in the dark beside a hostile lake. What the hell was she thinking? Why did she let Stuart talk her into leaving home? Why did she let herself be talked into it?

This wasn't all Stuart's fault, as much as she wanted it to be, she had to admit. She let herself be talked into robbing the bank and she came up with the idea of robbing the restaurant on her own. Inside her, somewhere, was the bad person she'd always been told she was; the bad girl, the whore, the lazy fat ass, they were coming out and having their way with her. Until she saw this sliver of lake, she was enjoying every bit of it, for the most part. Amanda Joan Heinemann Masamoli was every bit the useless piece of trash people pegged her as for twenty years.

Mandy sat back against a tree and let her view take her to the water again. It was still a dark, blank nothing. Like her. Just plain nothing. The lake glared back at her, black eyes on black water. You just don't get it, do you? The little slice of water and moonlight seemed to say. You don't just get happiness. You have to earn it.

She glared right back at it. I have earned it, she wanted to scream. Twenty years of living with parents making her feel like a pile of runny crap. Twenty years of an older sister outperforming her in anything she tried. A few less years of a little brother stealing any attention that might have once been hers and getting whatever he wanted, giving her nothing in return. Teachers who judged her stupid and ignored her, rather than helping her. Friends who gossiped behind her back and left her out of things. She lived through twenty years of bull and bullying with nobody but herself to rely on.

Nobody but herself, and Stuart. He was always there, from first grade until they left town together. He made Bascombe bearable. Maybe Stuart had faults, but he had reasons for them too, just like she did. He was always there for her, holding her, letting her cry, understanding her. He was the only one who ever made the effort to understand her, to love her. He did love her. Mandy had no doubt about that. And now she'd made him go away.

With a start, she realized he didn't stay away at all. He was sitting right beside her. Not touching her, not saying a word, not even looking at her, as far as she could tell. But Stuart was there, at her side, leaving her alone and being there with her at the same time. He didn't talk her into doing all of this. They were one. He wanted out of Bascombe, she wanted out of Bascombe, so they got out of Bascombe. Stuart was right. This was a one-time setback and they'd find their way through it. They always did.

Mandy reached across the sand and took Stuart's hand in hers. "Stuey, I'm sorry," she said softly. "I don't want you to ever go away. Never."

"It's okay, Angel. I'm never going anywhere without you."

She scrooched around so she could rest her head in his lap. From this angle, she couldn't see Lake Michigan, for which she was grateful. She could, however, see her husband, the man she loved and the only person to ever love her. "I could sleep right here and be perfectly happy," she told him.

"Kind of early for sleeping," Stuart said.

"I'm not doing any...honeymooning...here. There's too much sand."

Stuart stroked her hair. "Though that ain't a half-bad idea, it's not what I was thinking. Later, but not just yet." He hummed a few bars of "Earth Angel" before he spoke again. "You, my angel, wanted the lake, and it's right there. We should go in, enjoy it even if we can't really see it yet. It's what you wanted."

It's what I wanted, she reminded herself. To feel that water and the lake's embrace. If they slept out here tonight, she'd see the grand expanse of Lake Michigan in the morning. For now, the touch was what she needed. She looked toward the sky. "Do you think there's enough moonlight?"

Stuart glanced up. "I guess, if we don't go out too far." He leaned in and brought his voice down. "Ever skinny dip?"

"Stuart!"

He made a show of glancing about again before speaking. "Why not? We'll stick close to shore so we can keep an eye on our things. Ain't nobody gonna know."

"I don't know…"

Stuart had his shirt unbuttoned before Mandy could reconsider and they were quickly as naked as they were in the fancy hotel bed the night before. Stuart's excitement was obvious even in the dim moonlight, but Mandy was focused on finally touching that water and feeling its power embrace her. She could forgive the dead black first impression it made. She waited twenty years to be where she was.

Mandy savored the first kiss of lake water on her bare toes while Stuart ran in up to his knees. The water was colder than she expected, but Mandy didn't care. She couldn't remember a time she didn't want to be one with Lake Michigan. A chilled paradise, that's what it was. Near her, Stuart was bent over, splashing water on his face. She wondered if he was as enraptured as she was.

"Nice view," came a voice from the shore.

They both wheeled around and saw Bryce Strattlemeyer and another college-aged young man. Both were as naked as she and Stuart and Mandy suddenly felt very self-conscious. She didn't have enough hands to cover every part she wanted to keep hidden from view. The guys on shore didn't bother covering up. From what Mandy could see, they didn't need to be embarrassed. Not at all.

Stuart suddenly appeared in front of her, blocking the other guys' view. "What the hell you looking at, assholes?"

Bryce held up his hands. "Relax, Sport. Everything's cool. We got some cold beer back there if you want to join us."

Stuart visibly relaxed and started toward the shore. "C'mon, Angel. Private party."

The magic words, Mandy thought. Cold beer.

The last thing Mandy wanted was to leave the water behind, especially to go watch Stuart get loaded on cheap beer and talk with two horny college guys who already saw her naked, but she followed. Stuart was doing his best to keep her from being scared, so he deserved to have a little fun too. After all, she owed him her freedom, her life, and her love.

Back on the sand, Mandy quickly slipped into her dungarees and blouse. Stuart put on his boxer shorts, telling her he didn't want to plop his hairy ass directly into the sand and get grit in places where grit didn't belong. The other boys remained as naked as the day they were born as they led them to a collection of flat stones. On one, a bucket held ice and a number of bottles of Blatz beer.

Bryce spread his arms wide. "Welcome to Bryce's Beachside Beer Bar and Bistro. Immediate seating now available. My assistant, the one and only Troy E. Baldwin—"

"Troy Eric Baldwin the Fourth, to be specific," came the voice of the other boy from behind the rocks. He popped up with a large picnic basket. "We've got plenty of sandwiches and potato chips and pretzels and an apple pie swiped from my family's kitchen. All in all, a respectable bill of fare. Sit, sit," he instructed with a wave of his hand. "I, and my able-bodied bartender, will be honored to serve your every need." He bowed dramatically, which Mandy though looked silly, given his naked state.

They all sat and the beer and food were distributed in short order. The cold dampness from the stones seeped through Mandy's dungarees and she wondered how the boys could stand having their nude rear ends making direct contact. The guys were chatting like old friends. Baseball quickly became the topic, of course. Men and boys and sports. Mandy was far from being a tomboy, so she always tuned out these conversations. She had no interest whatsoever. Instead of talking sports, she studied the three of them. Her Stuart, the shortest of the three, was still the most attractive to her. The other two had clearly been friends for a long time, probably as long as she and Stuart. Despite not knowing where she was and having known these guys for such a short time, she felt very comfortable here.

Until Troy asked what she knew was a normal, natural question. "So how long are you two in town?"

Stuart took a swig of beer. "Just the night."

"My aunt's waiting for us. Downstate," Mandy said.

"Where?" Bryce asked.

"On her farm." Mandy hoped her smile was pure innocence.

Bryce drained his beer and laughed before opening another. "Where are you staying tonight?"

"We got a place," Stuart said, too quickly.

"I'm sure you do. I'm sure you two can afford whatever you want." Bryce looked off toward the lake. "Whatever you want."

Mandy tensed. "What do you mean?"

Both of the boys started laughing and Mandy was no longer comfortable. "Come on, doll," Bryce said. "Bank gets robbed up in Wisconsin, young couple, gorgeous blonde, nondescript guy, take off, steal a Buick, which just happens to be found at the festival where a young couple happens to buy new identities from a handsome young law student from Northwestern. No way it's just coincidence, especially when the couple uses the same names as the bank robbers."

Stuart jumped up. "You don't know jack. Nondescript could be anybody. It don't have to be me." He pulled Mandy up more than a little roughly. "Let's go, Angel."

"Sit down, Sport. We don't give a shit if you robbed a bank or knocked up the mayor's wife. We're not going to give you up to the law, unless you run off."

Though Stuart clearly did not believe or trust the young men, he did as Bryce directed. "What will you do?" he asked, his tone a mix of fear, distrust and anger.

A long moment passed with only the gentle lapping of the lake at the shore and the odd night sounds of the woods breaking the silence between them. "What will we do?" Bryce repeated at last. "Not a damn thing, Sport. You're rebels and you're getting away with it. We all need to break laws and rules and conventions sometimes to find our true happiness." Bryce gave Troy a look Mandy wasn't sure how to interpret. Could law students be law breakers too?

"Let me get this straight," Stuart said. "You—"

"Don't give a damn, Daddy-O," Troy finished for him. "Relax. Have another beer or a few, and we'll help you find a place to sleep tonight."

"Why are you doing this?" Mandy asked.

"What's in it for you?" Stuart added.

The two young men both smiled. "Seeing you get away with it,"

Bryce said. "My dad's an 'all young people are worthless delinquents so throw the book at them' type of prosecuting attorney. I root against him and his vigilante values every case he gets."

"And my dad's a county judge who convicts for anything Bryce's dad wants, true evidence of crime or not," Troy said. "Humanity never figures into his decisions, and I can't stand that."

"And we're both planning to finish law school and tell them to go screw themselves and become defenders of the poor and downtrodden," Bryce concluded. "Beats following in their Florsheim footsteps. We'll be poor but honest when we face St. Peter, if there is such a guy."

Mandy relaxed into Stuart. What would her father think if he found her sitting with Stuart in his underwear and two naked men a few feet away, and all of it happening outside for anybody to see? He'd crap his pants and then declare she'd fulfilled the destiny he predicted for her when she was asked to leave high school.

She would never, ever forget that day. "Well," her dad said once they were in the car. "What now? No more school, so you got to go to work and pay rent if you plan on staying in my house. Got it?"

The last thing Mandy wanted was to think about any of that, so she just said, "Yes, Daddy."

"And you will stay away from that little Masamoli bastard. Far, far away. That boy has always been a worthless little piece of shit. If you can't do better than that, then you're better off going without. He ain't worth the flesh he's made of. Mother Meatworthy's puts better quality in their sausage cans than the stuff Stuart Masamoli's made of."

Her father continued on like that all the way home, where her mother took over. "A useless slut. My younger daughter is nothing but a two-bit whore who don't remember to even collect the two bits. What were you thinking? Look at your sister. Good and pure and in college. Your little brother makes straight A's. And you, stupider than a box of rocks and a big enough tramp to screw a low-living piece of white trash like Stuart Masamoli."

At that moment, she knew for sure just how much she hated her parents. Linda was up at college, and from all accounts, doing a good job of humping at least two professors and Craig had more wads of crusty old cloths shoved under his mattress than any one teenage boy should, yet she was the one that was so horrible for loving a man who cared about her. Mandy promised herself she and Stuart would always be together and, one day, her family would be out of her life for good. Nothing and no one would keep her and Stuart apart. Ever.

She was so lost in thought it took her a moment to realize the boys were trying to get her attention. "Angel," Stuart said, once she mentally rejoined them, "these guys are going to show us a private cove we can sleep in tonight and then drive us to the next county tomorrow. Ain't that great?"

"That's wonderful. Thank you, guys."

"A pleasure, my lady," Bryce said, regally doffing an imaginary hat.

"My lady," Stuart corrected him.

Though his tone was light, Mandy knew he was sending a warning to the older boy.

"Absolutely," Bryce said. "Let's get to the cove and get some sleep."

"You're staying out here too?" Mandy asked.

"Sure. Nothing wrong with a little adventure."

The boys gathered their clothes, though no one dressed, and with Bryce leading the way and Troy bringing up the rear, the quartet walked along the shore. A little way away, Lake Michigan took a small turn to the west and back, leaving a little tree-encircled inlet. "Here we are," Bryce said. "There's a kind of cave-like thing over there that you two can use, and we'll flop on the other side of the cove so you can have a little bit of privacy."

Once they parted company and the college guys were about twenty feet away, Mandy and Stuart crawled into their home for the evening. "It is safe to trust them, isn't it, Stuey?"

He pulled her to him until she laid her head on his bare chest. "If they were gonna turn us in, all they had to do was get in their car and go call the cops. If they were gonna steal the money, it was right there on the shore while we was in the water. They could've took our clothes and run. So, yeah, I think they're probably okay." He let out a mighty yawn.

"I hope so," she said, snuggling up even closer and allowing herself to drift off to sleep.

It was still dark when Mandy's bladder woke her. She didn't want to wake Stuart, so she slipped out of his loose grip and left the little cave. She looked about to find the most private place to pee and spotted Bryce and Troy. Things became both very clear and very confusing. She heard about guys who liked other guys, though she was reasonably sure she didn't know any. Or maybe she did. When she was little, her uncle Edwin divorced Aunt Fiona and moved in with Clyde Bellnap. Her dad hadn't talked to his own brother since, and now Mandy understood what happened. Mandy's mother referred to the two men as having a "disgusting special relationship." If that's what Bryce and Troy had, and judging by their current, intimate activities, they did, they certainly seemed much more happy than disgusted.

A jolt from her insides reminded Mandy of why she was out here in the first place. She shook the mix of fascination and guilt in watching them and scooted along as quickly as she could. Behind a reasonably dense wall of trees, her sigh of relief had two causes. Peeing, of course, was one. The other was more important. Her failure to distract Bryce at the carnival earlier wasn't her fault. He wouldn't have been interested no matter what she did.

While pulling up her dungarees, another realization struck Mandy and she had to stifle a giggle. When Bryce saw the outline of Stuart's wallet against his butt, it wasn't sharp observation skills, but a definite study. Stuey wouldn't like that, she thought. And when Bryce said "Nice view" earlier, he meant bent-over Stuart, not naked Mandy. Stuart definitely wouldn't like that. Mandy, on the other hand, had to hold her breath to keep her laughter in.

On her way back to the cave, she glanced over at the college boys. They were too intent on each other to even know she passed by. Somehow, this made her feel safer. Their relationship and Mandy's knowledge of it would likely ensure their silence about her and Stuart's whereabouts. There was comfort in that.

Saturday

The morning sun jolted Mandy awake before she was ready. Her bladder called again as well, ensuring she'd have to drag herself out of the cave to the protective screen of trees a few feet away. On the shaded side of the cave, Stuart slept on. His slight snore blended nicely with the gentle lapping of Lake Michigan against its Illinois shore. Illinois. She was still away from Wisconsin. She sighed. Never to be in Wisconsin again was a dream just yesterday and now it was reality; her permanent reality.

Blue the orange bear was nestled in Stuart's armpit and Mandy carefully snatched him away. She loved Stuart dearly, but Blue couldn't be allowed to smell like guy sweat. The bear, once they settled into their lives, would have an occasional perfume spritz and sit on her pillow during the day. At night, he would be moved to her bedside table, available for a quick touch when she needed a boost of support. Not that she was likely to anymore.

She backed out of the cave, her body sore from a night on the hard ground. Thank God she and Stuart fell asleep before his bodily desires kicked in and took control of his brain. Being pounced on with the solid earth as a mattress would have left her too sore to move this morning. Even Stuart wasn't worth that.

Once clear of the cave, Mandy stood and stretched, amazed at how much cracking and creaking her body released. Once the popping stopped, she turned and caught sight of Bryce and Troy, still naked and blissfully sleeping. Their bodies were intertwined enough to leave no doubt as to why the boys came out here to be alone together. She made a note in her head to keep Stuart in the cave long enough to let the guys' morning excitement dissipate and for them to dress and look normal. She wasn't sure how her husband would react to the law students' relationship.

With all three young men still asleep, Mandy felt a little more comfortable with peeing outside during the day. She nestled Blue between two low branches of a nearby tree, slipped off her dungarees and panties, and squatted behind a huge, gnarled oak. This was one thing, she decided, where guys had it way easier than girls.

"Maybe they come over this way," came a loud, gruff voice way too nearby for comfort. "Them two can't be too far from the car the sheriff found yestiddy."

Mandy, who was nearly finished when the man's voice startled the rest out of her in a rush, quickly slipped on her pants. She grabbed Blue from his perch and took off for the others, praying they were awake and alert.

They were. All three men were in a frenzy of throwing on clothes and gathering belongings. Stuart, Mandy noticed, had himself between the other guys and her oversized, overstuffed pocketbook, where the bulk of their money was held. Even in a time ripe for panic, Stuart was thinking, looking out for her and for their marriage. Smart.

"I think I heard something moving over here." This was a second voice, even more gruff than the first. "If it ain't the bank robbers, maybe we'll find them two Nancy-boys you spotted out here last week, Papa Natey."

"Rewards or ass-kickings. Either way, something good's comin' out of this mornin'."

The third voice was younger and less gruff, but equally menacing. How the hell many of them were there anyway?

Mandy and the boys ran as quickly as the rough terrain allowed toward, she assumed, a car belonging to one of the boys. With the crunching of leaves and branches beneath their feet, she had no way of knowing if their pursuers were close behind or not. She was still sure she heard them back there, though, and willed her legs to move faster than ever before.

Finally, they came upon a fairly nice-looking newish car and the quartet quickly scrambled inside. Behind the wheel, Bryce fumbled with the key and, once he managed to slip it into the ignition, roared the engine to life and took off, forest debris flying behind their back tires. In the haze of shredded leaves and bits of bark and twigs, Mandy was positive she saw three mountain-sized male figures.

"Yesssssss!" Bryce cheered. "Got 'em good." He sped up and the car was quickly on the main road.

"What the hell was that?" Stuart asked.

"The McBrayers." Bryce hooted loudly. "Crazy Micah, who sells all the reefer around Waterport, Little Al, his stupid ass brother, and their meaner than hell father, Natey, who has no qualms about beating the living shit out of anybody who doesn't live by their rules. And," he added ominously, "they'd sell out their own mother if the price was right, so you know they wouldn't mean but trouble for us."

"That don't sound so good," Stuart said. "How mean-ass are they?"

A shotgun blast answered Stuart's question before the law students could. "Bastards are behind us," Troy said, a hint of panic in his voice.

"Yes. Yes they are," Bryce said too calmly for Mandy's comfort. "Troy Boy, should we pull over? Let the McBrayers have their rewards?"

"What the hell?" Stuart nearly screamed.

Bryce laughed. "Damn, Sport, calm down. I'm not that stupid. You don't get into Northwestern Law if you're stupid, no matter who your father is. Those jerkoffs would beat the shit out of me and Troy if we stopped for them."

"Beat the shit out of—" A look of realization came over Stuart and Mandy quickly grabbed his thigh and squeezed a warning to keep quiet. She doubted the guys in the front seat would kick them out, but there was no point in him saying anything to anger them and risk it.

Stuart swallowed hard. "What are you going to do?" His voice was barely a squeak.

"What are we going to do?" Bryce repeated. He was still using that too-calm tone.

"We're going to get away from them and their rusted-out piece-of-shit mobile. That's what we're going to do." He paused. "After we have a little fun with them, of course. Them acting like backwoods hicks from Arkansas or West Virginia or someplace brings down the whole quality of life in the beautiful Land of Lincoln."

A second shotgun blast again missed the car, but still terrified Mandy. She'd never been shot at before and it would be fine with her to never be shot at again. Her hand was still gripping Stuart's leg and she felt his tension as well. After last week with his father, gunfire in Stuart's direction couldn't be easy for him to handle.

Bryce slowed the car to a near-crawl and Stuart panicked. "What the fuck are you doing?"

"Having a little fun with a bunch of yahoos, Sport. Relax."

"We've done this before," Troy said. "Bryce always knows what he's doing. Always."

That was hardly reassuring, but Mandy stroked Stuart's leg and did her best to keep him calm while two more shots whizzed past. "It's okay, Stuey. These guys are like your dad. They're aiming to scare, not hit." She took a deep breath. "And it's working. Hold me, Stuey. Please?"

She adjusted her position so he could hold her tight. Truth was, she was scared, very scared, and she hugged Blue as hard and secure as her husband held her. She hoped the guys in the front saw Stuart as being strong and protective, rather than as frightened as she was.

"They're catching up, Bryce," Troy said. He was leaning over the front seat and watching out the rear window, seemingly oblivious of the couple in back. There was an odd half-smile on his face that Mandy didn't like at all. "About five hundred feet behind us." His voice rose up in pitch and beads of sweat were breaking out on his forehead. Mandy couldn't tell if he was nervous, excited, or both.

"Closing in," Troy said.

"Let's do it." Bryce peeled out, the smell of burnt rubber permeating the car's interior. "Time to play chicken with some ignorant farm boys."

The law students laughed heartily.

Mandy and Stuart didn't join in.

Troy stayed on his knees, looking out the back window and relaying information on the McBrayers' truck to Bryce, who was clearly trying to maintain a certain distance from the ancient Ford. "Looks like showtime up ahead," Bryce said suddenly.

Mandy tried to peer through the windshield, but all she could see was sky and trees. She scooted up to whisper in Stuart's ear. "What do you think he's gonna do?"

Stuart shrugged. He, too, was trying to see between Bryce and Troy to the road ahead. He tensed again when Bryce started to slow down. "Why—"

"Never question," Bryce said. "If you can't trust a Strattlemeyer, who can you trust?" He let out an odd sort of a laugh, then his face turned hard and serious. "You do trust me, don't you?"

"We got no choice," Stuart said.

"That's not an answer, Sport. You trust me? You have to say you trust me or I stop right here." Bryce slowed the car even more.

"Fine, man, we trust you, we trust you, we totally fucking trust you."

"That's better."

Despite Stuart's compliance, Bryce did not speed up. Instead, he continued to slow and moved them to the side of the road. Stuart opened his mouth to say something and Mandy squeezed his thigh again to shush him. She didn't have a clue what was going on, but it made more sense to play it out at this point—for better or worse.

When the car stopped, Bryce turned around. "You two, quick, pants down."

"Wh…"

"Do it now." Bryce turned away. "We've only got a minute at best."

Mandy undid her dungarees and Stuart did the same, leaving denim puddled at their ankles and their bare asses on the vinyl seat. "I don't know what this is, but if these queers are trying to get their thrills from me, I'll bust their asses myself," Stuart whispered.

"No worries, Sport," Bryce said. "Letting you two in on the fun is all, but only this part of it. Sex isn't on the agenda. At least not in any combination of us and you two."

"Bryce," Troy said. "They've pulled over."

"Perfect. Be ready, everyone." Mandy saw his glance move to the side view mirror. "Three…two…one…Bingo! Backseat, moon them! Now!"

Mandy and Stuart hopped up on their haunches and shoved their bare asses in the rear window. This was something they had plenty of experience doing back in Bascombe.

Bryce laid on the horn and peeled out once again. Mandy and Stuart practically fell out of the window. When they turned to look back, they joined in the laughter coming from the front. Behind them, way behind them, sat the Ford in a nasty-looking patch of mud. Mandy laughed harder at the sight of the three men, all up to their ankles in mud and clearly swearing profusely. She pulled up and fastened her dungarees long before her giggles subsided.

Once the McBrayers were out of sight, Bryce slowed down to a normal driving pace. "Maybe some time in the mud will teach them how to treat others," he said.

"Maybe," Troy said. "But I doubt it."

"Then we'll just have to keep teaching them, Troy Boy."

They turned on the radio and for about a half-hour, the foursome sang along with whatever song played. Stuart was the only one with a decent singing voice, but it was a good time. This was how our high school years should have felt, Mandy thought. Maybe she and Stuart would have finished school, had anybody given a good goddamn about their happiness.

A good goddamn. That was one of her father's favorite expressions. There was so much her father didn't give a good goddamn about, especially when it came to her. He didn't give a good goddamn about her being laughed at for wearing Linda's hand-me-down clothing when they were nowhere near the same body shape. Or that her mattress was so worn, it was more springs than cushion. Or that her bedroom window had so many cracks that winter winds came in more easily than summer sunshine. That he spanked her harder than he did Linda and much more often than he did Craig. And he didn't give a good goddamn that Craig ripped the head and paws off her favorite teddy bear, the only thing she ever loved in that house, because blue was a boy color and not a girl's. She hugged Blue a little tighter and closed her eyes, singing louder to drown out her tears.

At some point, she must have dozed off because Stuart's gentle nudge awoke her. "Angel, the guys figure we're far enough out of Lakeport to get some chow. You hungry?"

"Sure."

The car pulled to a stop at a red light that seemingly had no reason to exist. "So," Bryce said, "lunch is your treat, right, Sport? As a thanks for the getaway ride."

"Sure," Stuart said, the look on his face saying he was ready to be done with these two.

"Good choice. Oh, and Stuart?"

"Yo."

"You might want to pull those pants back up. Too much temptation might cost you your virtue and your sweet wife her future fulfillment." Stuart blushed and did them up faster than when her parents came home sooner than expected.

"We're about ten miles outside of Legion," Troy said. "If I remember right, that diner with the really good fried chicken is there."

"Sounds good to me," Bryce said.

"Do they have a decent used car lot?" Stuart asked.

Bryce inhaled loudly and his shoulders slumped. "Really, Stu? You ready to get rid of us now that you got your needs taken care of?" He shook his head. "Such a typical man."

Mandy couldn't help but laugh at the haughty way Bryce said this and she jumped in to speak before Stuart could. "No, no, it's not that. It's just that, well—"

"Relax, doll. Don't get your blonde beauty into an uproar," he said to Mandy. "I was just playing. Of course, you two want to be alone and do married people things. It's natural, I've heard. We need to get back to our beloved Waterport anyway. So here's the plan. Lunch, get us gas to get back home, and you're on your own in scenic Legion, Illinois, home of the Legion High Legends, who we beat every year in football, the Legion Glass Works, and some outstanding fried chicken. Sound good?"

"Works," Stuart answered.

Within minutes, the foursome rolled into a typical enough Midwestern town. The expected stores, Rexall, Woolworth's, Sears and Penney's catalogue stores, and a batch of little local ones, lined either side of the main street, which was, appropriately enough, named Main Street. A little place called Patty's Patterns caught her eye. The prettiest dress hung in the window and she knew it would look perfect on her. And it was royal blue, Stuey's favorite color. She'd have to get down there and get it to wear on their first night in wherever their first home would be.

A block and a half from the dress shop, Bryce pulled to a stop in front of Daly's Courthouse Diner. "This is the place," Bryce announced. "But don't get out just yet. I've got a business deal to discuss."

Next to Mandy, Stuart stiffened. "What's that?"

"To really establish a new life, you're going to need more than ID's. For a hundred dollars each, I can give you a reasonably authentic birth certificate and Social Security card. You'd be set for life with these." He smiled. "For life."

Mandy looked to Stuart, who nodded. She pulled two hundred dollars from her pocketbook and handed it to the law student. As soon as he had the money in hand, Troy hopped out of the passenger seat and went to the trunk. He was back in less than a minute with a manila envelope. He thrust it into Stuart's hand. "Check them over."

Stuart pulled out the papers and he and Mandy looked them over. As promised, there were two birth certificates, one for Stuart from someplace in Illinois and one for Mandy—Joan Amanda—from Michigan.

Why not? she thought. The new Mandy had to be from somewhere. There were also two Social Security cards and something extra—an Illinois wedding license joining them as Mr. and Mrs. Stuart Mason.

Mandy looked up from the certificate to Bryce. "Call it a wedding present from Troy and me," he said. "No charge."

"When we get out of this car, I am going to give you two the biggest hugs," she told him.

"We'll be satisfied with a kiss. Kiss for the bride," he clarified, obviously for Stuart's benefit. "It might be best if we part company now, though, before we're seen together by too many people and word gets back to the McBrayers or the police. Protects all four of us."

"Makes sense to me," Stuart said.

"So," Bryce said, "if you'll give us ten bucks for our lunches and gas..."

All four got out of the car. Mandy opened her pocketbook and slipped out a ten while Stuart muttered something about not-so-free wedding presents.

Bryce took the bill and shoved it in his pocket. "It's been a hell of a good time," he said. "And a real pleasure knowing both of you. You two be careful out there in the big bad world. If you ever need an almost-lawyer or two, my phone number is on the envelope."

Both men kissed Mandy on the cheek and shook Stuart's hand, then headed into the diner.

"Never woulda took them two for queers," Stuart said.

"Seems like such a waste," Mandy said absently, her mind on the dress shop up the street.

Stuart wheeled around and stood in front of her. "A waste, huh?" His tone was forced light and Mandy snapped back to the moment. "You didn't seem to waste anything on our wedding night."

She rapped him lightly on the side of the head. "Don't be silly. All I meant was they're nice boys, that's all. You're the only man I've ever wanted. But yeah, I didn't figure guys like them to be that way either. There just ain't that many of them out there and you can usually pick them pretty easy."

Stuart opened the diner door for her. "You'd be surprised. I can name five guys from school who play for the wrong team, and two are football players." He led her to a booth in the back corner.

As soon as they were seated, Mandy said, "Jimmy Wendler?"

"What about him?"

"You said two of the five were football players. I'm guessing Jimmy is one of them."

"Wendler's a kicker. Nobody cares about their puny little bodies anyways. He's never gonna get any action except with his right hand." Stuart handed Mandy a laminated menu. "Figure out what you want for lunch and don't worry anymore about the five."

"I'm not worried." Mandy held the menu in front of her face. "Just curious."

A hand on top of her menu surprised Mandy and she allowed it to be pushed down. "Pretty little thing like you shouldn't be covering your face with your menu or anything else."

Mandy looked up into the face of the sweetest grandmotherly type woman she'd ever seen. Her nametag identified her as Ellie, and she definitely looked like an Ellie. "Thank you," Mandy said shyly.

"You folks new to Legion?" the waitress asked.

"We might be," Stuart said without looking up from his menu.

Ellie raised a penciled eyebrow. "We were just married," Mandy said. "Our folks didn't approve, so we're looking for a place to settle down."

"Far enough away from your folks to establish your independence, but close enough to be like home." Ellie reached behind her and pulled up a chair. "Me and Ervin, God rest his soul, did the same thing more years ago than I care to think about." She raised her arm and flashed two fingers at an equally old guy in the kitchen, who scowled at her in return. She waved him off and returned her attention to the young couple.

"Your boss don't look too happy," Mandy said. "You ain't gonna get in trouble talking to us, are you?"

Ellie boomed a hooting old lady laugh from somewhere between her ample breasts and belly. "Daly? He can't lose me. I'm the best waitress he ever had. Besides," she lowered her voice to a conspiring tone, "his car's been known to be parked overnight in my driveway since a respectable time after Erwin's passing."

Mandy knew from the expression on Stuart's face he wanted to make a wise guy comment but, luckily for him, he held back. Mandy liked this old lady and didn't want Stuart to hurt her feelings. Instead, he said, "I'm ready to order."

Ellie pshawed that idea. "You already have. Two fried chicken dinners. Best in the Midwest. Eat all your vegetables and I'll give you free dessert."

Stuart shrugged. Mandy knew he'd try to shove the vegetable, whatever it was, onto her plate and take some of her chicken in return. She'd let him. Whatever it took to keep him happy.

"So, when did you two get into town?" Ellie asked.

"Little bit ago. Decided to stop when our car decided to," Stuart said. "We really need to get a better one."

Ellie laid her plump, freckled hand on Stuart's arm. "When you're done with your dinners, you two get on down the street to Dahlke's. I've known Justin Dahlke since he was filling his diapers. Tell him I sent you and he'll give you a deal on something reliable."

"Where is this place?" Stuart asked.

"Just up the road. Right behind Murphy's Market. And you best go today to find one. Can't sell no cars in Illinois on a Sunday." A bell dinged from somewhere and Ellie stood, her chair loudly scraping the green linoleum. "Looks like food's up for them two that came in before you. Look like nice enough boys." She turned to Stuart. "Best treat this one right or one of them might steal her clean away." She was gone before Stuart could answer.

"Now that we got a quiet minute, let's figure out what we're gonna do," Stuart said. "Stay here, move on, whatever we decide, we gotta start by getting us a car or we can't do nothing."

"Maybe we should look around, see if this is someplace we could live. We never really talked about where we'd go." Mandy's eye caught sight of a Mother Meatworthy's sign on the diner wall. "All I know is I wanted out of Wisconsin and we made it."

Stuart reached across the table and took her hand in his. "We've got time to figure it out, Angel. Right now, we live for today and for ourselves." He smiled that crooked smile that always melted her. "Now, what do you want to do?"

The royal blue dress commanded attention in Mandy's consciousness. "Why don't we do this? You go to the car lot. I wouldn't be much good there anyway. I'll walk around here, see if it feels like a place that's right for us." A vision of Stuart's eyes when he saw her in that dress teased her. "With our suitcase in the Buick, we're going to need plenty of stuff. I'm sure you don't want to be there while I pick up female doodads and whatnots."

"Uh...no."

"So, I'll get a head start on our shopping and by the time you pick me up, I'll know if this is the right town for us." She cocked her head in what she knew was a seductive way to him. "Maybe I'll even pick up something special just for you."

His smile told her the look hit the bull's eye. "Deal," he said. He sniffed at his armpit. "I don't think this shirt will make another day."

Ellie showed up with plates of chicken for the two of them. "Here ya go, kids. Two of Daly's finest chicken dinners. Folks live here in Legion just to come here for our dinners." She placed the food before them. "Plenty of opportunities here for a smart young couple." She waddled away toward a man just entering the diner.

"If you love this town half as much as she does, we'll be living here a long time." Stuart dug his fork into a massive mountain of gravy-smothered mashed potatoes.

Mandy bit into a crunchy-coated fried chicken leg and immediately agreed with Ellie that it was the best she ever ate. Granted, there was no way her mother would even attempt to make fried chicken. Chicken dinner in the Heinemann household meant rubbery chunks of dried-out bird parts, usually accompanied by a shriveled overbaked potato and whatever vegetables were on the marked down for quick sale table at Bebee's Thriftymart.

If they stayed, maybe Ellie would help Mandy learn to cook like this so she could keep Stuey happy. She never pictured herself as a housewife, but now that she was married and there was talk of a Stuey Junior, the idea was beginning to appeal to her. Some, anyway. At any rate, it would be far better than living with her family in Bascombe, Wisconsin.

The twosome ate in silence for a while. Stuart, Mandy figured, was probably thinking about their car. This would be the first car Stuart ever owned and that was a huge thing for a guy. Her brother could spend hours looking at pictures of cars and boring the family talking about his dream machine, despite being a couple years short of driving age.

As long as the car was reliable, unlike her father's, and looked slick, which was definitely not like her father's rust bucket, then she didn't care what he bought. Instead of spending her time worrying about that, she pulled a pen from her purse and a paper napkin from the dispenser. "Shopping list," she said in response to Stuart's puzzled expression. "We need everything."

Clothes—shirts, pants, socks, under wear. Mandy giggled a little. She'd never bought guy's underwear before and wasn't quite sure how to. She knew her brother's came in a package from Woolworth's or ordered from Ward's, but she had no idea about styles. Stuart's were always a dingy, baggy white, just like her little brother's. Her father's, which he often wore about the house and yard without pants over the top of them, were either striped or polka-dotted. Mandy wondered if Stuart would prefer some variety. He probably wouldn't care, she decided, so she'd choose for him when she got to the store, whatever store she ended up at.

Just as she scooped up the last of her vegetables, Mandy saw Bryce Strattlemeyer and Troy Baldwin head for the door. She gave them a smile and a discreet wave, which they returned before turning away to pay their bill. "Such nice guys," she said. "We were real lucky to run into them."

Stuart glanced over his shoulder. "Oh. Yeah. For homos they're a couple of regular guys. Least as regular as their kind can be." He tore into a chicken breast and continued talking around his chewing. "Let's just hope they keep their word and don't say nothing to nobody. I got a feeling we're almost home free, Angel."

Home. Free. These had always been just words to Mandy, and now they were within reach as real things, hers and Stuart's for the taking. Mandy always knew escaping Wisconsin would be her salvation. And she was right. She knew in her heart of hearts she was where she was meant to be, and it felt so good.

Ellie waddled back to their table. "So, kids, was the chicken everything I promised?"

"And more," Mandy said with more enthusiasm than even she expected.

"For sure," Stuart added, a small belch escaping with his words. Mandy added Life Savers to the list.

"Was it good enough to convince you to stay here in Legion?" Mandy couldn't tell for sure, but she thought there was a hint of hope in Ellie's voice. "We need more good people."

"If anything could convince us," Stuart said in his full-flirt mode, the tone that could make Mandy do anything, including robbing a bank on their wedding day, "this chicken is it."

Ellie's wide smile threatened to push her ears from her head. She fished in her apron pocket and pulled out a slip of paper. "My address," she said. "It's not the Taj Mahal, but it's clean. Two rooms, kitchen, and bath over my garage. Has a private entrance. Help with the yardwork and you'll be surprised how reasonable the rent will be." She left before either of them could answer.

"Well," Stuart said, "if we stay, it looks like we got a place to live." He looked thoughtful for a brief second. "Angel, what's this Taushma Hall thing?"

"I dunno," Mandy answered. "Some government building in Poland or something. I think Hitler lived there maybe. I know we talked about it in history once."

"I don't wanna live in Hitler's house. I left Mussolini's when I married you."

Mandy felt her heart blush. "You're sweet. I might be wrong about the Hitler thing anyway. It could have been the king of Poland or somebody."

"Well, my Polack queen, your Polack king needs to buy a car and you need to do some shopping, so we should pay our bill and make like geese and get the flock out of here."

Mandy slipped a ten dollar bill out of her purse so Stuart wouldn't have to pull out his overstuffed wallet in front of the entire diner. She kissed him by the cash register and said she'd be somewhere on Main Street for him to pick her up when the car purchase was done.

She almost made it outside when Ellie stopped her for a hug. "I can't help it," Ellie told her. "You two are just the sweetest looking couple I've seen in a long time. Make sure your young man don't lose my address. It's just a few blocks from here."

"He can't lose it. The paper's in my pocketbook."

Ellie hooted. "Honey, that's the best way. Let the menfolk think they're in charge and know that it's the women who get things done. I'll let you get on your way so you'll be home in time for supper. My Ervin's whole family gets together for Sunday supper. I'm hostessing this month, so you'll get to meet them all tomorrow."

She scooted Mandy out the door, the tinkling of the little bell fading as the door closed behind her.

Mandy made a left out of the diner toward where she thought the Woolworth's was. Might as well get the basics like socks and underwear out of the way first. She saw the five and dime across the street and started in that direction, then remembered Patty's Patterns and the beautiful blue dress. In the distance, she saw the clock above some bank; a few minutes before two. She'd have plenty of time to get the dress later. For now, she'd stick to the original plan and do the boring things first.

The store was busy when she entered and she was glad for that. It gave her a chance to locate the underwear and socks and face a new question. She had absolutely no idea what size Stuart wore. It looked like she had only four choices ranging from small to extra-large, so she decided Stuey was a medium. He wasn't football player-sized, but he was bigger than skinny, so medium made the most sense. She decided to get him one package for now, in case she misjudged, and picked up a couple packages for herself. Men's socks were easier. White and one size fits all. She added a package of t-shirts for Stuey and some bras for herself to the basket, then headed to the candy counter for the Life Savers, adding a few minor things along the way.

As the clerk rang up her purchases, Mandy asked her if there was a place in town to get a decent travel bag. The woman directed her to a little luggage shop on Main Street, "right next door to Patty's." Mandy took this as a sign from God that she was meant to have that blue dress. First, though, regular clothes for herself and Stuey. She stepped out of the store and scanned the street for anyplace that would sell slacks and blouses and men's shirts. She spotted a sign for a place called Taylor's Toggery that had a sign in the shape of a tie and decided to start there.

The window display, male and female mannequins posed to be playing volleyball in dungarees and various shirts, told her she found the right place. Toggery, she figured, must be Illinoisian for clothes. Illinois people, her parents always said, were weird, so they would have different words for normal things. Weird or not, she was starting to like it here.

As in Woolworth's, Mandy had no clue what size of anything to buy for Stuart. The clerk, a man she was certain would have been more pleased waiting on guys like Bryce and Troy than on a girl, helped her take a guess at what would fit her husband and promised that if he guessed wrong, he'd give her all of her money back or she could bring Stuart in for a proper fit. Somehow, she didn't think Stuey would enjoy that.

After a quick stop to pick up a suitcase, Mandy finally found herself in Patty's Patterns. That dress was going to be hers. No matter what it cost. She stepped over toward the display window, but was stopped by an older woman with a beehive hairdo large enough for all of the bees in North America. She looked to Mandy like a well-dressed cafeteria lady without the hairnet.

"May I help you, young lady," the cafeteria woman said in a disinterested voice.

Mandy realized that she probably didn't look so hot in two-day old clothes that had bits of Lake Michigan shore and forest stuck on them, and almost talked herself out of answering. But she so wanted that dress. "I was interested in that blue number in the window," she said, trying to match the woman's tone.

"Oh. That is a lovely frock." She looked Mandy up and down. "I'm not sure it would be right for you."

Before Mandy could come up with a smart-ass reply, Stuart burst into the store. "Got us a car," he whispered. "Buy whatever you're getting and let's go. We need to get the hell out of here."

"Wh…"

He kissed her on the lips and said as softly as possible, "I'll tell you later. Just move." He took her suitcase with the earlier purchases inside and sat near the display window.

Mandy turned her attention back to the woman. "About the dress?"

"Oh. Yes." She looked like she was about to be forced to drink sewer water. "We make some of our garments individually here at Patty's Patterns, and that dress is one of them." She launched into an explanation of how she believed every woman, "regardless of class or stature," deserved at least one dress made especially for them. Over by the door, she could see Stuart, obviously antsy, start pacing and muttering. "After we take your measurements, it will be at least a week before the frock will be ready. Will that be acceptable?"

Out of the corner of her eye, Mandy saw Stuart shake his head slightly and hook a thumb toward the door. No blue dress. She wanted to cry. That dress was for her Stuart to appreciate her in, and that dream was gone for some reason. Still, she thanked the saleswoman and turned about. "Are you ready, dear?" she asked in order to keep up appearances.

"Absolutely." Stuart went to the front door and held it open for her. "We'll be back," he told the woman, making Mandy's heart skip a beat.

On the sidewalk, Stuart led Mandy to a huge tank of a car. "Oldsmobile," he said. "Ain't she a beaut?" He unlocked the back and deposited the suitcase on the seat. "Didn't cost too much. We'll still have cash to live on." He held the passenger door for her. "M'lady. Your chariot."

Mandy hesitated. This scene would have been so much better if she had the dress. Her dress. The dress that clearly would never be hers. "Amanda Joan Masamoli," Stuart said. "Do me a favor."

"What?"

"Open the suitcase and show me what you got."

"What?"

"Show me what you got in there."

"Just stuff," she said, but she opened the rear door and unlatched the suitcase. There, laying on top, was the blue dress. Mandy stole a quick glance at the window, where a mannequin stood in the altogether, then back at the dress, then at Stuart. "How did you..."

"Later. Right now, get in the car. We got to fly."

His words were clipped, but his expression was all little boy eager to please. And she was pleased. Very. She got in their car and Stuart sped away from the curb and into the light traffic of Main Street, Legion, Illinois.

"Angel, we almost had a big problem on our hands," Stuart said.

"What's that?"

"I went to the car place like that waitress said. Guy there asked how I heard about him and I told him and he said, 'That Mrs. McBrayer, she sends me more business than anybody.' I kept my face straight as can be, but I knew right then it was get a car and get the hell out of there, which is just what I did."

"Mrs. McBrayer," Mandy repeated slowly.

"Yeah. I don't know if she's related to the bozos who chased us this morning, but I ain't planning on waiting around to find out. Name's not that normal."

"She seemed so nice."

"Yeah, I know, but we can't take chances now. We're too close to free, Angel. Too close to totally free."

They were outside of Legion by this time and headed Mandy didn't know where. She was no good with directions to begin with and didn't know her north from her south. Somehow, leaving Legion behind made her feel a little less sure of their future. Legion just felt so right to her. What could possibly be next?

"Do you think they knew?" Stuart said suddenly.

"Do I think who knew what?"

"Do you think those two homos knew that that waitress is a McBrayer?"

Mandy took a second to make sense out of Stuart's question. "Bryce and Troy? Nah. They'd be taking too big a chance, knowing the McBrayers want to beat them up for being...what they are."

"Yeah, maybe, but I don't know. I think they're both nuts. Look at the way they played chicken with those McBrayers. The way they slowed down like they was gonna turn us over to them for the reward. Just makes sense to me either way."

"I see what you mean, but I don't see them doing that. They were too nice."

They lapsed back into silence then, Mandy staring out the window at the seemingly endless forests broken only by the occasional small town. With Legion no longer a possibility, all of the questions she had before came rushing back, flooding her brain and heart. Where were they going to end up? What place in this world was right for them? Were they going to end up back in Wisconsin? No, they wouldn't end up in Wisconsin. She'd rather die than go back now.

"How far do you want to go tonight?" Mandy asked, not looking forward to long hours in the car again.

"Well, after missing out last night, I figured we'd go all the way a couple times at least."

Mandy playfully slapped Stuart on the back of the head. "You know what I meant. Driving, silly. How far?"

"Not too far. When we find the right place, we'll know it. In any case, we stop whenever we find sup..."

A thumping noise interrupted Stuart. "Stuey," Mandy said, "is there something wrong with the car?"

"I don't know. Cars ain't my specialty, Angel, but it didn't feel like anything in the engine." Stuart flipped on the radio. The soft voice of Doris Day seeking her Secret Love filled the interior of the car. Just as the music changed to the McGuire Sisters Sincerely crooning about love, the thumping came again, three quick knocks, a dull, pounding sound.

"Stuey, I don't like that sound."

"Me neither, Angel. It wasn't doing that back at the car lot at all."

More knocks, six of them, beat out a rapid staccato. "Stuey, did that sound like it came from under the hood to you? I swear it was in the back."

Stuart pulled off to the road's shoulder. "I thought the same thing. Must be something loose or rattling around in the trunk. Easy fix." He opened his door. "You stay here and be gorgeous. I'll have this taken care of in a shake or two."

Despite Stuart's instructions, Mandy got out of the Olds. They were only about two hours or so out of Legion, but she was convinced her legs and body were as stiff as if they'd be on the road for days.

"Holy shit!"

Stuart's voice squeaking like it did in junior high startled the lethargy out of her and she rushed to the back of the car, where Stuart stood staring down at the open trunk. She looked down and saw not a loose item, but a grubby little blond kid, around nine or ten, she guessed, looking as petrified and confused as Stuart did. "Wh-wh-who is that?" she asked.

"Fuck if I know."

"Stuart, language," she admonished.

"Sorry," he mumbled. "It's just that, well, you know...Kid, who are you and how did you get in our trunk?"

"C-c-can I g-get out, please?"

"You better believe it." Stuart lifted the boy out and stood him between himself and Mandy. "Now, spill it."

Mandy caught Stuart's eye and gave what she hoped was a 'be gentle' look. He nodded. "Whattya say we go sit in the car and get out of the sun? After being in the trunk, you got to be hot," she suggested. The scent of sweaty, grimy kid left no doubt.

The boy silently turned about and headed toward the passenger side. He opened the door and climbed into the backseat without saying a word. "Stuey," Mandy whispered. "What are we going to do?"

"Play it by ear right now, I guess. One thing I know for sure. There ain't no way we can take him back to Legion. Not with McBrayers roaming around."

"Stuey, we got to. It's got to be his home."

"We'll figure something out. But we got to think about us too. We can't let that little bast—" His grip suddenly tightened on her arm for a split second before loosening into a loving squeeze. His face and voice softened. "We'll protect him, Angel. You just watch and see how safe that kid is gonna be till we get him home."

Mandy chalked up Stuart's sudden change of heart to his nice side taking over. He'd be a great father one day, and that day would be soon. Mandy just knew it. She rubbed her belly. One day soon, but not too soon, she hoped. She sat in the backseat next to the boy, who still looked ready to cry. "Hey, little guy," she said. "You're not in trouble. Really. What's your name?"

The kid studied his scruffy, mud-crusted sneakers as if the answer was somewhere in the worn out Keds logo. Eventually, he schnurfled out, "Denny."

"Denny. That's a great name," Mandy said in her best sweet-girl voice. "Can you look up at us, Denny?"

Slowly, the boy raised his head and looked at Mandy, studiously avoiding eye contact with Stuart. "I'm sorry," he said. "I was playing hide and seek with Harry and George and Wally and the guys and I saw this trunk open and thought if I hid there, the bigger guys wouldn't find me right away and I wouldn't have been the first one found and gotten the business from the other guys for being the first one found again and all." Denny took as deep a breath as his snot-clustered nose would allow. "And somebody closed the trunk."

"That might have been the car seller," Stuart said. "He'd shown me the trunk and left it open. I remember cause he said he should close that after we looked under the hood."

"It was probably Gary McBrayer. He was playing too and he would do that." There was more than a little bitterness in Denny's voice.

"Another McBrayer," Mandy said. "How many of these McBrayer people are there?"

"About a bazillion," Denny said, wiping his nose on his sleeve. "They're everywhere. And none of them are good."

Stuart shook his head. "Kid, you—and us—we got a problem. You need to get home and there's no way we can just go back to Legion. Definitely not with a bazillion McBrayers all together at that waitress' house. The McBrayers we know aren't very nice."

"Ain't none of them are. I told you that."

"Still, we need to figure out what to do with you."

The boy looked hurt by Stuart's words, and even though Mandy knew Stuey wasn't trying to scare him or upset him, she wished he said it differently. There was something going on with this kid, something he wasn't going to just spill. Mandy was sure if they tried to bring Denny back to Legion, he would run. She didn't believe for a second he got trapped in the car while playing hide and seek. If he had, he would have pounded to get out immediately. No, this boy needed to get away from something in that town, and Mandy definitely understood that need.

There was an uncomfortable silence in the car. There was no way they could keep this boy with them. He belonged to somebody, after all. She knew Stuart knew too. This was going to be a complicated problem. She hated to think of Ellie sitting in her house, surrounded by a bazillion mean-ass McBrayers, waiting for her and Stuart to come and make a family she could love, but Stuart was right. There was no way they could go back to Legion, Illinois, let alone settle anywhere near there. Yet this boy needed to be home, not in the middle of nowhere with them.

"So, what do we do?" Stuart asked.

"Well, we can't turn around and head into the McBrayer nest," Mandy said. "And we can't head to Wisconsin."

"Why not?" Denny asked.

Mandy looked down at him, hoping her smile looked reasonably sympathetic. She definitely was. "You know how you feel about Legion?"

"Yeah."

"That's how we feel about Wisconsin."

"Oh." Denny clearly wanted to ask more questions, but kept quiet. Mandy figured he thought that asking questions would invite being asked questions.

"Stuey, if we keep going this way, where would we end up?" Mandy asked.

Denny started laughing. "Stuey? Like beef stewy?"

"Stuart," Stuart corrected him. "Only Mandy can call me Stuey. You got it?"

The laughter ceased. "Yes, sir." The kid looked suddenly scared.

"That's better." He turned his attention to Mandy. "Now, if we keep heading how we're going, we'll be in Iowa—" He looked at his watch. "Sometime tomorrow morning. If we head south, we'll end up in Kentucky or Tennessee or something, but it'll take longer than Iowa. If we go around Chicago, then we'll be in Indiana or Michigan."

"Chicago!" Mandy and Denny said in unison.

"As good a direction as any," Stuart said. "But we got to get rolling to do that."

The adults slipped out of the back seat and Mandy caught Stuart's eye. "What are we gonna do with him?" she asked over the roof of the car.

"We'll figure it out. There's always Greyhound if nothing else."

"Stuey, he can't ride alone on a bus. They wouldn't let him."

"Then we'll come up with something. Get in. We really got to get moving."

They got into the front seat and Stuart started the Olds. "Next stop, uh...somewhere for supper and a hotel for the night. We could all use showers." He took an exaggerated whiff. "Especially the boy beast."

"I don't have any clothes to change into," Denny said.

"Next town we come to, we can take you to a store to get a few things," Mandy said. "I didn't finish my own shopping back in Legion anyways." Mandy twisted around so she could lean over into the back seat. "So, Denny, how old are you? Ten?" She unsuccessfully tried to swat Stuart's hand from her rear end.

"I'm twelve," he said, his tone saying he was underestimated many times before.

"Sorry. Anybody looks younger alone in the backseat of a big car like this. We'll be stopping for supper eventually. What's your favorite food?"

The boy's face lit up. "I can have whatever I want?"

"If we can find a place that has it. Now, what's your favorite?"

"Hot dogs!"

Stuart laughed. "I like this kid. We'll find us a drive in for chili-cheese dogs and onion rings and fries."

Mandy sat back down. She hoped there were enough Life Savers in the suitcase to get them through the night, if Denny was anything like his father—Father? Where the hell did that come from? Mandy and Stuart were eight when this kid was born. No way God sent him to them to be their Stuey Junior. Did He? Could they really keep Denny with them? Would that be weird? No weirder than robbing a bank on the day they got married. Would Stuart let her keep him? Would he want to? Would Denny want to stay? Was it meant to be? Well, the boy had her blond hair and blue eyes and Stuey's, well, man and boy could both use a bath. That was one thing they had in common. Mandy stifled a giggle. She closed her eyes and let the rhythm of the tires on the pavement lull her into a soft, contented sleep.

She was awakened by Stuart and Denny singing with the radio. "Earth Angel" was playing and she was as comfortable as she had ever been in her entire life. Her husband and her boy were serenading her with the family song. She corrected herself. Her song. From her husband. She couldn't let her heart get ahead of her brain. After all, somebody was missing this boy back in Legion. They weren't going to be able to keep him with them. They didn't even know if the police were still looking for them, let alone him.

Still, Denny didn't seem to be missing anyone back in his hometown. What was his story? Was he just ignored or beaten down to nothing by his parents, like she was? Or did someone hurt him the way Stuey's father hurt him? She opened her eyes and smiled at them both. They harmonized well, if off-key, and sounded for all the world like they belonged together. If she had to be stuck in a car for hours again, this was a great way to be stuck. When the time was right, they'd find a family song. Together.

"Kid, listen, it ain't 'in my behind.' It's 'earth angel, earth angel, would you be mine,'" Stuart said. "That there is a special song and it's got to be sung just right. It's for a special lady."

"Are you sure that's the words? My friends always sing it the way

I did."

"Your friends are little nerds. You're better than that."

Mandy closed her eyes again. It was a weird father-son type moment, but Stuey did say she was a special lady and he was sharing some wisdom with Denny about how to treat a woman, so there was that. She closed her eyes again as her men performed a duet of "The Ballad of Davy Crockett." That one fit the boys perfectly.

"Time now for the top of the hour news update," said the announcer on the radio. "Our top story at six o'clock concerns the search for a missing boy from the town of Legion. Sources say that Dennis Wilfred Underwood was last seen playing with some friends near Dahlke's Car Lot in downtown Legion and disappeared shortly after breaking away from the group. The boy's mother, Ruth Underwood, says Dennis has been known to slip away from his friends and go off on his own, but that he always returns long before his five-thirty suppertime. The boy is described as twelve years old, blond, on the small side at four foot-six inches tall, weighing around seventy pounds."

"Sixty-three," Denny said.

"Shush," Mandy scolded.

"He was last seen wearing a blue and white striped shirt, cuffed dungarees, and black sneakers. Police say there was only one stranger in the area at the time, a nondescript man purchasing a car at Dahlke's, but Dahlke vouched for there being no one in the car when the man pulled away. If anyone has any information on the whereabouts of Dennis Wilfred Underwood, they are encouraged to call the Legion Police Department. Meanwhile, in Washington—"

Stuart snapped the radio off. "Well, kid, they know you're missing."

"Yeah."

"And they still got no clue what I look like," Stuart said to Mandy.

Mandy turned around and knelt on the front seat so she could see Denny. "It doesn't sound to me like you were playing hide and seek with anybody."

"Yeah, kid," Stuart said. "What gives?"

"Other guys were wrong. That's what we were doing. At least, that's what I thought we were doing." Denny sounded sincere, but Mandy wasn't so sure.

She tried to look him in the eye, but he kept his glance low. "Denny, no matter what got you into our trunk, it don't matter. What matters is what we do with you now. You've got a mother looking for you and—"

Denny looked up at her. "What?"

"Your shirt is solid red."

"So?"

"Kid, even I can figure this one out. The radio guy said you were last seen wearing a blue and white striped shirt. Blue and white striped ain't red, far as I know."

Denny again shifted his gaze to his lap. "Mama wouldn't know what I was wearing. I get out of the house as fast as I can before she wakes up. Besides, she don't pay me no attention anyways. She guessed what I had on, probably. I only got three other shirts and those were handed down from my brothers. There is a blue and white one."

Hand-me-downs. God, how Mandy hated hand-me-downs. "Well, the rest of the description, cuffed dungarees and black sneakers, was right, so we're going to have to be careful."

"Pants are too long. My brothers are a lot bigger than me."

Mandy could relate to that too. Linda's build was different than Mandy's, more stick than curve, and she was always having to adjust her clothing to make it work. She figured Denny, like her, probably never had new things of his own in his entire life.

After a short silence, Stuart snorted a laugh. "Hey, kid, I gotta know" he said. "Wilfred? What kind of a middle name is Wilfred?"

"I dunno, Beef Stuey." Denny giggled.

"Wilfred, I warned you about that. Only Mandy calls me Stuey."

"Ain't nobody calls me Wilfred." Denny's voice cracked a little when he said this, but he tried to sound as tough as his sixty-three pounds would allow. "Well, what's your middle name?"

Out of the corner of her eye, Mandy saw Stuart tense. He probably regretted bringing the question up. "Don't matter," Stuart said.

"Come on. Give. What is it?"

"Gaylord," Stuart said softly, throwing Denny into a fit of giggles again. "And there ain't nothing funny about that." There was a hint of lightheartedness in Stuey's tone. "Tell you what. You forget the Gaylord and the Beef Stewy crap, I'll forget the Wilfred. Deal?"

"Deal."

Mandy heard a rumble from Denny's stomach. "How long has it been since you've eaten?"

"Breakfast. Half a bowl of Cheerios. They was kinda stale, so I didn't finish."

Mandy turned to Stuart. "Any idea how long until we are going to be in a town?"

"Sign back a ways said five miles. Probably more like two or three now."

"You think you'll make it another two miles, Denny?"

He grinned. "Sure."

Mandy sat back down and turned the radio on again, hoping for another song her guys could sing together. Unfortunately, the next song was "Mr. Sandman" and neither of them really knew the lyrics, but they gave it a shot anyway. Though painful to listen to, the laughter in the car wasn't.

Before long, the Olds entered a smallish-looking town proclaimed to be *Fountain Grove, Illinois—The Small Town with the Big Heart.* It looked like any other small town to Mandy, but she was grateful to see it. Her brain, legs, and bladder all fought over who needed to be out of the car first.

"I see a hotdog stand up ahead," Stuart said. "Still game for chili-cheese dogs, little buddy?"

"Hell—heck, yeah," Denny answered.

"Stuey, I know we're all starved, but maybe we should find a hotel first," Mandy suggested. "I think we can all stand to stop for the night."

Despite the hunger protestations from the backseat, Stuart drove past the hotdog stand for another couple of blocks before finding the Grovesway Motor Court.

"Look," Stuart said after parking the car. "The sign says they have television."

"Cool," Mandy and Denny both said. Mandy had seen glimpses of television, but never had the opportunity to really watch it, so this was definitely the place she wanted to stay. "Why don't you go get us a room and we'll figure out after what we're doing from there. I'll stay here with Denny."

Stuart hopped out of the car and went into the motel office. "Denny," Mandy said, "you know what you did wasn't real smart? You didn't know when you'd be getting out of that car or even that you'd be out of Legion."

"I know, but I just had to try. I just had to."

"Do you want to talk about why?"

Denny shook his head. "Just didn't want to be there."

Mandy let it drop, for now. The boy was scared and confused and hungry, three things that wouldn't make it easy for him to relax enough to trust her. Instead, she decided to try to earn his trust. "For now, you can stay with us. None of us have any choice and you seem like a decent enough kid."

"I do my best."

"I know you do. So, here's the deal. If we let you stay with us for a while, you're going to have to live by our rules, do what we say, and be a good boy."

Denny started to say something, but Mandy kept talking.

"We won't ever beat you and we'll treat you like you should be treated. Both me and Stuart were twelve once. We get it." Boy, do we get it, Mandy thought. "We're going to have to get you some clothes and stuff. Do you know what size you wear of anything?"

"No."

Stuart came out of the office, whistling and jingling a hotel key. He stuck his head in Mandy's window. "Get our stuff, Angel. We're in room nine, on the far end. We'll get all moved in and get some hot dogs in our boy." Stuart rubbed his stomach. "Pappy could go for a dog or four himself."

Pappy? Stuart never called himself that before. Our boy? As always, their thoughts were in sync. "I think, while you two are chowing down, I'm going to run down the street and see if any stores are open, get our boy here something else to wear."

"New stuff?" Denny asked.

"Absolutely. And I'll be back in time to join you guys for your second helping. But first, I'll need sizes, so you two go in the bathroom so Stuey can read the tags in your clothes."

After the bathroom door closed, Mandy sat on the end of one of the beds and made a quick mental shopping list. Pants or shorts, shirts, underwear, socks, stuff to keep Denny occupied in the car and in the hotel room, stuff to keep her occupied, toiletries, and more Life Savers. And maybe a nice gift for the whole family.

A few minutes later, the guys were out. Stuart handed her a sloppily scrawled list. Mandy made sure she could read it all before they went back to the car. Stuart drove the block to the business district and dropped Mandy off in front of something called Horvath's Discount City, where a large sign proclaimed the store carried *Everything for the Entire Family...and More.*

The store was brightly lit and bigger than any Mandy ever saw before. As soon as the door closed behind her, a man with too big a smile and a very pink carnation in his lapel stopped her. "Young lady, would you like to apply for a Horvath Super Card, hmm? If you meet certain requirements, you'll be able to shop tonight and pay later. Can't beat that, hmm?"

Mandy had no idea what the guy was talking about, but pay later sounded good to her, so she let Mr. Carnation lead her to a table and chair. "Are you a married lady, hmm?"

"Yes."

"Excellent. Fill out the form, let me see your identification, and you can charge up to fifty dollars' worth of merchandise. Quite the deal, hmm?"

"Umm...quite," Mandy said.

She pulled out her new ID and showed it to the man, then quickly filled out the form, copying the address information on the card and listing Stuart as having his own business. In a way it was true. In a way. When she gave Mr. Carnation the paperwork, he explained that once her information was verified, which took about two weeks, her credit limit could be as high as two hundred dollars. She indicated she understood and stood. The man scanned the form, wrote some things on it, then thrust a card in her hand. "Congratulations, Mrs. Mason. Here is your temporary card to use today for up to fifty dollars. Welcome to the Horvath credit family. Enjoy your shopping, hmm." He shot out his hand.

Mandy shook his hand with as little contact as possible and quickly scooted away from the guy with the creepy, leering smile and into the store. She spotted the boys' wear department and pulled out the list of sizes. She quickly filled a shopping cart—the store was big enough to have shopping carts—with three changes of clothes for Denny, as well as pajamas for all of them and more jeans for Stuart and herself. She added some books, activity pads and toys for Denny and picked up two of her favorite board games, Sorry and Parcheesi, for them all to share. On an impulse, she added three baseball caps, one for each of them, and some baseball cards for the boys to have something to talk about.

She brought her purchases to a row of cash registers at the front of the store and when everything was rung up, Mandy was amazed that the cashier simply took the card Mr. Carnation gave her, had her sign a slip of paper, and packed up her merchandise with a cheery, "Have a nice night."

Outside of the store, Mandy realized she forgot to grab the room key from Stuart, so she would have to carry all of her purchases three blocks to the hot dog stand. She offered up a silent thank you for the flatness of Fountain Grove's main street and started to walk. She'd barely gone a quarter of a block when a police car rolled up beside her. There was no way Mr. Carnation could have checked up on her background already. Or was there?

"Evening, Miss," the policeman on the passenger side said. "Quite a load you've got there. Have far to go?"

"J-just to the hot dog stand. My husband's there and I forgot to tell him how much I needed to buy. Silly me," she added with a self-deprecating giggle.

"Hop in," he said. "We'll save you some trouble."

The last thing Mandy wanted to do was ride up to Stuart in the back of a police car, but what choice did she have? If she turned down the kind offer, it would look suspicious. So, with a deep breath, she gathered up her courage and her bags and accepted.

The policeman jumped out of the car and opened the back door for her. "It's a slow night," he said, "so any courtesies we can offer, especially for a pretty, young lady, we do. It just isn't right to watch you struggle with all of that stuff and for us to drive on by." His smile revealed slightly uneven teeth, but seemed sincere. Mandy settled her purchases on the seat and got in.

The driver cop spoke for the first time. "Are you new in Fountain Grove? I don't know everybody here, but I never forget the pretty ones."

"Just passing through. We stopped for the night at the motor court. I forgot to get the key so I'm having to bring everything to where my husband is." So far, no lies. Easy to keep track of what's what when you stick to the truth, Sister Mary Dymphna told her and Stuart when she caught them playing I'll-show-you-mine-if-you-show-me-yours. Of course, Sister also warned them both about the evils of premarital sex when they were just six years old, so they didn't pay much attention to her advice.

"It's our pleasure, ma'am," the driver answered. "It's a constable's sworn duty to protect all citizens and visitors to our environs." He punctuated his comment with a wink and they took off.

Constable? Environs? One thing was sure. If she ended up becoming an Illinoisan, she was going to have to learn this new language. She already had three words, constable, environs, and toggery, so that was a start. Why didn't they teach this in school if Wisconsin was just over the border?

Mandy's heart sank when, instead of just pulling into the parking lot, the officers parked. "Suppertime for us," the cop who spoke to her first told her. "Even policemen have to eat. Would you like a hand with your things?"

She saw Stuart walking toward them and shook her head. "No," she said, maybe a hair too quickly. "Thank you, but my husband's coming over now." Mandy fished around in her shopping bags and brought Denny's new ball cap to the top before opening her door.

"As you wish. He looks like he can handle it." He sounded a little disappointed.

"Angel—"

"Hi, sweetie. I'm afraid I bought more than I should have. These nice officers gave me a ride when they saw me carrying all these things down the street. Wasn't that nice of them?"

"Sure." Stuart took two of the bags. "Very." He rushed off toward a table, clearly trying to block the officers' view of Denny.

Mandy took her time getting the remainder of her bundles, letting her rear end sway from the open door, which she hoped kept the cops' attention away from Stuart and Denny until, she hoped, Stuart found the hat. The boy's clothes didn't match the description the police had, but his blond hair was definitely too easy to spot.

She pulled herself out of the car and tried to thank the officers for their time, but they wouldn't hear of it. They insisted on helping her with her remaining bags and she knew it would look funny if she protested too much, so she had to let them. Mandy prayed they would just dump the stuff and go, and hoped she could steer them to do just that. "How much time do you get for supper?" she asked.

"Half-hour," the driver replied. "If we're lucky."

"Then why don't I just take these things and let you get your food. You must be starving."

Mandy glanced over at Stuart and saw him putting the ball cap on Denny's head. Thank God he figured out her hint. She breathed a little easier.

"Already heading to your table," the first cop said. "Only take a second." He speeded up a little and Mandy had to rush to keep up.

A few seconds later, both cops and Mandy arrived at the table, which was covered with hotdog wrappers and a couple of empty Coke bottles. "Hello, sweetheart," she said, kissing Stuart on the cheek.

"Hello, Angel," Stuart said. "And hello, officers. Thank you for helping my wife."

"A pleasure, sir. And who's this little guy?"

No one spoke for a moment, then Mandy broke the silence. "William, the nice policeman is talking to you. Can you thank him for helping your aunt with all these bundles?"

Denny hesitated for just a split second, then said, "Thank you for helping my aunt. We didn't know she was gonna buy so much junk." He never looked up from his hotdog.

"Where you folks headed?" the cop who first helped Mandy asked.

"Downstate," Mandy said, giving the by now familiar story about visiting an aunt and uncle, but changed the reason for the trip. "Got to bring this little fella back home. We've had a grand two weeks, but they have to be missing him."

The driver cop looked from Mandy to Denny to Stuart. Before he could say anything, though, his partner reminded him that they did need to eat and get back on duty. The two policemen wished the threesome a good evening and good night's stay in Fountain Grove and went to the window to place their orders. The cop who asked all the questions looked over his shoulder at them twice before he and his partner reached the order window.

"What the hell was that about?" Stuart asked once the officers were out of sight.

Mandy shrugged. "Nothing, Stuey. They saw me carrying all these bags and pulled over and asked if they could help. There was no way I could say no without looking suspicious, so I had to accept."

"I think maybe we should get out of here, just in case," Stuart said. "We'll blow this town off and go somewheres else. Maybe find an all-night diner to make sure you get some food."

From where she sat, Mandy could see the Grovesway Motor Court and the illuminated *Television in Every Room* sign. "Stuart, I'm hungry. I'm getting something to eat, then I'm going to the hotel room we've already paid for and I'm going to look at the television. There's no reason for those officers to suspect us of anything."

"What about William here?" Stuart looked at Denny. "And I haven't forgotten your middle name is Wilfred, not William, by the way."

"Whatever you say, Beef Stuey."

"What about him?" Mandy asked.

Stuart pulled the bill of the ball cap over Denny's eyes. "Don't call me Beef Stuey. And, Angel, about him, just cause nobody's probably looking for us round here doesn't mean nobody's looking for this dust mite. I didn't like the way that one cop was looking at us like something was wrong. We got to be careful now that we got this miniature person with us."

"Stuart, we have a believable story and I don't think either cop was looking at us in any special way. And I'm hungry." She said these last three words slowly to add emphasis.

She didn't realize how hungry she even was until she saw the empty wrappers on the table. Scared as she was Stuart might be right about the policemen, she didn't want to live her life in fear. They'd gotten this far, they'd get farther.

"Fine." He stood up. "Let's get you some food."

"I don't need help, Stuey. Stay here with Denny."

Stuart took her arm. "No, I want to help you." He pulled her toward the order window the police officers were just leaving.

"Do you think it's a good idea to leave Denny there alone?" Mandy whispered.

Stuart stopped walking. "I wanted to get away from him for a minute to tell you something."

"What's wrong?"

"Angel, when I had that boy in the bathroom and he took his shirt off so I could check the tag, I saw it."

"Saw what?"

"Somebody's been beating the shit out of that kid. And it ain't being done by other kids. Tell you the truth, I'm pretty sure he wanted me to see it."

Mandy thought Stuart looked ready to cry, if Stuart was one to cry, that was, which he wasn't. "We got to protect him," she said.

Stuart nodded. "We can't let him get sent back to people who hit him. That...that's no life for a boy." He spat on the ground. "Not for our boy," he mumbled barely loud enough for Mandy to hear. "Not like we can take him back to that town anyways. I still think," he said in a louder whisper, "that we need to get out of here. Do you think you can hold off on eating until later? We'll find another hotel a town or two from here and figure out what to do with him later."

"What about the hotel here? If the cops check, they'll know we checked in and out today and that'll look more suspicious."

Stuart spat again. "That's true. Dammit, we got to protect that kid." His tone made it clear the decision was made.

"I can wait until we find someplace else to eat and sleep, Stuey," Mandy said.

He used the words 'our boy' and he was right. They had to protect him. "We could just leave the key on the bed with a note saying we left real early before the office opened," she suggested. "There's no reason for nobody to come to that room before morning."

Stuart took her face in his hands and kissed her forehead. "Angel, you're a genius."

While the three of them cleaned up the table and packed Mandy's purchases away in the car, Mandy thought about the first time she saw marks and bruises on Stuey's back. Second grade swim lessons at St. Andrew's. The school required the lessons and would allow no exceptions, boys separated from the girls, of course. Stuart faked illness to get out of it when he heard the plans for the afternoon, going so far as to vomit on Sister Mary Clementine's classroom floor. No soap, even with his lunch all over the place. When the Bascombe PD found him hiding out and delivered him to the school, Father Paul, the boys' gym teacher, ordered him to strip naked with the rest of the boys. Stuart had no problem losing his pants, but clung tightly to his shirt. Father, already upset over having his precise planning interrupted, ripped Stuart's white button-down shirt right over his head, revealing cuts and bruises he ignored and no one else missed.

Mandy not only saw all the boys in her class naked that day, through a hole in the lavatory wall, she also saw the warzone that was Stuart's back. She made him tell her where the bruises came from despite his reluctance to do so. Every time new welts and bruises appeared in the intervening years, Mandy vowed she and Stuart would find a way to escape Bascombe. Now they had, and they had the added bonus of saving Denny along the way.

After leaving the key and a note explaining their early departure, the trio was on the road again. Once they were settled and moving, Denny, who'd been quiet since Mandy showed up with the police, piped up from the backseat. "You sure you ain't hungry, Aunt Mandy?"

Mandy could hear the "is it okay if I call you Aunt Mandy?" in his voice.

It was. "I'm fine, sweetie. Don't worry about me." Mandy's stomach grumbled in protest at this lie. "I'll eat when we stop for the night."

"Aw, what was wrong with the place we was gonna stay at?"

"Your bed was too close to ours, kid," Stuart said. "Your snoring woulda kept us up all night."

"Hey, I don't snore, but I bet you do, Beef St—Uncle Stuart."

"Pulled that one back just in time, didn't you, kid?" Stuart laughed and reached for the radio knob. "Let's get some tunes going here."

Instead of music, the car filled with crowd sounds and talking. "Hey, yeah!" Denny said. "The Cubs are playing in St. Louis tonight. Leave it there, Uncle Stuey—Stuart. Please?"

Stuart took his hand away from the dial. "Love me a good ball game. We're gonna get along great. But one thing."

"What's that?"

"Uncle Stuart sounds too formal and fancy to me. Uncle Stuey's fine. But no Beef and no Gaylord. You got it, Wilfred? You screw up and I'll make you into a Winifred with my bare hands."

"Yessir...Uncle Stuey."

Mandy patted Stuart on the thigh and snuggled into him. "That was a nice thing you just done," she said low enough for Denny not to hear over the broadcast.

"What? I like baseball."

"You know what I mean, Uncle Stuey."

"Yeah, well, was no big deal."

It was a big deal, Mandy knew, but she shut her yap about it. Stuart was her strong, silent man who didn't need glory when he did the right thing. Mandy glanced back at Denny, who was clearly immersed in the game, then whispered to Stuart, "I'm starving. Any clue when we'll hit a town?"

"Probably about fifteen minutes at least, Angel. Why don't you grab a little shuteye? It's been a pretty long day."

As soon as the words were out of Stuart's mouth, Mandy realized how welcome a catnap would be. She closed her eyes and let the rhythm of the car and the babble of the radio lull her into a contended near-sleep. She thought about the police back in Fountain Grove and decided Stuart was actually wrong. They didn't suspect anything about Denny being the kid missing from Legion. Of course, Denny wasn't that kid anymore. He was theirs, at least for now, and man and boy were her family and everything would be just fine from here on out. The three of them, and maybe some little Stueys and Mandys, would be a perfect set.

A sudden lurch nearly sent Mandy to the floor. "Sorry, Angel," Stuart said. "Traffic stopped sudden. Roadblock." He sounded nervous.

"Roadblock?" Just repeating the word tied her stomach in a knot and the thought of food flew from her mind. "Why? Do you think it's for us?"

"Nah. Why would people in Illinois care about a couple of Wisconsiners?" As he spoke, Stuart jerked his thumb toward the backseat, out of Denny's sight.

"What are we gonna do?" Mandy asked in a panicked whisper.

"Bluff," Stuart said. "And if that don't work—" Stuart brought his left hand up enough for Mandy to see his gun. "We bluff bigger."

"Stuey, no. We can't."

"We can. And we will." He put his hand back where Mandy couldn't see it, a move which brought her very little comfort. "Hey, kid. Keep your hat on and pretend to be asleep."

"Why?"

"Just shut your yap and do it."

Mandy heard shuffling in the backseat and knew Denny was doing as told. Good boy. Now if they could just get out of this without the gun.

Stuart rolled to a stop as directed by a state patrolman. "Evening, young man," the officer said with a yawn. "Where are you two headed tonight?"

"Downstate, we're—"

"Going to visit my aunt." Mandy held up her left hand. "We were recently married and she couldn't make the wedding because she was in the hospital and my folks have been watching her son. She's never even met my husband and, well, she's my favorite aunt and all and it was cheaper and safer to drive little William back than putting him on a train alone."

The patrolman also held up his hand. "I won't hold you up for long when you're on such an important mission. We're just looking for a missing boy. Blond, around twelve. Any chance you've seen him?" He never even glanced into the back seat.

"Nope," Stuart said. "Only kid we've seen is the one we've got."

"Afraid not," Mandy added. "But we really haven't stopped except for gas and such. We'll keep an eye out for him though."

"Damn kid...uh, sorry, ma'am. Darn kid probably fell asleep by a stream or something and is back home with his folks by now anyway and has no clue he's making me work a double shift." He tipped his hat. "You folks have a good evening now." He yawned again and waved them through.

Stuart rolled them away slow and steady, every inch the good young man who followed the rules of the road at all times. Once they were far enough away, he whooped. "That was so easy! Damn fool didn't even look in the back. And kid, you did great. No snoring or nothing."

Denny leaned forward, forcing Mandy to move her head to the right. "I'm not stupid. I know when to play possum. And..." He brought his right arm up to reveal he held Mandy's cute little gun. "...I was ready if things went bad, just like you, Uncle Stuey."

"Give me that!" Stuart said, making a grab for the weapon. He had to reach up and behind himself to get at Denny's hand and smacked the gun rather than taking it, causing the thing to fire loud enough to rattle Mandy's eardrums. Mandy saw rather than heard her side of the windshield shatter and glass rain down onto her and the front seat. She let out an involuntary scream and gripped Stuart tighter as he pulled to a stop on the side of the road.

"Wowee." said Denny softly, punctuating it with a small whistle. "Wouldya look at that."

"I am," said Stuart. Mandy didn't like the flatness of his tone. "Angel, look back and see if those cops back there heard that."

"That was really cool!"

"Was it?" asked Stuart.

Mandy recognized the monotone question as Stuart's father style, a question asked just before a punishment was doled out to Stuart or his brother. She hated seeing Stuart acting like Mr. Masamoli in any way.

"No one heard, Stuey. Nobody's coming."

Oblivious to Stuart's anger, Denny said, "Hell—heck yeah, that was cool! I never fired no real gun before." He reached over to the far end of the seat and picked up the little pistol.

"And you ain't ever gonna again till you're old enough," Stuart said, snatching the gun from the boy's hand.

Reality must have finally settled into Denny's brain. He lowered his arm, sat back, and meekly said, "Yes, sir."

"That's better." Stuart turned his attention to Mandy, who relaxed once her husband looked her way rather than glaring at Denny. "Are you okay, Angel?" he asked.

"I—I think so. More shook than anything. But no matter if the next town has an open restaurant or not, we better stop. We can't go too far like this." She waved her hand at the windshield.

"Why don't you scoot out and sit in the back with Billy the Kid," Stuart suggested. "You can't be sitting in a pile of glass chunks like that." He opened his door and slid out of her way.

Carefully, Mandy got out of the Oldsmobile and stopped herself just before she tried to brush the glass pieces from her clothes. Instead, she shook them off as best she could and gave herself a quick inspection for cuts, not that she'd be able to see them well in the growing darkness, then climbed into the backseat.

She gave Denny what she hoped was a kind, but stern motherly look. "As for you, young man, when we find a hotel, it's bath and bed for you. No fooling around."

"But it's not even nine o'clock yet. And it's summer. And it's Saturday. And—"

"Enough," Stuart said. "If you're gonna stay with us, you're gonna remember who's in charge."

"Yes, sir. Yes, ma'am." The boy sounded resigned to his fate.

Mandy put her arm around his shoulders. "Doesn't mean we don't like you, Denny. We just need and want you to be a good boy." She gave him a one-armed squeeze.

"Ow!" Denny exclaimed.

Mandy pulled away from him as if he were suddenly electrified. When she did, she saw why the boy cried out. A small piece of glass was embedded in the back of his neck. She reached for her pocketbook for a handkerchief and realized that not only did Denny find her gun in there, but he saw the large amount of cash she carried as well. She'd have to find a way to tell him to keep quiet about it. She managed to get the glass out of his flesh and sat him back into her handkerchief to stop the bleeding. He tried to protest, but with the wind rushing in where the windshield used to be, she couldn't hear him. Probably better for him at the moment, she thought.

About ten minutes later, the trio passed a sign welcoming them to *Brownstalk, Illinois—A Piece of Prairie Paradise.* Just beyond the sign was a very small business district with, thank God, a motel with an open restaurant attached. Stuart brought the Olds to a stop right at the door of the Starlight Chalet.

Chalet, Mandy thought, must be another one of those foreign Illinois words she'd have to learn. If the owner hadn't put the translation, motel, in big letters on the sign, they would have driven straight past. Hopefully, when they did pick a place to live, it would be someplace where people spoke plain American.

She let Stuart see to checking them in. While he was gone, Mandy had Denny sit forward and she pulled the handkerchief from his neck. The bleeding had stopped and the cut was pretty small. "You'll live," she told him.

"Unless Stuart kills me."

"Uncle Stuey," Mandy said.

"Sure."

Gently, she pushed Denny back and took his face in her hands. "Listen. That was a stupid thing you did, okay? Your punishment is straight to bed once we're in our room. We all do stupid things and we all pay for them. That doesn't mean we're not gonna take care of you still. You and us, we're a team, and we are the team leaders. You have to do a better job of listening. Got it?"

"Got it." Denny gently wrestled away from Mandy's hold. "Aunt Mandy."

Mandy was glad to see Stuart coming back before the subject of the money could come up. She wasn't ready to explain that to the boy. At the restaurant, they were greeted by an older woman who didn't appear to have a functioning smile. Other than the scowl, the hostess reminded Mandy of Ellie at the diner back in Legion, and she felt guilty all over again. This woman's bobbing nametag identified her as Gert. She never made eye contact with any of them while she seated them and handed out menus.

"Welcome to the Brownstalker Restaurant," she recited automatically. "Special tonight was pot roast, but it's gone, so ignore that. Urban's closing the kitchen in fifteen minutes, so I'd pick something fast, I was you." She turned and walked away.

"She seems sweet," Stuart said.

"No kiddin'," Denny added.

"Best order fast, Angel, or you'll end up with whatever's scraped off the grill."

Gert was back, order pad in hand. "You folks ready to order?"

Mandy opened the menu. Her eyes landed on hamburgers and decided that would be good enough. "Burger, well done, fries, and a Coke," she said.

"Pop's shut down for the night," Gert groused.

"Fine. Chocolate malt then."

Gert grumbled something Mandy didn't catch and started to lumber away, but Stuart stopped her. "Make it three malts, and three slices of chocolate cream pie."

The waitress rolled her eyes. "I'll see what we got left." She took off before anyone could stop her again.

"This is great," Denny said. "Pie and a malt before bed. Never been allowed to do that before. I'm liking this."

"That reminds me," Mandy said, "of something I'm not liking. If I ever catch you in my pocketbook again, young man, you're in more trouble than one night of going to bed early. You got it?"

"Yes, ma'am."

Mandy decided against talking about the money just then. Instead, she looked at Stuart. "When the waitress comes back, ask her if there's an auto body shop around here. We got to get a new windshield."

"Me? Ask Gargantuan? Why me?"

"I think she likes you," Mandy teased. "I saw how she looked at you."

"Yeah. Like she'd like to roast me alive and have me for dinner."

"Sorry, kitchen closes in fifteen minutes and Beef Stuey takes longer than that," Denny said through giggles.

"Kid—" Stuart abruptly cut off his retort when Gert showed up with a tray.

"One burger with fries," she said, banging a plate in front of Mandy. "Three chocolate malts." Three bangs. "And three pieces of chocolate cream pie." One bang of a dinner plate with three slices of runny pie on it. "Small plates is washed up and locked away for the night. I didn't think you'd mind sharing. Here's your bill. Bring it up and pay when you're through. We close in twenty minutes."

"Miss?" Stuart said, earning a fresh crooked-toothed scowl.

"Yeah?"

"There an auto body shop in this town?"

"Yeah. Other side of the building. Opens at seven. Ask for Urban."

"Isn't Urban the cook here?"

Gert looked in no mood to bother with details. "Yeah, my Urban works real hard."

Mandy watched the waitress return to the kitchen before speaking. "I think Urban uses what's leftover on the grease rack to cook the fries. These things are nasty."

"How can you mess up fries?" Stuart and Denny both took one, sampled them, and spit them into napkins. "Damn, that ought to be a crime," Stuart said.

"Yeah, damn." Denny paused. "I mean, darn."

"Eat your pie," Stuart said. "And shut your pie-hole."

Denny shoveled in a huge forkful of pie and made a face like he'd just been kissed in front of everybody by the ugliest girl in his class. "Uncle Stuey, don't eat it," he whispered. "It's a trap."

As Mandy knew he would, Stuart had to take the dare. His look said he regretted it instantly. "Dessert's out," he declared.

Though the burger managed somehow to be both half-raw and dry, Mandy choked it down anyway, knowing breakfast would be a town away in the morning, if they could get the windshield fixed and the glass out of the front seat. If the rest of Brownstalk was as friendly and helpful as Gert, she didn't hold out much hope of leaving town soon.

Burger finished and fries and pie ignored, Stuart paid the bill and the trio left the Brownstalker for their room at the far end of the Starlight Chalet. Stuart unlocked the door and found the light switch and said, "Holy shit."

Denny squeezed between Mandy and Stuart to take a look. "Wowee! It looks like winter threw up in here."

Mandy couldn't disagree with the boy. Every wall, every surface of furniture, had hand-painted pictures of snowy mountain peaks with snow falling above them. The ceiling was the grayish blue with ominous clouds. The bedspreads matched the walls and Mandy wondered if the walls were painted to match the spreads or if the owner found bedding to match the walls. Even the dresser, night tables, and chairs were part of the freakish winter wonderland. "Hopefully, this will be the strangest place we ever stay," Mandy said.

"Is it me," Stuart said, "or is it really cold in here?"

"Freezing. Maybe the room has an air conditioning unit?"

"How the hell could we tell?"

"Hey, what's the Donner Party Expe...exped...ex...pe...whatever. What is it?" Denny asked, pointing to a scene near the bathroom door.

"Bunch of fools who like to have parties in blizzards, I guess," Stuart said. "Forget about that and help Aunt Mandy bring in the stuff from the car."

"Musta been a pretty crummy party. One guy and a bunch of skeletons. They got a fire and no food."

"It was Halloween, okay? Get moving."

In just a few minutes, the suitcase and the bags from the bargain store were on the bed Stuart claimed as his and Mandy's. "Okay," Mandy told the guys, "I want to get all of the new clothes in the suitcase. Until we get a second, we can use these bags for dirty laundry." She rummaged through bags until she found pajamas and underwear for Denny. She threw them to him and said, "Bath and to bed. Aunt Mandy doesn't forget."

Once the boy was in the shower, Mandy set about her task. "Angel, how come you only got one suitcase?" Stuart asked.

"All I could carry. We can get another later. We'll have to, now we got Denny with us."

Stuart sat next to Mandy. "Do you think we should keep him?"

"Stuey, you make him sound like a puppy who followed us home."

"I didn't mean to. But...can we? I kinda like the little brat."

"Of course we can keep him. We found him."

"Now you're making him sound like a puppy."

Mandy laughed. "Have you smelled him? He smells kind of doggish. He needs to stay under that shower a good, long time. Then we can keep him." She laughed again.

"I know I could use a shower myself," Stuart said. "Once the kid's out, what say we hop in there?"

Mandy stifled a yawn. "In front of Denny?"

"We ain't gonna invite him in to watch, Angel."

"I mean with him in the room."

"Angel, we're married. He's twelve. He's gotta have some clue what married people do. I'd bet he's heard all about it by now. When I was twelve, I knew a lot. You know that."

The yawn Mandy stifled burst forth. "Maybe tomorrow night. I'm for a quick shower and bed."

Stuart's hand slid up her thigh. "Bed's an even better idea," he said with a grin.

She pushed his hand back down to her knee. He immediately moved it back up. "I am definitely not doing that with Dennis in the same room," Mandy said. When she saw Stuart's face melt into a pout, she added, "At least not while he's awake."

The shower turned off and Stuart's hand slid back down again. "I hope he's a fast sleeper," Stuart said.

Mandy did too, but she didn't say it.

Instead, she reached for a pile of clothes she left out of the suitcase. "These are for you," she said, handing Stuart a pair of red plaid pajamas.

"I don't think so, Angel," Stuart said, pushing them back toward Mandy. "I ain't worn pjs since I was in a crib and I ain't starting now. I sleep in my shorts or nothing at all."

"Stuart, what about Dennis?"

"He's a boy. He knows what a guy looks like in his underwear. All he's gotta do is look down at himself."

The bathroom door opened and Denny came out in identical plaid pajamas. "Please, Stuey," Mandy whispered. "I bought a red nightie. We'll all match. Like a family."

The pajamas moved slowly back toward Stuart. "For tonight," he said. He stood up. "I'm gonna take my shower. You get the kid to bed. And kid, you best be snoring when I get out." He winked at Mandy.

Denny pulled back his spread and clambered into bed. "I don't snore," he said just before Stuart closed the bathroom door.

Mandy moved the suitcase off the bed and looked over at Denny. All alone in the full-sized bed and with the blanket pulled up to his chin, he looked even smaller than just small for his age. "Dennis," she said softly, "are you too big for a good night kiss?"

"I dunno," he answered. "Don't get them." The blanket did a poor job of hiding his smile.

She went to him and gave him an awkward but fulfilling hug and kissed him on the cheek. "From now on, you're getting one every night." She kissed him on the other cheek, marveling at how soft his skin was. She'd only have five or six years until stubble replaced soft, and she wasn't planning on missing out.

Denny yawned and turned on his side. "Goodnight, Aunt Mandy, and thank you." Once Mandy was settled on her own bed, he added, "I love you," in a barely audible whisper.

"Love you too, kiddlywink," she answered in just as soft a voice.

To her surprise, she realized she already truly did.

She was fighting sleep when Stuart came out of the bathroom. "Looks like I did pretty good on getting the right size," she said when she saw him in the pajamas.

"Not really a lucky guess. You've had your hands all over me plenty of times. Go take your shower quick. I'll be here waiting for you to measure me up again."

Though she knew Stuart was eager, Mandy took her time under the near-scalding shower. Bathroom time was precious in her family's house and hot water even more so. This, then, was a luxury she had to allow herself. Judging by how long Stuart's shower took, he did the same thing.

When she emerged a half-hour later in her new nightie, no underwear, her feet got entangled in something on the floor. She looked down and saw red plaid pajamas, boy-sized. A matching man-sized set was crumpled up at the foot of their bed. Both guys were sound asleep. Her mama, ignorant about most things, was right about one. Boys were sure strange creatures sometimes, no matter their age. She picked up the pajamas, folded them neatly and put them in the suitcase, and got into bed.

~ * ~

A loud moan startled Mandy out of a sound sleep and it took her a moment to get her bearings. Hotel. Somewhere, Illinois. Another moan. Stuart and Dennis. Were they okay? She reached her hand out for Stuart and found his shirtless stomach. "Stuey?" she said as softly as she could.

"Yeah, I hear it."

A third loud moan followed by what sounded like smacking filled the pitch-black room. "What is that?"

"Don't know." Stuart yawned. "But it best stop soon. We got a lot to do tomorrow."

After another couple of moans and odd smacks, the noises stopped as suddenly as they started. Mandy and Stuart snuggled under the blanket, Stuart's protective arm draped over Mandy's middle. Within a few minutes, Stuart was snoring lightly and Mandy was just drifting off to sleep when another moan, this one definitely higher in pitch, filled the room, punctuated this time by a loud knock.

"What the hell?" grumbled Stuart.

Moan. Knock.

"Stuey—"

Moan. Knock.

"What is that?"

Moan. Knock.

"It's two people screwing," came a little voice from the other bed. "My folks do it all the time. Sometimes even together."

"Told you the kid was smart," Stuart said over the noise.

The moaning and banging increased in intensity until Mandy couldn't take it anymore. She made Stuart bang on the wall several times, to which he added a yelled, "Shut up in there!"

"Shit! My wife!" came a male voice.

"Urban, don't stop," was the protested reply.

"Urban?" Mandy started to laugh.

"That jackass thinks I moo like that troll of a waitress," Stuart said. "I oughta go over and kick his ass for him."

"Beef Stuey's a cow! Beef Stuey's a cow!"

Stuart flipped on the light and pointed at Denny. "And you're gonna be creamed Wilfred on toast if you don't cut it out."

Despite being momentarily blinded by the sudden flood of light, Mandy got out of bed and stumbled to the window in time to see a naked man retreating across the gravel parking lot into the darkness beyond. "Show's over, you two. Let's get back to bed. We'll have to get an early start in the morning." She snapped off the light, went to her side of the bed, and climbed in.

Before the lamp went out, Mandy caught a glimpse of the bruises and marks on Denny's bare back for the first time. With that image in her head, Mandy couldn't get back to sleep as easily as she thought she would. While man and boy snored and breathed, Mandy thought back on Stuart's many hurts at the hands of his father. She had no clue how many times over the last fourteen years she saw that aftermath. Now she saved him from that and, together, they saved Denny, and now they would never face that again. Life was near perfect. Once they found a place to live, it would be completely perfect. She yawned and pressed into Stuart. Life couldn't get much better than this.

Sunday

A pounding at the door startled Mandy back to the living. Hints of sunlight at the edges of the window drapes told her it was at least morning again. Before she could gather her thoughts, another pounding, followed by a growl that sounded something like "Hrrzbrrzig," shook the room.

"What the hell is that?" Stuart grumbled.

"S-sounds like a mad bear," Denny squeaked.

Stuart rolled out of bed. "I doubt there's one out there, but there's gonna be one in here if they don't knock that shit off." He went to the door.

"Stuey, you only got underwear on!"

"I don't give a shit." Stuart flung the door open wide. "What?"

Despite the strong glow of sunshine, Mandy could see the bulk of Gert in the doorway. "I said, housekeeping. Time to clean up after you folks."

Stuart rubbed his eyes. "What time is it?"

"Half-past eight." She tried to squeeze in the room past Stuart.

Stuart stood his ground. "We got the room paid for till eleven and we might need another night, so you're gonna have to come back."

"You ain't staying here another night. Not after last night."

"Huh?"

"All the noise you two were making last night kept the honeymooners two rooms over up all night cause of all the ruckus." Gert looked Stuart up and down. "Don't surprise me none. You never heard of pajamas and a robe, young man?"

"Thought I'd give you a thrill. And so you know, we were sleeping last night. Nothing more."

"Uh-huh."

Stuart tried to close the door into Gert's bulk. "See ya at eleven sharp."

"Before I forget," Gert said, seemingly oblivious to the door smacking into her, "I told Urban you'd be coming about your car. I'd suggest you do it this morning while half the town's in church and the other half's having breakfast at the Brownstalker. Warn you, though, that Urban's in a foul mood. Didn't sleep none too good. See ya as soon as you're packed."

She turned and stomped away, leaving nearly-naked Stuart exposed to the motel parking lot.

"Stuart, close the door. Keep your secrets in here with me," Mandy scolded.

"Huh? Oh, yeah." Stuart closed the door and went back to the bed. "You know, Angel, I don't know if I'm more mad at that cow for waking us up so early and mooing at us about noise we weren't making or more amazed that so many people would want to eat at that tar pit we ate at last night.

"If King Kong's grandma is the type that lives here, it ain't no surprise," Denny said. "She's downright scary."

"Dennis! That's not nice, even if it is true," Mandy said. "Let's get dressed and get out of here. No matter what, this won't be our room tonight."

Thanks to Mandy's organizing of their things the evening before, the trio was dressed and packed in short order. "Why don't you two take the car over to the garage and see if they'll be able to do anything today and I'll get us checked out of here. I'd rather sit in shattered glass with wind blowing me in the face than spend another night in this place."

"Amen to that," Stuart said. He and Denny headed to the restaurant/body shop.

Mandy walked toward the motel office, stopping short at the door when she heard Gert's raised voice. "You two done stayed the night," she was saying when Mandy arrived. "You can't get a full refund when you didn't bother to complain until this morning. You used the room all night."

"You mean we stayed awake all night listening to animal rutting," a man's voice answered.

Mandy peeked in the door and saw a middle-aged couple dressed more for a funeral than a honeymoon. Both wore black and both had faces that looked like sucking lemons was their idea of a good time. Their honeymoon had to have been a huge joy.

"All night long, wall banging and vile moaning and cursing," the man said, pleading a clearly lost cause.

"And that female," the woman said. "Screaming vulgarities like a whore."

Mandy could hear the blush in her voice.

"And over and over yelling 'Urban, Urban, oh Urban' and all manner of filth aft—"

"Urban!" Gert's growl increased to an intensity that shook the building, and possibly the entire town. "Urban!"

The middle-aged couple darted out of the office so fast, Mandy wondered if Gert hadn't sprouted horns and a pitchfork. Mandy wouldn't put it past her, that was for sure. In their haste, one of the two dropped something on the ground. Rather than face Gert in her current state, she picked up the object. *Procreation with God, for God's Needs*. A religious tract. Figured.

After a few deep breaths to steel her courage, Mandy meekly stepped into the office, only to find it empty, a door on the other side still flapping from Gert's wrath. Outside, she heard a car take off, spewing gravel in its haste to leave the Starlight Chalet. The religious folks speeding to salvation, she decided.

Mandy debated going off in search of Stuart and settling up the bill later, but her eye was drawn to the hotel desk, where a cash box sat open and unattended. The other couple may not have received a refund, but she and Stuey would, and then some. Quickly, she emptied the contents into her pocketbook, added a couple of postcards for her collection, and started to leave. Then a last bit of inspiration struck and she left the religious tract with its proclamations of a guaranteed Hell for sinners in the void where the money had been. She decided she'd innocently come back later and give Gert some of her own cash back, blissfully ignorant of what the other couple did when they left the hotel in such a hurry. Stuart would be so proud of her. Hopefully, this would cover the cost of the windshield and make up for last night's horrible supper.

Mandy walked toward the Brownstalker and was surprised to find cars in every parking spot and in a vacant field across the street. Sure enough, the restaurant was jammed and it appeared there was a line of folks waiting to get in. A few men and boys gave her appreciative looks as she passed, but no one said anything more than hello or good morning and she quickly found herself on the other side of the building.

The mood was vastly different here. Stuart and Denny stood stock still against the wall outside the open garage door. Gert's voice boomed from within, picking up grease and venom as she berated a sliver of a man, the naked man from the middle of the night.

"And from now on, the only sticks you better be dipping for women will be to check their oil, not to rev their engines!" Mandy heard Gert yell as she approached.

Stuart furtively waved her over and pulled her against the wall. "Ain't safe around here, Angel," he said. "She's already chucked a couple of wrenches and a fender at him. Hell only knows what's coming next."

He no sooner spoke the words than a brick sailed through the doorway and shattered on the street beyond. "Pissed as she is," Stuart said, "if anything she throws connects, old Urby's a dead man."

"He'd be better off," Denny said.

"And another thing, Urban Flockhauser, if I ever, and I mean ever, catch you with that whore Mabel Whippet or any of them other tramps down at the Bowl and Tap, I will personally rip your balls off and put them through the grinder." Gert's threat was followed by a huge crash somewhere inside.

A moment later, Gert was outside and facing Mandy, Stuart, and Denny, who had his ball cap pulled down way low and was practically welded to Stuart's leg. "You poor children," she said in a surprisingly soft voice. "I'm so sorry I accused you so unjustly. Urban will have your car ready soon. The repair, the stay, and breakfast are all on him for the inconvenience he caused you. Follow me and I'll see that you get seated right away."

She led them to the back door of the restaurant and brought them to a table that was clearly just deserted by prior customers. Gert grabbed a dishtowel from a passing busboy, waved off a waitress who was heading toward the table with four lumberjack-looking men, and wiped crumbs and water rings from the Formica before allowing the trio to sit. "Again, I'm so sorry for what you've been through. Let me tell the chef to prepare three specials right away."

Mandy watched the waitress/maid/desk clerk head toward the kitchen and thought that, maybe, somewhere under that tough Gert shell was a soft-hearted Ellie trying to burst out. She almost felt guilty about taking the cash box money, then she remembered it was Urban's too and she felt much better.

"Hey, Angel," Stuart said. "See that waitress over there?" He pointed with his chin toward a woman with a tray of food emerging from the kitchen.

"What about her?"

"Who you think she looks more like, Humphrey Bogart or Edward G. Robinson?"

"I vote Frankenstein," Denny said.

"Stuey, you're teaching this boy bad things." Mandy giggled. "But I'd say the Wolfman. She's got five o'clock shadow and it's not even ten a.m."

The three were still laughing when the woman brought the food to the table. Up close, Mandy was certain she saw an Adam's apple. "Gert said I should bring ya this and take you back to the garage when you're done. She said she don't wanna see Urban no more today." She started placing plate after plate of food in front of them, plus juice, milk, and coffee. "If ya need anything else, just flag me down or ask somebody to get me. Name's Flora." She left them to their breakfast.

"Don't Flora mean flowers?" Denny asked.

"Not no more," Stuart answered.

Mandy laughed. "You two are terrible, you know that?" She took a tentative bite of the omelet placed before her. "But this...this is fantastic."

"Really?" Stuart and Denny asked simultaneously.

"Yeah. It's really good."

The guys both looked doubtful, but gave their eggs a try. "Holy crap," Stuart said. "They need to keep Urban out of the kitchen, and outta other places."

"No kiddin'," Denny said around a mouthful of food. Mandy doubted he understood all that Stuart meant.

They tore into their food with gusto. As they ate, Mandy watched her men. For being new to buying clothes for guys, she did pretty good. And the duo cleaned up okay too. Like all boys, they talked sports in a language she didn't bother to understand and for all the world they acted like they'd known each other forever, rather than for less than a day.

From somewhere deep in the recesses of her mind, she pulled out a phrase from a long-forgotten story. Kindred spirits. That's what they were, the three of them. They were a family now, yes, but they were something bigger, something deeper. You could hate your family, Mandy knew this firsthand, but she and Stuey, now she, Stuey and Denny, no way they could ever be like her parents and her.

"Earth to Mandy. Come in, Mandy." Stuart's voice and gentle nudge brought her back from her thoughts.

"Sorry," she said. "Lost in thought."

Stuart leaned his head to her ear and whispered, "Save those thoughts for tonight after the kid's asleep," he said. "I ain't missing out again."

She slapped his thigh under the table. "Looks like we polished every—"

At the counter, a man sat, obviously trying not to be obvious about staring at them. For a brief moment, their eyes locked and, to the guy's credit, he didn't guiltily look away. Mandy had a feeling she'd seen this guy somewhere, but she just couldn't place him. From his expression, Mandy wondered if he was thinking the same thing.

"Denny, boy, we lost transmission," Stuart was saying. "Mandy, Mandy, come back to Earth, Angel. Earth angel, will you be mine? My darling dear, love you all the time."

Stuart's transition from speaking to singing derailed Mandy's mental train. "Sorry again," she said. "Thought I saw somebody I know. But the only Illinois person I know is Denny."

"Oh, he's Illinnoying alright." Stuart laughed at his own pun. "Anyways, there's no food left, so I guess we're done here. Let's find that waitress and make like geese and get—"

"Going," Mandy finished for him. "Do you see Flora anywhere?"

Stuart pointed. "Over there at the counter, talking to the jasper in the old man hat."

Mandy looked over and saw Flora talking to the man who had been looking at her. The waitress shook her head vigorously and turned in their direction. Stuart waved her over.

"How were your breakfasts?" she asked when she arrived at the table.

"Great," Denny said.

"Good. I'm glad you liked it. Gert will be so pleased." Flora swiped a stray strand of hair from her forehead. "And we all have to please Gert, don't we?" she muttered. She brushed at the strand again. "Follow me and I'll take you back the way you come."

The group went back through the kitchen to the garage, where Urban stood as if he were waiting for them. "Flora, darlin, you take your pretty self back in before my dear wife misses you and I'll take care of these folks now, okay?" He gave Flora a pat on the ass and a wink. "And you later."

"Sure, Urban, honey." She headed back for the kitchen.

Urban wiped his hands on his grimy coveralls. "This way," he said. "Got your Oldsmobile right over here." The new windshield glinted in the bright summer sun. "Now, she ain't perfect. Din't have no Olds windshields around the place, but she'll hold and that's all she's got to do." He opened the passenger door. "Also done vacuumed out all that glass so you won't cut your shapely...self." He flashed Mandy a tobacco-stained smile and Mandy instinctively scooted sideways to avoid the grope she knew would come otherwise. Her stomach recoiled at the thought that she actually ate food prepared by those hands.

Mandy looked the front seat over carefully before sliding in, just in case Urban's vacuuming skills matched his handwashing and cooking skills. The guys went to the other side of the car and climbed in. Just as Stuart went to start the car, Gert burst out of the kitchen door. "Urban! Urban!" Her voice was a high-pitched screech rather than its usual growl. "We been robbed! Them damn Jesus people done robbed us!"

Urban said a hasty goodbye and ran to his wife. Stuart got the car going and headed them out onto the highway again. "At least that robbery's one thing we can't be blamed for," he said.

"Uh...Stuey?"

"Angel?"

Mandy pointed to her bag. "Yes, we can."

"Angel? You? Again?" He laughed. "And you called me a bad influence." He hit the gas.

Mandy started to laugh with him, but then caught sight of Denny out of the corner of her eye. He was laughing along with Stuart, but this wasn't funny or fun anymore. He already knew about the bank money. He knew about the guns. And now he knew about this. If he stayed with them, they were going to have to change their ways. If he didn't stay with them, they ran the risk of him telling somebody about this someday. Mandy and Stuart were going to have to have a serious talk with Denny, and they were going to have to have that talk soon.

Once they were out of Brownstalk, all they saw were trees, fields, and the occasional house. After about an hour, Denny yawned loudly. "I'm bored."

"Look out the window," Stuart said.

"I am. And I'm still bored."

"I'll turn on the radio for you. Kiddo, next time we stop, we'll get the stuff I bought out of the trunk. I forgot all about it this morning."

"Okay, Aunt Mandy. See if you can find a ballgame."

"Kid, there ain't no games at eleven-thirty in the morning, especially on Sunday. Music, news or God. Only choices you're gonna get."

"No news and no God."

Mandy worked her way through the dial until she found what he wanted and for fifteen minutes, the car was filled with music. At eleven, the station started a news broadcast and Denny groaned.

"Pipe down, kid. It's only a few minutes out of your life. You'll live."

"Good day," said the radio newscaster. "This morning's top story is a daring daylight robbery in Brownstalk. The popular Starlight Chalet

Motel, Brownstalker Restaurant, and Urban's Country Auto Body lost a week or more's worth of receipts to the robbers. The Plum County Sheriff's Department is on the lookout for a middle-aged couple, Ephraim Elijah Gideon and his wife, Delilah Damaris Gideon. We don't have a description of the couple yet, but Starlet Chalet owner Gert Flockhauser recalls overhearing the Gideons talk of the weekly meetings at the revival tent church, Genesis Reborn, which is a popular attraction over in Valhalla, and police are aiming their search efforts in that direction."

"Looks like you pulled it off, Angel."

Mandy felt a flush of pride mixed with shame and decided they would have to have that conversation with Denny sooner rather than later.

"Meanwhile, today in Legion, local authorities have called off the search for missing twelve-year old Dennis Wilfred Underwood after his mother found the boy's shirt just outside the culvert beneath the Illinois, Iowa, and Indiana tracks near Legion. Local police have warned citizens to stay away from the III tracks for years, but it appears young Dennis Wilfred Underwood willfully chose to ignore those warnings. A candlelight service will be held tonight for the Underwood family."

"I'm not willful," Denny complained. "And what's a culvert? And what's willful?"

"Cool your jets, kid. We wanna hear this."

"The Cubs are in action this afternoon against the Cardinals down in St. Louis and the Sox square off against the Yankees on the south side later today. The stock market will open—"

Stuart turned the radio off. "Well, kid, looks like we're stuck with you and your stink now."

There was no response from the back. When Mandy turned to talk to Denny, she saw him stretched out, his back to them, and his shoulders shaking slightly. He had to be crying, and Mandy was at a loss for words. She sat back in her seat.

Stuart reached over and put his right hand on her arm. "It'll be okay," he said softly.

Mandy wasn't sure if that was meant for him, for her, or for Denny, but she wasn't so sure he was right.

There were so many decisions to make and so many things to learn, and all of them were bigger with her and Stuart being responsible for Denny. She thought of the bruises on Denny's back and how that made her think that the two guys had more in common than Denny had with her. But learning the boy's mother faked her son's death to avoid having him around felt more like something her own useless parents would do. Denny really was a combination of Mandy and Stuart after all. He had the worst of all worlds. Now he'd have the best. She silently promised him that.

"Guys, for lunch, what do you say we try to pull together a picnic," Mandy suggested. "Maybe we can find us a nice park or playground."

The guys agreed with her idea and she set Denny to watching both sides of the car for any signs of an upcoming town. She turned the radio on again and the three went back to their mostly off-key harmonizing. Eventually, another welcoming sign came into view. This time, they were greeted by Valhalla, Illinois—*The Lord's Love in the Land of Lincoln.*

"That's a lot of L's," Denny said.

"An L of a lot," Stuart said, laughing as always at his own pun.

Within minutes, they found themselves surrounded by trailers and vans of food vendors and sellers of all sorts of things. All sorts of mostly religious things, Mandy realized. "This is where the people who they think stole the hotel money were coming. That revival meeting."

"Screw that," Stuart said. "Let's find the food we want and then find a place for the picnic."

After some discussion and Mandy's clincher comment that she wanted an edible burger, they settled on getting a sack of burgers and fries. They found a stand and Stuart parked, jumped out, and placed an order. He came back with three sacks and three bottles of Coke. "Lady said there's a park with a playground and a lake up ahead. All we have to do is drive past the big tent where that preacher guy will be and round the bend and we'll be on the other side of the lake from it. She also said that the afternoon service is in about an hour, so we might have the place to ourselves. She was trying to tell me we should eat fast and get back to get a good seat, but the hell with that."

As promised, just after the enormous tent was a bend in the road, then the park, playground and lake. Stuart parked the Olds in a spot just vacated by a Chevy and the three climbed out, each carrying some part of their lunch, and headed toward the water.

A well-dressed family was coming from the opposite direction. "Hello, brothers, sister. You folks are heading the wrong way. Reverend Pickering is delivering his afternoon sermon at the other end of the lake just like always."

Stuart held up his bag. "Lunch."

The man checked his watch. "You don't got much time, brother. You don't want to miss a blessed word of Reverend Pickering's sermon."

"I'm sure we don't," Mandy said, picking up her pace a little to both show the guy they would rush and to get away from him.

After a few furtive glances and judgmental looks, the crowd was past them and Mandy, Stuart and Dennis had this part of the lake to themselves. Mandy led them to a picnic table with a nice view of the water. "Can we dig in?" Denny asked. "I'm starved."

"Me too," Stuart said, opening his bag.

Mandy shook her head. "Guys, we just ate a huge breakfast a few hours ago. How starved can you be?"

Stuart pulled burgers out of the sack. "Driving all morning's hard work, Angel. Makes a guy hungry."

"Being bored in the backseat's hard, too," Denny said. "Besides, I'm growing. And I'm starved."

"You already said that. Stuey, feed this child before he passes out."

Stuart passed out the burgers and opened the Cokes and put Denny in charge of passing out the fries.

"Stuey," Mandy said, "if you got the burgers and Denny's got the fries, what's in here?" She held up the bag she carried.

"Dunno. Lady said it was a surprise. Maybe it's dessert."

Mandy opened the sack and looked inside. Then she reached in. "Mini Bibles," she said, holding one up. "A whole bunch of them."

"Give them to the kid. He can read them one by one when we hit the road so he won't be so bored."

"No thanks," Denny said around a mouthful of burger. "I read enough of that to last me a life and a half."

They sat in silence for a while, eating and watching the breeze slightly ripple the water's surface. Back in Bascombe, a picnic meant old

Mother Meatworthy's Canned Sausage on stale bread, wrapped in wax paper and thrown in a brown bag. It meant sitting on the bank of Kellnor Creek, called Smellmore Creek by Mandy, Stuart and their friends because of the thick green algae that blocked any view of the water beneath.

But this? This she could get used to real fast. The lake was big enough to be more than a puddle, but small enough for a leisurely lover's stroll around it. The breeze was gentle and refreshing. The trees provided plenty of shade with nice sunny patches of grass between. There were flowers and birds and music and—

Music? "Stuey, do you hear—"

"Yeah, I hear it. Must be coming from that big tent. Hey, kid, why don't ya do a dance for Aunt Mandy?"

"Yeah, right." Denny belched loudly. "I'm all done. Can I go look around a little?"

Stuart looked at Mandy, who said, "Sure, but stay nearby. There's plenty to look at right around here."

Denny took off toward the deserted playground. He was soon happily climbing on the monkey bars. Watching him, Stuart said, "I gotta admit, he's been pretty good for a boy cooped up in a car all morning."

"Yeah, he has. You know, I forgot I got him some puzzle books in that store yesterday. They're still in the trunk. Remind me to get them out later."

Stuart sat back. "I'm finished. How about you?"

"Couldn't eat another bite, and there's not another bite left even if I could."

"Let's go sit by the lake then. There's a little bench down there right at the water and we'll just have to turn around once in a while to keep an eye on the kid."

While Mandy cleaned up the mound of paper wrappings from their lunch and threw it and the bag of Bibles away, Stuart brought the three Coke bottles to the car. "Fifteen cents deposit is fifteen cents in our pocket," he explained when he came back.

Hand-in-hand, they walked down to the lakeside bench. The sun was nice and warm on her arms and Mandy wished she could sunbathe for a little bit. Instead, she said, "Stuey, I've been thinking."

"A thinking blonde is a dangerous blonde," he answered with a snicker. "What's up?"

"Denny. Since we're gonna keep him, we got a lot of stuff to consider."

"Like what?"

"Like making sure wherever we settle down has good schools. And making sure he goes."

"Yeah, one thing I'll always regret is not finishing school."

"Really?"

"No. I don't miss old Poppin-Snot one little bit. But maybe one day, we can both go to night school. Don't want the kid to be more educated than us."

"Still, we're responsible for him now and we're gonna do a better job than our folks did."

"Of course, Angel. Of course."

Out on the water, a duck Mandy was watching suddenly dove for something beneath the surface. "And we got to learn stuff about him."

"Like what?"

"What grade he's in, when's his birthday? Oh, and he's gonna need a new last name. He can't be Dennis Underwood anymore."

"No. But he can't lose the Wilfred. Got to have something to hold over his pointy little head."

Mandy laughed. "You're good with him, you know that? You're a natural dad."

"Maybe we should practice some baby-making tonight. We ain't for two nights now and this is our honeymoon."

She kissed him and said, "Stay focused on this a little longer, Stuey, and you'll get that later. I think we got a good story of Denny being my cousin. We look enough alike to pull it off. But we got to have charge of him since we won't be traveling forever. We can't always be taking him back home."

"Yeah, well, we'll kill off his parents. Least we can do after his real mom killed him off. Maybe we can get them two queers to make up a couple of death certificates for them and a birth one for the kid."

Mandy sighed. "We can't go all the way back to Waterport, Stuey.

Those McBrayers are looking for us and it's heading in the wrong direction."

"You don't get me, Angel. That Bryce guy gave us his phone number. All we got to do is get on the long-distance blower and while our money's on its way to him, them Nancies can be getting to work on what we need."

"Sounds like it makes sense. Maybe we should get Denny and ask him what he wants for a last name. We all may as well get used to it."

They turned toward the playground, where they saw unused equipment and no boy. "Where the hell is that kid?" Stuart said. Mandy wasn't sure if he was panicked or mad. "Dennis!" he yelled.

"What?" came the reply.

"Where are you?"

"Over here!"

Stuart spat. "Over here. Yeah, big fat gob of help that is," he said to Mandy.

If he was panicked before, he was definitely moving toward pissed now.

From the corner of her eye, Mandy saw a blond head bobbing in the lake. She tapped Stuart on the shoulder and pointed.

"That little dumbass. What the hell is he doing?"

"Swimming," Mandy said.

"I can see that, but did we say he could?"

"Did we say he couldn't?"

Stuart exhaled loudly. "Angel, don't get technical. He should know the answer's no till we say yes." He stomped over to the water, Mandy on his heels, and moved closer to where Denny was. "Kid! Get out of that water!"

"I...I can't."

"Why not? Alligator got your foot? What?"

Denny blushed. "Well, I wanted to go swimming and I didn't want my clothes to get wet, so..."

Stuart hooted loud enough to disturb Mandy's duck. "You naked in there?"

"Uh, yes, sir."

"Where are your clothes?" Mandy asked.

"Behind that rock over there."

"I ought to take them over to the car and make you dress there," Stuart said.

Mandy went to the rock and grabbed the pile. Jeans, shorts, shirt, socks, sneakers. Everything accounted for. "Got them." She placed everything as close to the water's edge as she could.

"Get out of there and get dressed. Now," Stuart said.

Denny looked straight at Mandy. "I can't."

"Stuey, can you come talk with me for a second. In private. I know Denny can get dressed without our help."

Mandy led Stuart to a nearby bush, which she hoped would be enough of a privacy screen for Denny. She kept her back to him and the water as she spoke. "Stuey, don't be too mad at him, okay? He just wanted to have a little fun is all. Besides," she moved closer to Stuart and put her hand on his chest, "swimming makes a boy tired. We could use him being tired later." She toyed with the collar of Stuart's t-shirt and let her nail lightly scratch the skin beneath.

"Aw, I'm not mad at the kid, Angel. Hell, he didn't do nothing we didn't do the other night. But he's got to listen to us if we're gonna be in charge, right?"

"Well, yeah. A little scare'll make him think next time. Just not too much of a scare."

"You know I won't." Stuart looked over Mandy's shoulder. "He's got his jeans on. We can go back over there now."

"Remind me when we shop again, swim stuff for all of us," Mandy said. "We can't be skinny dipping no more either."

The couple rejoined Denny, who was just putting on his shirt. "I'm sorry, Aunt Mandy, Uncle Stuey. I just hadda—"

"Don't sweat it, kid. Just remember next time to ask."

Mandy looked at a dark spot on Denny's shirt. "Too bad we didn't have a towel," she said. "Not being able to dry off is good reason not to go in the water."

"And there's another." Stuart nodded toward a rusted sign hanging crooked on a more rusted pole. *No swimming by order of Valhalla Police*

Dept. "Congrats, kid, you're now a lawbreaker."

Denny beamed. "Well, we are family, ain't we?"

"Dennis!"

"Sorry, Aunt Mandy."

Stuart put his arms around Mandy's and Denny's shoulders. "Listen, kid. The little things we all done are like a sale on bananas at the grocery store. This week only. Once we settle down, we settle down for good. And you'll swim where you're supposed to, and not bare-assed naked."

"Yeah, but at least I can say I done it once."

So can we, Mandy thought. The threesome headed to the car. "Stuey," she asked, "where we gonna go?"

"Good question, Angel. Find a place to stay, I guess. Maybe see if there's a store open somewhere so Johnny Wisenheimer here can have swimming trunks in order to keep his privates to himself until he's old enough to need them. Nobody needs to be seeing his naked butt."

"Oh, I don't know," Mandy said. "I thought it was kinda cute."

Denny blushed the deepest red Mandy ever saw. "You didn't see, did you?"

She tousled his wet hair. "Nah, just teasing you. Can't say for sure the group of girls who were on the swings didn't though."

Somehow, Denny managed a few shades more scarlet, which quickly cleared. "Not a chance. There weren't no girls there. No group of girls would keep quiet enough not to be heard."

"He's got you there, Angel."

"Shut up and get in the car," she said.

Once inside, Stuart said, "Which way you think we should go to find the town?"

Mandy pointed to the right. "That way. The God people are the other way and there might be a lot of traffic."

"You point, I follow."

Stuart pulled onto the street. The business district of Valhalla was just a few blocks away and the trio quickly found themselves faced with a choice of two motels, The Heavenly Rest and The Pearly Gate. "Both these places sound like old folks' homes," Stuart said.

"Well, Heavenly Rest is on this side of the street, so let's try there," Mandy said.

Stuart pulled in and parked and the three went to the hotel office. The office was all dark, heavy wood and low lighting. The counter was trying hard to look more like marble than Formica. From somewhere, an organ droned behind a choir screeching hosannas and hallelujahs.

"Is this a church?" Denny whispered.

"Shut your yap," Stuart whispered back.

Mandy noticed a woman sitting at a desk on the other side of the counter. She looked to Mandy like she weighed less than Denny. Her hair was pulled back in a bun so tight that her roots appeared to be painted on her skull. She was reading a book, following the words with her finger and whispering, the same way Stuart did whenever he had to read something difficult in school. Apparently, she was so engrossed in her novel, she didn't hear them come in.

"Excuse me," Mandy said softly.

The woman startled as if the angel in the painting behind her jumped down and tapped her on the shoulder. "I'm sorry, brothers and sister. I didn't hear you enter." She placed a red ribbon in her book and closed it. Mandy saw *Holy Bible* in gold on the cover. "Welcome to the Heavenly Rest. I'm Ruth. How may I serve you?"

Stuart gave Mandy a look that said you handle this nut job. "We, my husband, my cousin, and myself, need a room for the night."

"I."

"Pardon?"

"My husband, my cousin, and I. Not myself."

"Oh. Well...the three of us need a room for the night."

"Certainly." Ruth put on the pair of glasses dangling from a chain around her neck and consulted a book on the counter. "It appears I have one available." She tsked. "It's next door to a single gentleman who checked in a little bit ago. Will that be okay?"

"Sure," Mandy said. When she saw Ruth scowl, she said, "I mean, certainly. We'll be okay."

Ruth spun the hotel register in her direction and Mandy reached for the pen. "If your husband will just fill in the registration, I'll give him the key." The woman's emphasis on husband and him almost made Mandy turn and walk out the door. She could read and write as good as Stuart could, even if she did say myself instead of I.

Stuart wandered over and registered them as Mr. and Mrs. Stuart Mason of Chicago. "Don't forget the boy," Ruth said. "Just put his name there after yours."

Mandy watched Stuart write Dennis and something for a last name, which he managed to smudge when he brought his hand back across the page. Ruth handed Stuart the key, told him how to find their room, and blessed him for his business before blessing each of their days. "And don't forget," Ruth said as they were leaving, "Reverend Pickering is having his evening service at six-thirty sharp. You won't want to miss the reverend. He has a way of making everything so right, no matter whether it truly is or not."

"We'll probably be having supper about then," Mandy said.

"Then you'll definitely be at the revival," Ruth replied. "Only things open when the reverend is on stage is police, fire, and us. But the Pickerings serve up a fine fish dinner for their believers for only two dollars."

"I'm allergic to fish," Stuart lied.

"There are always other dishes, brother. The flock wouldn't let a traveler starve. Reverend Pickering's wisdom and generosity knows no bounds. He's the reason the Presbyterians and the Methodists closed up shop here in Valhalla. Folks are wondering who'll see the light next, the Lutherans or the Catholics." She blessed them all again, the organ music swelling in the background as if to punctuate her sincerity, and they left the office.

"I know one town I don't plan on staying in for long," Mandy said once the heavy door was closed behind them. "This one." She took a look back at the office. "Let's quickly find our room. Hopefully, the single gentleman next door will be able to control himself."

The room was the last in the row. Mandy was grateful to be as far from the weird woman in the office as possible. Stuart carried the suitcase in one hand and the key in the other. Denny had the bundles that spent the previous night in the car, and Mandy carried the sack of yesterday's laundry. Other than finding supper and a map and possibly placing a long-distance call to see about a birth certificate for Denny, they were, Stuart declared, done for the day.

Stuart unlocked the door and found the light switch. "Are there any normal hotel rooms in this state?" he asked no one in particular.

This room, like the office, had walls made of the darkest wood Mandy ever saw. All of the fabrics looked heavy and scratchy and everything—bedspread, drapes, and towels—were a gray-soaked army green. There was a duplicate angel to match the one in the office on the far wall, with a crucifix on either side of the picture.

"Twin beds?" Stuart said with disgust.

Mandy was so overwhelmed by the depressing décor, she hadn't noticed the unwelcoming military spreads covered single mattresses. "We'll make it work, Stuey. Maybe we can push a couple of them together. We got four of them in here."

He put down the suitcase and tried to move the closest bed. Despite his clear strain, the thing didn't budge. "I don't think the three of us together could do it. Maybe we—"

"We will make it work," Mandy said slowly, emphasizing each word.

"Fine." He flopped down on the bed closest to the door. "Bed's not too soft, that's for sure." He cocked his head. "Do you still hear that damn organ music?"

Mandy listened for a second. "Yeah, I think I do."

Denny laughed and pointed. "Could it be the radio over there on the desk?"

"Smart ass," Stuart muttered. "Kid, find another station."

The boy jumped up and went to the radio. "Dial's stuck," he announced.

"Then turn it off."

"It's stuck on."

"What the hell?" Stuart moved over by Denny. After checking the dials himself, he climbed under the desk and unplugged the radio. "No way any of us are gonna be able to sleep with that funeral music going on."

"Well, we're not sleeping now," Mandy said. She reached into the sack from the discount store. "Anybody up for a game of Sorry?" She held up the box.

"Never played it," Denny said. "But sure."

In a few moments, the three of them were on the floor, sitting around the game board while Mandy explained the rules to Denny. The boy won the first game and quickly declared them to be playing the Sorry World Series, with the first to win four games to be crowned the family grand champion. They were just about to break a three-way tie at two wins apiece when there was a knock at the door. Mandy jumped up and answered it.

Ruth. "Just stopped over to remind you folks about the evening services. And the fish dinner before."

"Still allergic, but thanks," Stuart said from the floor.

Ruth talked in that same combination of scolding and pious as she did back in the office. "Again, there will be other items available. If you'd like, you can follow Mr. McChesney and me."

I, Mandy thought. Or maybe myself. She wanted to correct the old prune's grammar, but instead she said, "That's okay, Mrs. McChesney. We were out that way earlier today."

Ruth's face brightened to a lower intensity thunderstorm, approaching near-human in quality. "Oh, then you're already familiar with the Reverend Pickering. I am so relieved to hear that." She turned to leave, then reversed. "It's not Mrs. McChesney, but I am hopeful. It's Miss Simmons. Enjoy tonight's meeting."

This time, she did leave and Mandy closed and locked the door. She wished she could bolt it and board it up as well. There was something about that woman that terrified her.

"You know, I been thinking," Stuart said. "What that crazy dame says about not getting food don't make no sense."

"What do you mean?" Mandy asked.

"If every place shuts down when this Reverend Pickyournose is yammering, how were we able to buy burgers for lunch?"

"Yeah, how?" said Denny, sounding like a radio detective's sidekick. "That's a good question, Uncle Stuey."

"Natch. I asked it, didn't I?"

Mandy started cleaning up the Sorry board. "I'm not all that hungry yet, but those stands were closing up before the afternoon service started. Since the next show is in a couple hours, we should probably get moving."

"Smart thinking, Angel. Maybe we can get some popcorn or something so we can have a snack later if we're gonna have supper so early."

"Yeah, Uncle Stuey, good idea," said his trusty blond assistant.

"Then help me clean up," Mandy said.

Five minutes later, the Olds and its passengers were back on the road to the lake and the big revival tent. When they arrived, there were food and merchandise vendors lining the street just as before. "Knew we'd be able to get food without a bunch of hell-fired yibberyabbering," Stuart said as he pulled into a space far from Reverend Pickering's huge tent. "Let's get on out there before it's all closed up." They left the car and headed toward the crowd.

"Angel, you see anything you like in one of these places," Stuart said once they reached the vendor area, "just sing out. You, too, kid."

The threesome strolled for a little bit. Despite the carnival-like atmosphere of the roadway, Mandy doubted she ever saw a more miserable looking group of people in her life. No one smiled and no one laughed, except Stuart and Denny, who drew scornful glances every time they did.

Between a man with a table of tacky Noah's Ark statuary and a woman offering hand-knitted blankets with crosses worked into the patterns was a large booth that clearly didn't belong. There was all sorts of junk on the tables, none of which looked remotely religious. Mandy headed in that direction, Stuart and Denny following.

"Hel-lo, little lady, gentlemen. I've got to tell you, it does my old heart good to see folks wearing colors other than black or gray. Tells me there's life in the world somewhere. Clearly, you folks are strangers in Valhalla, am I right?"

"Definitely," Mandy said.

"I can tell. You don't have the hollow, glazed look these fine, God-fearing people do." The guy laughed.

Mandy liked the way it reached all the way to his eyes. "Gil Tattinger's my name, by the way, and you are..."

"Mandy and Stuart Mason and this is my cousin, Denny," Mandy said.

"Pleasure to meet all three of you," Gil said. "A real pleasure seeing actual humans on a Sunday in Valhalla. Staying here long?"

"Probably just tonight," Stuart said.

"Smart. Get out of this town before it sucks the life from you, too."

Denny cocked his head. "How come it ain't sucked you yet?"

"Dennis!"

Gil held up his hands. "No, no, the boy's right. I don't fit in here. I'm not selling religious claptrap. No chunks of the Cross or glow in the dark Christmas mangers or any of that other buy-a-piece-of-God's-love-and-spend-your-way-to-heaven crap. Gilbert John Tattinger's way too practical for that. If you folks lived here, I'd give you a good price on a television set like nobody here claims to own, but which I've sold at least twelve of this year. Not a good idea for travelers though. Equipment's too delicate. But I'm sure I got something here to make your trip more palatable. Take a look around. I'm sure you'll find something you need. Prices are better than God's."

The three started to browse. Mandy was amazed at the variety of stuff Gil had crammed in his tent. She pulled Stuart aside. "Do you think we can get some extra things for Denny to do? Kid lost everything he had when he became ours."

"Whatcha got in mind?"

"A transistor radio with one of those little things that go in your ear. Maybe some more games for at night, that sort of thing."

"You fix the kid up, Angel. Let him pick out whatever he wants. He'll know what he wants better'n anybody."

"True." She called Denny over and told him to scout around for special things for himself.

Gil Tattinger approached Mandy and Stuart. "You folks have any questions about the merchandise or about the gentle, boring folks of Valhalla? I got plenty of time on my hands. Closer it gets to show time, the fewer shoppers I get."

"Why is that?" Mandy asked.

"Because these good people don't want to be seen by the reverend and his shrewish wife or his weasely children. Old Picky Pickering doesn't approve of commerce on the Sabbath, unless he gets a piece of the action, of course. Then it's the Lord's work, or some shit."

"I'm surprised this priest guy even lets you set up shop here," Stuart said, fingering a pair of red fuzzy dice.

"Reverend, son, not priest. Not ever. Catholic and all the other religions are sinful to old Picky."

Mandy nodded when Stuart held up the dice. "Well, it's still surprising he lets you be here."

The vendor laughed from somewhere way deep inside. "Lets me? No, little miss, it is I who let him set up here. I own all the land at this end of the lake. He and all these other fools pay me, though the righteous reverend accepts a hefty kickback in exchange for not telling his people not to shop here. For me, it's a tax-deductible donation. For him, it's more cash in his overstuffed pockets."

"Then how come you let him tell all these people to shut down? We're gonna need food soon."

"Son, he doesn't tell them to shut down. They do it because he's sold them a bill of goods that says they're heathens if they stay open during worship. You just stick with me and once the Godding starts over in the tent, I'll see you get a proper meal."

"Hey, Aunt Mandy."

Mandy turned and saw Denny holding up an orange teddy bear.

"Don't you think Blue needs a little brother?"

"Don't see why not. Hold on to him."

"Which mortuary you folks interred in tonight?" Gil asked. "The Heavenly Rest or the Pearly Gate?"

"Heavenly Rest," Mandy said.

"And yeah, it's restful. Like a tomb without the laughs," said Stuart.

"Only laughs you're going to find in Valhalla on a Sunday are right here in this tent Might just as well stay here while the sheep head off to be forcefully told how horrible they are for three hours or so."

Mandy felt her eyes grow wide. "Three...hours?" She thought her weekly forced hour in Mass was bad enough.

"Oh, yeah. If the reverend keeps it short."

Denny approached with an armload of stuff. "Hey, mister, you got a place I can put this stuff down so I can keep looking?"

"Dennis, we are not buying all of that for you."

Gil pointed to a table. "Just put it all there, son, and get back to looking."

Denny did as he was told and scampered off again. "Mr. Tattinger," Mandy said, "we are not getting all of that for him."

Gil laughed. "Why not? I'll give you a surprisingly good deal. Besides," he lowered his voice to a near-whisper, "don't you think a boy whose mama lied to the police to have him declared dead deserves a hand-picked Christmas at the very least? Besides, from Wisconsin to Illinois, I'm sure you can afford it now, can't you?"

Mandy's entire body flushed cold. How could he know all he implied? Next to her, the fuzzy dice slipped from Stuart's hands.

Tattinger put up his hands, looking for all the world like the picture of innocence. "Folks, don't worry. There's no love lost between me and the law, for a variety of reasons I feel no need or desire to explain. You've gotten away with so much that you're to be admired, not betrayed. I pay close attention to the news of the world for a reason. The pious out there have their God guild. We scallywags have to stick together too."

Words wouldn't come, though Mandy certainly tried. Stuart was mute as well.

"If you're wondering how I know, it's simple," Tattinger said. "I listen to the radio all day long, and I don't listen to the station here in town. I don't need God all day every day. There's news coverage about you two. Just because you didn't hear it maybe doesn't mean there isn't. The boy, too. But you got to know, I'm not going to report you. Got no reason to. You done nothing to me. I do have one question, though. What do you intend to do with the boy?"

"We're keeping him," Mandy said evenly. "He's my cousin."

"Makes more sense if you say nephew, since he calls you Aunt Mandy. You plan on raising him up right?"

"Of course."

Gil Tattinger waved Denny over. "Boy, you want to live with these folks?"

Denny seemed confused by the question. Mandy smiled at him,

willing him to say yes. He did.

"And they've been good to you?"

The boy's gaze went from the man to the table of merchandise. "They're great."

"Okay, then. When's your birthday, boy?"

"May seventh."

Tattinger looked him up and down. "And you look to be around twelve. Am I close?"

The expression on Denny's face said no one ever took the undersized boy for his actual age. "I'm exactly twelve," he said proudly.

"Tell me, Denny, what do you think of the last name of Ulrich?"

"I dunno. Better than some, I guess."

"Good enough." He bent down to Denny's level. "Now, you go pick out whatever else you want, up to five dollars' worth. On the house."

Again, Denny disappeared into the maze of shelves. "What the hell was that about?" Stuart asked.

Tattinger leveled his eyes at Stuart. "If you're keeping the kid, you need a cover story. Ulrich is my Clara's maiden name. She's got a dead brother. You get in any trouble with the law, we can back up your story and keep the kid safe."

Stuart let out a low whistle. "Cool, man, but why you doing this for us?"

Tattinger shrugged. "During the Depression, I was an orphan on the streets of Chicago. It's no life for a boy." He looked away and Mandy got the impression that subject was not only closed, but locked up tight. She thought maybe she was glad of that. "Anyway, if you folks will do me the honor of having supper with Clara and myself..."

Mandy knew using the word myself was right, despite what Prune Face Ruth said. "Of course we will."

"Fantastic. Let me go tell Clara to throw on some extra steaks and burgers. I'll be right back."

Just after Tattinger left, thunderous organ music rumbled the air and people began running toward the big tent. Mandy watched them as they scurry-marched toward the music and thought about how obedient they all seemed to be. And how stupid. They spent Sunday doing this because some reverend guy told them to? They followed all these boring rules because this guy said doing it would get them into Heaven?

Well, Amanda Jean Heinemann Masamoli Mason had Heaven right here on good old Earth. She didn't need or want some funeral music and an old guy yelling at her to stay boring during this life because the next one was better. No sir, no ma'am. This life was just fine now and if she didn't like the next, she'd just fix it to her liking, just like she did with this one.

What these people didn't have, she decided, was nerve. It may have taken Mandy twenty years to find hers, but once she did, once Stuart put that cute little gun in her hand back in Bascombe—was that really just four days ago?—she took control of her life and she'd be damned if she ever looked back.

"Hey, Angel," Stuart's voice intruded. "Gil's got a couple duffle bags back there. Till we can find another suitcase, think those'll do the trick?"

"Sure," she answered. "We can put clean clothes in one, dirty in the other, and save the suitcase for all of Denny's new things."

A few minutes later, Denny was finally finished scrounging and set to weeding through the many items he pulled from the shelves. "You gotta have fifty smackers worth of crap there," Stuart told him. "Cut it in half."

"I'll take twenty-five for the lot, sight unseen," came Gil's voice from behind the three of them.

"We couldn't do that, Mr. Tattinger."

"Little lady, you're not a kid anymore. The name's Gil. You want to talk to Mr. Tattinger, go track down my father. Second, I don't take advantage of anybody but the yokels. Never take advantage of a friend."

Friend. That was a good word to hear.

"Twenty-five, minus the five I promised him, so twenty plus twelve for the things you two picked up. Call it thirty and we're square. And one of my associates will have the boy's birth certificate done and ready by the time we're done with supper. Get you back to the hotel before the harridan comes out of that meeting. That Ruth Simmons woman isn't exactly inspiration to join God's team, that's for sure."

Stuart handed over a ten and a twenty. "She def ain't."

"Clara will have food here any minute, so just settle in and watch the rest of the faithful parade by. It can get pretty interesting sometimes. Especially the hats and the facial expressions. Enjoy, folks." He disappeared toward the back of the tent.

"Seems like an alright guy," Stuart said.

Mandy nodded. "But..."

"But what, Angel?"

"But it scares me that he knew who we are and who Denny is."

"So? He's on our side."

"Or so he said. Look at these people." Mandy indicated the passing parade. "Do you think any of them would wait half a second before calling the cops?"

"Them out there? Hell no," Stuart said. "But Gil's different. Look around in here. He ain't selling God crap. He's got a stack of girlie magazines back there that would last your little brother a month. He ain't like them jaspers out there."

"How can we be sure?"

"Simple, Aunt Mandy," Denny said. "We been in here for a little while and ain't nobody else came in at all. Like he said, nobody wants to be seen with him."

Stuart rubbed the top of Denny's ball cap-covered head. "Our boy is one smart kid, Angel. He's exactly right."

"Yes, he is," Gil said. "And he looks strong enough to grab these two chairs so his aunt and uncle can sit, then come help me with the other chairs."

Mandy smiled at Gil. "Go ahead, Denny."

"Thank you," Gil said. He led Denny away.

"Angel, we got to trust somebody sometime, right? Those two pansies, even though they were weird and, I think, maybe not right in the head, helped us and, far as we know, kept their yaps shut. This guy will too."

"Yeah, seems like he will," Mandy concluded.

"He will." Stuart put his arm around her. "Gotta trust instincts sometimes."

Denny came back, carrying two chairs, with Gil behind him with a chair and a card table. "Supper in ten minutes, folks. Clara's got a feast going and, if you don't mind, I'm going to take Muscles here to help haul food out. We always eat out here on Sundays. Keep the tent open after the services so the yokels can buy after the reverend inspires them not to. Besides, it's too nice to be cooped up inside."

"You should see back there, Aunt Mandy. The back of the tent goes right into Mr. Tattinger's garage. Mrs. Tattinger's got a ton of food cooking on a grill. We're gonna eat real good. Let's go, Mr. Tattinger." He grinned and headed back.

Gil leaned between Mandy and Stuart. "Piece of advice. Always trust a child's instincts. They can see through bullshit and hypocrisy faster and more accurately than any adult because they've got none of their own." He clapped them both on the shoulder and left.

Mandy turned her attention to the passersby. The parade was down to a trickle now and the few who bothered to look their way had faces that said Mandy and Stuart were the only ones in the area whose shit ever stunk. Mandy hated them on sight and remembered her vow outside of the Heavenly Rest office that this was one town they would never, ever settle in. Even meeting Mr. Tattinger—Gil—wouldn't change that.

"Supper's on the table, folks." Gil's voice made Mandy jump. "So, turn around and let's dig in."

"Gilbert, mind your manners. Introductions first."

"Yes, dear."

Mandy and Stuart turned to meet Clara Tattinger. Mandy didn't know what she expected Gil's wife to look like, but this wasn't it. Where Gil was tall and wide with jet black hair, Clara was what the ladies back in Bascombe would have called a mere slip of a thing. As blonde as Mandy, attractive for sure, with a more than pleasant enough demeanor. Any lingering doubts Mandy had about Tattinger trustworthiness vanished when she saw Clara.

"So," Clara said, "everyone grab plates and serve yourselves. We've got steaks and burgers and plenty of other things and there's pop on ice in the cooler. Nobody leaves our place hungry, that's my rule."

As instructed, everyone took plates and loaded up. There wasn't enough room at the card table for them to eat, so they set Denny up at the table and the adults formed a semi-circle next to him and held their plates

142

in their laps. Not an ideal set-up for cutting into a thick slab of steak, Mandy quickly realized, but the melt-in-your-mouth goodness of the meat more than made up for it.

"So," Clara said around a mouthful of tenderness, "tell me about yourself, sister Mandy."

Mandy felt her eyes widen. "Sister?"

There was a split-second of silence before Clara burst out in laughter. "Hell, girl, I don't mean sister in the Lord or whatever crap the Pickering crowd spews. I mean, if Denny here is supposed to be my dead brother's son and you're supposed to be his aunt, that would make me his aunt too and make the two of us sisters. So tell me both stories."

"Both stories?"

"Yeah, both stories. The truth, and the story you want me to tell if I'm ever asked. Always best to be prepared, that's my rule."

Mandy and Stuart launched in, alternating the storytelling role as needed. After polishing off his second burger and loading a third with ketchup and relish, Denny added his part of the narrative as well. By the time they were through with both the meal and their stories, as well as listening to Gil and Clara's life highlights, Mandy felt a kinship with her newfound sister and brother-in-law and was sorry she ever doubted their sincerity. She tried to tell the Tattingers this, but Gil cut her off.

"Hell, Mandy, you got to be careful. I learned that growing up in the streets."

"Absolutely," Clara added. "Watch out for you and yours first, that's my rule. And you three are family now."

A man appeared at the tent entrance, a brown envelope in his hand. "Stuart," Gil said, "give the gentleman fifty dollars. That is, if you want receipts for the boy to prove he was born and been to school and that he's now yours and Mandy's problem—I mean, property—now."

Stuart fished the cash out of his wallet and handed it to the man, who quickly pocketed it and took off. Hefting the envelope, Stuart said, "Heavy."

"Wait till you see what's all in there. Young Mr. Ulrich has a whole new life in that envelope."

"Who?" Denny asked.

"You, mush head," Stuart answered.

He started to open the envelope, but Gil stopped him. "Later for that. It's coming up on nine and the freaks will be out of the monkey house soon. You don't want to get caught up in that ungodly God traffic. Besides, the lingerers will be stopping in after the Pickering clan clears out so they can do the Sabbath shopping they aren't supposed to do."

Mandy was surprised to see tears welling up in Clara's eyes. "I'm sorry," she said. "All my life, I wanted a little sister. And chances are good I won't be seeing you again anytime soon. I didn't expect it to hit so hard though. Keep emotions close to the vest, that's my rule."

The two women hugged, inspiring hugs all around. Clara pressed a slip of paper into Mandy's hand. "Don't you lose that," she said. "Got our address and phone number on it. Now that we're family, we'll need regular updates from you."

That started Mandy's waterworks and the hug chain started up again. Eventually, the trio pulled away, Stuart and Denny each with a duffle of stuff and Mandy with the all-important envelope and slip of paper.

Back in the hotel room, Mandy decided to find out what, exactly, they purchased from Gil Tattinger. Once Denny was settled in playing a game of four-player Sorry by himself, she opened the first duffle. On the very top was a small, wrapped package with a note attached.

> *Mandy,*
> *While we were eating, I noticed you are missing something very important. This isn't much in money value to be sure, but is huge in the hearts of every couple truly in love. Please remember to keep in touch with us, wherever you wind up. Family is more important than anything, that's my rule.*
> *Love,*
> *Clara*

Dying of curiosity, Mandy opened the package. She gasped, catching Stuart's attention. "What did Wilfred buy that's got you so shocked, Angel?"

Denny looked up from his game. "Watch that Wilfred stuff, Uncle Gaylord. We got a deal."

"Stuey, look what Clara gave us." Mandy held out her left hand.

"What?"

"An engagement ring. She saw I didn't have one." She looked down at it. "I wonder if it's a real diamond."

Stuart stared at the floor. "You know I was gonna get you one, don't you?"

"Oh, Stuey, I know. And one day, we'll replace this one. For now, though, this is a family ring and I'll love it as that, okay?"

"Sure, Angel. But I will get you one. One day."

The ring fit almost perfectly and, while Mandy knew it upset Stuart that Clara beat him to the punch, she also knew she wouldn't take it off until her husband replaced it with one he picked. And she knew he would do so one day. She knew how much her Stuart loved her.

The sound of paper tearing got her attention. Stuart opened the envelope they paid fifty dollars to obtain. "Angel, we def got our money's worth here. Look at all this stuff. Birth certificate for the kid. Say, you were a skinny little jasper when you broke out of your mama. Six pounds." Stuart laughed. "I was twice that much."

"What else is in there, Uncle Stuey?"

Stuart pulled out a handful of small squares and shook his head. "I'll be damned. Monster pictures."

Mandy stopped pulling toys out of the duffle and went over by Stuart. She plucked one out of his hand. "Monster pictures. Stuey, you're so mean. These are baby pictures." She flipped over the one she held. "Even says Dennis, May, 1943, on the back."

"Hey, how'd they swipe those?"

"That's not really you, stupid. That's some other goofy-looking diaper wearer. They just wrote that on there."

"Oh."

Stuart dug in the envelope again. "Would ya look at this? Report cards. First through sixth grade. Looks like you're starting junior high come September."

"Yay." Denny's tone was completely flat.

"Aw, junior high ain't so bad, kid. That's when the girls start getting their ti—their bazoombers."

"Stuart!"

"Uh, let's take a look at last year's report card." Stuart opened one of the little booklets. "Not bad," he said. "Mostly B's. Couple of A's. But a C in science. You need to work on that, young man."

"I hate science."

"I think our boy is able to make honor roll. What do you think, Aunt Mandy?"

She smiled at Denny. "He can do anything."

"'Teacher comments,'" Stuart read. "'Dennis is mostly well-behaved, though he tends toward talking a bit too much at inappropriate times.' Boy, ain't that the truth. 'He's come a long way this year and he's going to develop into a fine young man. He's been a pleasure in class and he'll do well next year in junior high school.'" Stuart put the bogus report card down. "See, I told you. You'll be big man on campus, little man."

The boy didn't answer, but Mandy saw a small smile on his face. "Hey, Denny. Over on the bed in that blue box. Got something special for you."

He stood and got the package. When he opened it, there was definitely a smile. "Thanks, Aunt Mandy. I saw these, but I didn't think you guys would let me get one." He hugged the transistor radio as if it were his first girlfriend.

"Why don't you get ready for bed and then see if you can find a ballgame to listen to? I put a toothbrush in the bathroom for you."

"Sure." He ran into the bathroom, where the sounds of splashing soon emerged.

Mandy took the rest of the two duffel bags' contents and divided them into two piles—items for the backseat of the car and items for wherever they settled down. Mandy was glad to see the second pile was bigger than the first. Denny was theirs, this told her. They weren't just a quick stop on his way to someplace else.

Sitting atop the pile of Denny's stuff was the orange teddy bear, slightly darker in color than her own, and she wondered why the boy wanted it. Did boys his age sleep with teddy bears? Remembering the night in the woods by Lake Michigan, she decided the answer might be yes. After all, at some point that night, Blue shifted from her arms to Stuart's. Just in case, she moved the bear so it sat upon Denny's pillow.

She no sooner returned to her own bed when Denny came out of the bathroom. He was clad only in shorts and Mandy decided the pajama purchase was a waste of money. Still, she'd keep them for both of the guys. They might actually wear them again someday.

Denny went to Stuart and gave him a stiff-armed hug. Stuart surprised Mandy by pulling the boy to him and scooping him up into a proper bear hug. He even, she noticed, took care not to squeeze Denny where the worst of the marks were on his back. Stuart kissed his adopted nephew on the cheek. "Get a good night sleep, little man. We're back on the road in the morning."

"Yes, sir." Denny got down and headed to Mandy, but stopped and turned to face Stuart. "Thanks for all the stuff today."

"Better'n listening to you whine you're bored all day in the car."

"Yeah." Once again, he turned away, then turned back. "Good night. Love you, Uncle Stuey."

"Love you too, kid." Mandy was glad Stuart didn't hesitate before saying it back.

Denny had a smile he clearly couldn't contain when he reached Mandy. She, too, gave him a big hug. "Love you, kiddlywink," she whispered in his ear.

"Thanks, Aunt Mandy. I love you, too." She thought she heard him whisper "more than you know" as he headed to his own bed, but she wasn't sure.

Mandy watched Denny move the bear from his pillow and stuff it under his blanket. He put the earphone in place and started to fiddle with the radio dial. Once he seemed to find a station he liked, he settled into his pillow. He slid the bear up next to him and put a protective arm around it.

For the next hour, Stuart read a copy of *Sports Illustrated* Gil had in his store tent. Since a basketball player was on the cover, Mandy figured it wasn't too recent an issue. She read a romance novel she bought that evening. It was nowhere near as racy as the cover suggested, much to her disappointment, but it was something quiet to do while Dennis fell asleep.

Once she was sure Denny was asleep, she joined Stuart on his bed. "That was very sweet of you, Mr. Mason."

"Which of my many sweet but manly acts are you talking about?"

"Hugging Denny and telling him you love him."

Stuart shrugged. "I guess I do." He paused. "I really do." He seemed stunned to realize it, let alone admit it out loud.

Mandy kissed her husband on the cheek, then moved around to his lips. "And I love you."

Stuart tossed his magazine on the floor and turned off the light. "Why don't you stay here for a while and I'll show you how much I love you too."

So she did. And he did. Twice. As she drifted off to sleep still snuggled in his arms, she knew she finally figured out just what love was truly all about.

Monday

Monday morning was clear and bright as the Mason family loaded up their Oldsmobile. Mandy had no sooner put the last duffel bag in the trunk when Ruth appeared in front of her. The older woman's hair was again pulled back tighter than the laws of nature would seem to allow and her expression was as pleasant as ever. Mandy figured the sun was frantically searching the skies for a cloud to hide behind until she was gone.

"You people checking out?" Ruth asked.

Stuart stepped up beside his wife. "That's right. We need to get back on the road."

"Please wait until the inspection of your room is complete." She marched smartly off to their room.

"Room inspection?" Stuart said. "What the—"

"Cleanliness is next to godliness, I guess." That cleanliness/godliness crap was one Mandy's mother pulled out whenever her father bitched about the filthiness of the Heinemann house. Then Linda would come up with some stupid reason why she couldn't possibly be expected to contribute to the workload and Craig would be excused because he was a boy. Mandy never understood the connection between having a penis and not being able to work a broom or dust cloth, but she never asked. Her family hated her enough as it was.

"She's coming back," Stuart said.

Denny darted into the backseat and locked the door. Mandy wanted to tell him not to bother, that the old woman's face could dissolve steel and there was no place safe to hide, but Ruth was before them too quickly.

"There will be additional charges for damage," she proclaimed.

"For what?" Mandy asked.

Ruth pointed a finger heavenward. "One, the radio was unplugged."

So? Mandy thought, though she said, "It was too loud."

"And we couldn't change the station," added Stuart.

"As it says in the rules of the establishment, which are clearly posted on the inside wall of the closet, any tampering with the radio will result in a one-dollar charge for damages."

"Lady, you're nuts," Stuart said. "Nobody wants to listen to that crap all night."

What little color Ruth's face possessed drained so quickly that Mandy half-expected her to snag a bird out of the air for a snack to replenish her strength.

"Young man, vulgarity and blasphemy are not welcome in my presence nor on the grounds of the Heavenly Rest. The radio station which delivers the Lord's word and His music goes off the air at ten o'clock, an hour when decent folks perform their ablutions and say their prayers and devotions and retire to their separate beds." She looked Stuart straight in the eye when she said this and emphasized the word separate. "Number two. There are stains in the middle of one of the beds. If I'm expected to save the bedding after that sort of...activity, the rules state we are entitled to just compensation."

"Lady, you're goddamned nuts," Stuart said. "The nuttiest nut in the goddamned—"

"We're sorry, Miss...uh...Ma'am," Mandy said quickly. "We didn't know there was a time limit, so we abluted late." Mandy had no idea why this was any of Ruth's business, but she felt she should try to explain.

"Yes," Ruth answered, her tone venomous ice. "The total damage fee is four dollars."

Stuart gave her the cash for the room, then added another bill. "And there's an extra five for the damage. Take the change and make a donation to Reverend Prickinface."

"Stuart," Mandy said, "it's not Prickinface, it's Prickinher."

"Prickering...I mean, Pickering," Ruth said, sounding both mortified and angry at the same time. "The Mission of Genesis Reborn thanks you." She turned about and strode off.

"What a piece of work," Mandy said.

"Let's get the hell out of here, Angel, before they cast some kind of spell and we become one of them."

They joined Denny in the Oldsmobile and made a fast exit from the Heavenly Rest. Stuart announced they would get breakfast in the next town they came across, a decision that brought a sigh from Denny.

"I'm hungry now, Uncle Stuey."

"Shut your yap."

"It's Monday. Stuff'll be open."

"Shut your yap."

"But I'm hungry."

"Kid, one more word and we're going back and leaving you with that old lady to be her altar boy or her lunch or something." He turned on the radio and filled the car with The Chordettes begging Mr. Sandman to please, please bring them the man of their dreams and, in short order, Valhalla, Illinois was in their past.

They made it through five more songs before Denny piped up again. "We gonna be stopping soon? I'm starving. When's the next town?"

"Do I look like a road map, kid?"

"No. When's the next town?"

"When we get there. Now, shut your yap and play with some of that crap we bought you." Stuart turned up the radio and Denny fell dramatically into the backseat.

"Stuey, he's kinda got a point. We should get ourselves a map and start figuring out where we're going."

"I was thinking the same thing, Angel. We're gonna run outta money at some point otherwise. Time to settle down. Runt's gonna need a home and so are we."

Mandy was impressed that Stuart was thinking like a father and husband. "So," she said, "when is the next town?"

Stuart laughed. "Angel, shut your yap."

As they drove along, Mandy thought about the towns they'd stopped in since they got married the Thursday before. Bascombe, of course, where she spent most every day of her life before the wedding. Cloverdale, Devlin's Crossing, and Bordertown in Wisconsin. Waterport, Legion, Fountain Grove, Brownstalk, and Valhalla in Illinois. They were certainly on a sightseeing tour, but it was time to think about finding someplace permanent. Someplace home.

"Sign up ahead," Stuart said. He slowed the Olds some.

"Welcome to Penobscot—"

"Poppin'-Snot!" Stuart snorted.

"Welcome to Penobscot—A Shore Bet You'll Love," Mandy read. "Shore! Stuey, have we circled back round to the lake?"

"Be honest with you, Angel, we done twisted and turned so much I got no idea. Maybe we have. Find out soon enough."

Stuart pulled the Olds into a Phillips 66 and had the attendant fill it up. All three got out of the car to stretch their legs. "Hey, Mister," Mandy said to the gas station guy. "Where's the best place to get a decent breakfast around here."

The man, who looked old enough to be her father, looked her up and down carefully before looking out toward the Penobscot business district. "You got two, three good places I'd recommend, but since you got a kid with you, I'd go Shamrock Café, I was you. Old Mrs. Evans, she runs the place, Old Mrs. Evans'll spoil him rotten. She loves kids, Old Mrs. Evans does." He looked her up and down again.

His leer made her skin crawl. "Where's this place at?" she asked.

The guy pointed at the road they came in on. "You take a right out onto Bixby Street there, go a couple blocks to Wabash, take another right, and go up two blocks. It'll be on your right. You can't miss it none. Round building, all green. Looks like a scoop of mold during the day. Lights up pretty at night, though, the Shamrock does."

"Hey, pal," Stuart said from behind her. "My wife's ears are up higher than where you're aiming your answers."

The attendant put up a hand. "Calm down, son. Just window shopping. Not looking to buy."

Stuart moved around in front of Mandy, blocking the attendant's view. "You got any maps around here."

"Course we do. Company puts out the best maps of anybody, the company does. You want Midwest?"

Mandy felt Stuart thinking the same thing she was. Stupid question. "Yup," he said.

"Surely. I'll get'm for you soon's the gas gets done, I will. And that should be right about...now." The guy shut off the pump and hung up the hose. "I'll go get you that map."

"When we get the map, we'll figure out just where we are and where we want to go." Stuart said after they slid into their seats.

"Breakfast," Denny said.

"Kid..."

"I'm hungry."

"Denny," Mandy said, "Shut your yap." Stuart looked surprised at her and was clearly trying not to grin. "We'll look at the map while we have breakfast."

"Oh."

The attendant gave Stuart the map he requested and gave Mandy a last appreciate look before sending them on their way with a friendly wave. Stuart followed his directions and they found the Shamrock Café right where the man said it would be.

"Guy was right," Stuart said after they were parked and out of the Olds. "It does look like a giant scoop of mold."

"Maybe somebody popped a snot and this is what happened," Mandy said, giggling.

"Must be." Stuart took in a large inhale. "Smells like a mess of bacon. That works no matter what the place looks like." He led the way to the front door.

The inside of the Shamrock was as green as the outside, green tile floors, green upholstered booths and chairs, green Formica tables and countertops. They even had a green Sprite sign on the menu board above the counter instead of the usual Coke red. "Looks like a leprechaun got slaughtered in here," Stuart said.

"Still smells good," Denny answered.

A kindly-looking older woman wearing, naturally, a green uniform approached them, menus in hand. "Three for breakfast?" she sing-songed. "Right this way." Her smile and tone were extremely welcoming. Mandy was certain she saw an actual twinkle in the woman's eye.

The hostess arranged the menus and invited them to sit. "My name's Em and I'll be taking care of you this morning."

Mandy had a feeling she really would take care of them, given half a chance. "Can I start you off with some fresh orange juice or some milk?"

Denny practically bounced out of his seat. "Both, please."

"A please from a young man on a Monday morning. What a wonderful thing. Of course you may have both."

"Thank you very much," Denny said, clearly sucking up the attention.

"We'll have the same," Mandy said, adding a quick thank you.

Em assured them she'd be right back with the drinks and did an efficient waitress scurry away. Stuart put his menu down. "Already know what I want. The number one breakfast."

"Me too," said Denny.

Mandy hadn't so much as looked at the menu and marveled at how her men decided so quickly. The number one—three eggs, four pancakes, four slices of bacon, hash brown potatoes, and toast—was a bit too much for her, so she glanced further down and chose the number four, a meal with a little less of everything.

Stuart pulled the Midwest map out and folded it so the region was visible. He'd just started to trace their route from the border of Wisconsin when Em arrived with nine glasses. "Juice, milk, and water all around." Stuart pulled the map out of her way so she could set the drinks down.

Em glanced at it and said, "Didn't think I'd seen you three before. Where are you headed on such a nice day?"

Mandy launched into their rehearsed story of taking in Denny and searching for a place they could live, adding in details about how a fresh start would benefit all three of them.

Like Ellie, the waitress back in Legion, Em recommended her town as the perfect place for the new family to settle. "We got a lot to offer here in Penobscot," she said. "Friendly people, good jobs and schools, nice stretch of beach down by the lake. You could do worse." She took their orders and read them back. "Two Hungry Man Platters and a Princess Plate. Most popular breakfasts in Penobscot. You folks'll fit right in. I'll get your orders to the kitchen. You think about what I said." She was gone without waiting for an answer.

Stuart held up the map again and showed the others the route they'd taken. From Bordertown, they'd basically made a backwards letter C around Chicago and were indeed again near Lake Michigan.

"We gonna live here?" Denny asked.

"Who knows," Stuart answered.

"It's early-ish," Mandy said. "No reason we can't take a look around, maybe take a dip in the lake. We got to end up somewhere and we got all of Chicago between us and Wisconsin."

"And between me and Legion," Denny said.

Something from a long-forgotten geography class clicked in Mandy's brain. "Stuey, let me see that map again."

He pulled it from where it was wedged between his leg and the wall of their booth. "What you wanna see, Angel?"

She pointed. "Look, here's Bascombe, in this pinkish part. And here's Valhalla, in this green part."

"Right."

"And here we are now in Penobscot. In this blue part."

"So?"

"So, Wisconsin's the pink and Illinois is the green."

"So?"

"So, Penobscot's here, in the blue. We aren't in Illinois no more. We're in Indiana."

Stuart peered at the map. "I didn't see no Indiana sign. You sure there ain't two Penobscots?"

"Sure isn't," Em said. Mandy was so intent on looking at the map she hadn't noticed the older woman appear with a huge tray of food. "You must have come up from the south. You'd definitely know you crossed over if you came through Chicago and Gary. Sign out on the south highway blew down last year and I guess the state hasn't fixed it yet. Only been about seven months."

She started passing out plates. When she gave Denny his breakfast, she said, "I added a fruit cup. Growing boy needs his vitamins."

"Thank you," Denny said, clearly charmed into remembering his manners.

Em patted Stuart on the head. "Don't worry, big boy. There's one for you, too. On the house."

"Uh...thanks," Stuart said.

"You three really are footloose and fancy free if you didn't know you crossed the state line," Em said. "If you got time, why not take a look around here? I can call my sister and get you a place to stay tonight. Sapphire runs the Blue Waters Motel. It's right on the beach."

"Beach?" Denny said.

Em laughed. "I think the little guy is sold. How about you folks?"

"Stuey..."

"Angel, it's all falling into place. How can I say no? We'll spend our day here in Poppin...uh...Penobscot."

Mandy didn't answer. It wasn't the town that bothered her, it was the name. Something inside her said to avoid Penobscot, but she couldn't give voice to it.

Denny frowned. "We don't got swimsuits. No way we can swim."

"You found a way before."

"Uncle Stuey!" He blushed furiously.

"Well," Em pointed out the window, "LaRue's Department Store is right across the street. They can fix you up in no time as soon as you're done here."

"Thank you," Denny said yet again, as if he just discovered the two words buried within all the green and liked the way they sounded.

Em turned her attention back to the adults. "One last thing. If you do decide to become a Penopscotan, you come see me or talk to Sapphire. We'll get you in touch with our brother, Stone. He's in real estate and should be able to find you a decent place to rent or buy when you're ready." She laughed. "I'm done prattling on now. I'll let you folks enjoy your breakfasts before they get any colder. I'll be back later to check on you."

The threesome dug in. As they ate, they decided to do just as the waitress suggested and hit the department store. Mandy reasoned that a day spent not cooped up in the car would do them all some good and, if they liked what they saw, and if Mandy could tamp down that little voice in her head, maybe they'd stay. If not, they'd move on and see what the rest of Indiana had to offer. Either way, she and Stuart were out of Wisconsin and Denny was out of Illinois.

"Stuey, do you think maybe we can find some dressier clothes for you and Knucklehead while we're at that store?"

"Whattya mean, Knucklehead?"

"She means you, Knucklehead, so pipe down. How come the fancy duds, Angel?"

Mandy squirmed a little. "I want to find a nice place for supper, wear my new dress. You know, like a regular family does."

"Well, I don't know, Angel. I mean, I clean up pretty good, but Stinkbomb here, well..."

"Hey!" Denny said. "I just took a shower the other night and I bet I look just as good dressed up as Beef Stuey does. I just don't like getting all fancied up is all."

"Little man, no guy does," Stuart explained after shoveling in a forkful of eggs. "But we gotta keep the ladies happy or they won't want us around, dig?"

Denny shrugged. "You guys say dress up, guess I got to." He finished off his milk. "But I won't like it."

The rest of the meal passed quickly and, as each of them finished, Em was right there to take away the empty plates. She escorted the group to the register and took Stuart's money, but refused his tip. "Hell, son," she said. "I own this place and you can see it does a pretty good business, so I'm not looking for tips. You save your money and buy the lady a little something." She tossed Denny a mint. "That's because you were good."

"Thank you," Denny said.

"You're welcome, kiddo. I'll be seeing you folks around town, I'm sure."

Once they were outside again, Stuart said, "Thank you. Thank you. Thank you. Oh, and thank you too. Kid, when did you get manners?"

"Don'tcha think somebody should have them around here?" he said and raced away before Stuart could swat him.

Stuart glared at Denny. "Kid, at some point you're gonna be in reach and then...pow!"

"Thank you," Denny said.

"You," Stuart said, "are one strange kid."

Denny took an exaggerated bow. "Thank you."

Stuart started to chase after him, but Mandy grabbed his arm.

"Boys, we're about to cross the street and go into a store where actual people shop. Pretend like you fit in and try to behave."

"Yes, Aunt Mandy."

"Stuey..."

"We were just having fun."

"Stuey..."

Stuart made his sad puppy face that always worked on Mandy. "Yes, ma'am," he said in a small voice.

She rolled her eyes and sighed. "You're too much."

"That's why it takes a special woman to handle me."

"Oh, gross."

"Shut your yap, kid. This here's called romance. You'll learn about it in about fifty years." He started to cross the street. "Let's go."

Mandy yanked him back. "Stuart!"

"What!"

"There's traffic. Don't just walk into it. Wait for a break."

"In school, they say we're supposed to cross at the corner."

Stuart scowled. "Look, kid. We're here. The store's right there across the street. There ain't no reason to go all the way down to the corner, wait for the light to change, cross, and come all the way back."

"It's called jaywalking. It's against the law."

"Naked swimmer boy, you got no place talking about the law. We already know you're a criminal." Stuart shook his head. "Let's go."

They crossed the street and entered the store. A man with a carnation approached and Mandy recoiled, remembering the creepy credit guy at the discount store a couple of days earlier. But this man's smile seemed genuine and all he wanted was to make sure they could find the department they needed. He directed them to the escalator and told them men's and boys' wear was on the third floor. Denny used his sweetly polite thank you and they headed off.

On the third floor, Mandy left Stuart to find his own things after giving him a list of what he was looking for and headed off with Denny to the boys' department. There, another man with another carnation offered his assistance. The salesman didn't bat an eye at the unusual combination of needs and led Denny to a mirror surrounded area.

"First, young man, we'll need to take your measurements."

The man pulled a tape measure from his pocket. He wrapped it around Denny's t-shirt clad chest and had him breath in and out. He then measured his arms and jotted something on a little notepad. When the man started to move his hand up the boy's inseam, Denny pulled away. "Watch what you're doing, mister. Ain't nobody touching me down there."

Mandy startled at the boy's reaction and wondered what else of Denny's past they didn't know. "Don't worry, sweetheart. He just needs to know how long your legs are. Nothing else will happen." She hoped the guy noted the threat in her voice.

The salesman got the measurements he needed and went off to pull some clothes from the racks for "the little gentleman to sample." Denny stayed close to Mandy's side while they waited for the guy to come back. When he did, Denny snatched the clothes from him and raced off to the dressing room. From where she still stood, Mandy heard the door lock. "He's a little shy."

"It happens. Especially at his age."

"I suppose."

Denny was back quickly. His button-down shirt was untucked and his sneakers looked silly sticking out from brown dress pants, but Mandy still thought he looked pretty darn adorable. Knowing how boys were, she resisted saying so. Instead, she said, "Not bad."

The salesman nodded. "I agree. Young man, I think we picked well. Why don't you show your aunt one of the swim trunks? That's definitely an item you don't want too large or too small."

Denny took off and Mandy used the time to ask the clerk about socks. All she had for the boy were white, and white socks with dress clothes reminded her too much of her father. She wouldn't have that. Hopefully, Stuart would remember to get some for himself.

The boy was back quickly, white dress shirt still on and hanging over the trunks, which she thought looked ridiculous. She went to him and lifted his shirt just a little to check the fit, ensuring she revealed none of his bruises. She declared the size perfect and the clerk agreed.

"Can I put my jeans back on now?" Denny asked, a hint of a whine in his voice.

"Sure."

"You just leave the merchandise you aren't taking right there in the dressing room and I'll restock it later," the clerk said. Denny went back to change and the salesman went for the socks Mandy requested. Stuart appeared at her side while she waited, wrapped packages in hand. "Shirt, pants, socks," he said, holding up his bundles. "And trunks and, for you, I even got a tie. Def don't expect that to be a regular thing." He looked around. "Where's the kid?"

"Getting dressed. We're done here."

"Good. Then we can hit the beach."

"Uh, Stuey, you're forgetting something."

"What's that, Angel?"

"Aunt Mandy needs a swimsuit too."

"Not as far as I'm concerned she doesn't. You looked damn good without one last time we was at the lake."

"And you looked damn good to Bryce and Troy."

"Don't remind me." He laughed. "Okay, you need one too. No telling who might be out there."

Denny came back with the pants, shirt, and trunks in a heap on his arm. He dumped everything on the counter for the clerk. "Beach next?"

"My swimsuit next."

He grinned. "Oh. Yeah."

"Yeah, Squirt," Stuart said. "Some people actually wear clothes when they go swimming."

The clerk presented them with Denny's wrapped packages. Mandy paid the bill, thrust the purchases into Denny's arms, and led the way to women's swimwear on the second floor. Denny lagged behind a little and Mandy couldn't believe he'd be having problems carrying his few items. She rushed him along, but he didn't look happy doing so.

When they reached the second floor, Mandy wasted no time in finding just the suit she wanted. Blue, with green accents, the two colors that looked best on her. "Aunt Mandy, you gonna get one of them ladies hats that look so stupid."

What was he talking about? A moment later, it dawned on her. "A swim cap? No, I don't care if my hair gets wet. But we do need one more thing."

Both guys sighed. "What?" Stuart asked.

"Towels. Oh, and a blanket to sit on. It'll only take a couple of minutes." She snapped her fingers. "And we all need shoes for tonight." Both guys sighed again. "We'll go quick, I promise."

Mandy was true to her word and in less than an hour, they were jaywalking back to the Oldsmobile. "Son of a fucking goddamn bitch!" Stuart said, earning a glare from a passing woman.

"Stuart! What's wrong?"

"We got a fu—"

"Stuart!"

"Sorry. Look." He pointed. "We got a parking ticket."

"So what?"

Stuart ripped the slip from the windshield. "This ruins my perfect driving record, that's what."

"Stuart, you've gotten lots of tickets," Mandy said once they were in the car.

"Not as Stuart Mason. I just wanted—never mind. Doesn't matter." He roared the Olds to life and they took off.

The beach was located just a few blocks beyond the business district, alongside a small but well-maintained park. A fortunate bend in the shoreline shielded the area from having too much of a view of the industrial buildings they'd just passed. Mandy was grateful for that. She wanted her lake to be as pretty as possible.

"There's some restrooms right over there, Angel. You and me can go change in there. Raw swimmer there can just strip and go."

"Uncle Stuey, it was one time."

"You just remember that. One time."

They headed toward the restroom and Mandy noticed Denny lagging and doing his odd little walk again. Not quite limping, but clearly something was wrong. She whispered to Stuart to find out what it was while they were changing.

Mandy separated from the guys when they got to the little building. She was just out of her blouse and bra when Stuart's laughter boomed from the other side of the wall. "Amanda Joan! Come here! You got to see this!"

He had to be joking. "Stuey..."

"Aw, there's nobody in here but us. Come over."

"Don't!" Denny squeak-shouted.

Her curiosity piqued, Mandy threw on her newly-purchased swim wrap and headed to the guys' side. Both were shirtless, Denny in swim trunks and Stuart still in his shorts. In her husband's hand, he held a piece of striped cloth that appeared to disappear in Denny's trunks.

"Go on," Stuart said. "Tell Aunt Mandy."

Denny looked at the tiled floor. "When...when I heard Uncle Stuey say he'd wear a tie for you tonight, I thought I should too. Only you didn't buy me one, so I swiped one." He looked up at her with a sad, hopeful smile. "I wanted to clean up good for you too."

"Well," Mandy said, "that was wrong, but kinda sweet."

Stuart was obviously trying not to laugh. "Go on. Tell her the rest."

The hopeful expression melted and the boy's gaze returned to the tile. "Well, the guy brought two swim trunks, so I kept one under my pants."

"And over your shorts," Stuart said. "Go on."

Denny hesitated, but Stuart gave him a look that urged him to finish. "So, I quickly grabbed a tie and stuffed it in there and now...now it's stuck."

"What's it stuck...oh, oh, I get it." The boy looked so pathetic Mandy had to bite her cheeks to stop herself from laughing. "You go in that stall and, uh, untangle yourself and you two finish getting ready. We'll deal with the stealing later."

Denny took a step toward the stall then stopped suddenly. "Uncle Stuey, let go," he whined, his voice squealing.

Stuart looked down at the tie as if he forgot he still held it. "Sorry, kid." He let the strip of cloth flutter away and Denny disappeared into the stall. "What a maroon," Stuart said after the door clicked shut.

"Is that really any worse than when you and Paul Holowitz were trying to light your farts with your dad's Zippo lighter and you set your own butt on fire?" Giggling came from behind the stall door.

"Ancient history," he said. "Go get changed. I'm for hitting the water all day."

Mandy went back to the ladies room and marveled for a moment at the huge event of this morning. Stuart bought a tie and was willing to wear it. Mandy recognized that for the sacrifice it was. Stuart hated dressing up, going so far as to rip his tie off at First Holy Communion and cry that the Lord was using it to choke him. God, she loved her husband. And her boy, who wanted to look his best for her.

She finished changing and hurried outside, where the guys were waiting for her. Stuart let out a low wolf whistle. "Looking good, Angel."

"Yeah, real good," Denny added.

"Well, since you both approve, let's get out there. I need my lake and I need it bad."

They found a spot in the sand, spread the blanket, weighed it down with the towels and clothes, and splashed into the cool water of Lake Michigan. The boys wrestled and tumbled and Mandy joined in for some of it and watched some of it. The three of them swam and floated and just enjoyed the water and the sun and, most of all, each other. When they settled into a world of work and school, these would be memories Mandy knew she would hold onto and cherish. Her family, together and without a care.

Mandy had just decided to stretch out on the blanket when somewhere nearby a church bell chimed. "Stuey, we gotta get going. We need to find the hotel and get a room."

"Then eat somewhere special. Kid," he called out. "Haul it in."

"Lunchtime?" Denny asked after swimming up to them.

"Nope," Mandy said. "We swam through lunch. Supper. It's after five."

"No way." Denny looked up to the sky as if judging the time by the sun. "Cool. I never swum all day before."

"None of us have, but now we need to scat."

As they waded back to the shore, Mandy made a silent promise to the lake to come back just as soon as she could. There was something about that water that called to her and reassured her. She would never lose that.

They made quick work of gathering their belongings, changing into their street clothes, and getting into the car. "What's the name of the place we're looking for?"

"The Blue Waters Motel," Denny said.

Stuart started the car. "Which way should we try? Left or right?"

"Left," Denny said. "I can see the sign."

"Can't argue with that." Stuart pulled out from the beach parking lot and, in less than two minutes, into the driveway of the Blue Waters. The motel was as blue as the Shamrock Café was green, with dolphins and assorted friendly looking fish gracing the perimeter. All-in-all, it looked like a giant cinderblock aquarium.

Together, they entered the hotel office, which was done up in lighter blue tones. A woman who had to be Em's sister Sapphire greeted them as if they were long-lost kin. "Em told me you'd be here when you were done playing at the beach and, sure enough, here you are. I've been holding Room 118 for you. It's the best we got. Just down by the pool—"

"You got a pool?" Denny interrupted.

"Wouldn't be the Blue Waters without a pool, and just a few steps outside your door. We keep it lit and unlocked till eleven at night." Sapphire bent slightly and said directly to Denny, "If you want to take a peek, just go outside. You can see it from the end of this building."

Without asking permission, Denny took off. "And for you two, the boy's bed is in an alcove. Impossible to see your bed from his. After all, married folks stay in a hotel, got to expect them to do what comes natural, right?"

Stuart grinned. "I like the way you think."

Mandy felt herself flush. She enjoyed special time with Stuart, but that was really nobody's business but their own, far as she was concerned. She was relieved when Denny barreled back into the office.

"The pool looks great," he announced.

"Glad to hear it," Sapphire said. "Wouldn't want to disappoint our guests."

"Maybe after we eat, you can swim for a bit before bed," Mandy told him. "If you're on your best behavior."

"That's the best way to do it," Sapphire said. "Good behavior means good rewards. Bad behavior, well..."

She busied herself with some paperwork on the counter and had Stuart officially check them in. She gave each adult a key to the room and thanked them for their business. Before she could turn away, Mandy said,

"Do you think you could recommend a decent restaurant here in town. We've been on the road and eating at stands and diners the whole way. It's time to fancy it up a little."

Sapphire reached under the counter. "Here's a list of restaurants in the city, good and bad. If you want a nicer place with good food and reasonable prices, I recommend The Embers. I'm partial, I admit, since my brother Garnet owns and runs it, but it's busy enough without my recommendation. Would you like me to call him and make a reservation for you? Say seven fifteen-ish."

"Sure," Mandy said.

"Thank you," said Denny.

Stuart shook his head. "Thanks for your help."

The room was nicer than Mandy expected. Unlike the mountain mural room they had back in Brownstalk, the theme, nautical, didn't overwhelm her. As promised, there was a twin bed tucked in an alcove around the corner for Denny and a huge bed for her and Stuart.

She put the department store packages on their bed and directed the guys to unload the car while she set up the room. She laid the guys' new clothes out for them and, when the suitcase came in, she immediately opened it and pulled out the special blue dress Stuart got for her in Legion. Finally, she was going to get to wear it.

Only, it was more than a little wrinkled from being packed in the suitcase for two days. She told Stuart to leave everything not yet put away in the corner. She planned to take a shower, a good, long, hot one, and let the steam get the worst of the road weariness out of the dress. She put it on a hanger and hung it on the back of the bathroom door, and then gathered other clothing she'd need. On a whim, she gathered up her makeup and shoes. When she came out of the bathroom, she wanted to knock Stuart's socks off.

As she had with every shower on the trip, she made the water as hot as she could stand it. Days of traveling melted into billows of steam, rejuvenating her and, she hoped, her dress. This, she told herself, would be the first of many nights like this. She'd get herself dolled up and go out on the arm of her handsome man, handsome men if Denny was with them.

And Denny was a good-looking boy. Definitely a little small for his age, but so was Stuey at twelve and he eventually had a growth spurt up to five-eight. They'd get Denny enrolled in junior high and she would go to parent-teacher meetings and the PTA and contribute to the bake sales, when she learned how to bake, and do all the stuff her own mother never did. She was sure Denny's mother didn't do those things either. Any woman who could fake the death of her own son, just to not be bothered with him, was unlikely to.

As much as she didn't want her shower to end, she was more than eager to be out and about with her family. She shut off the water, toweled dry, and put on her bra, hose, and panties before checking on her dress.

The steam worked wonders. The wrinkles were pretty much gone and the dress looked as good as it did in Patty's Patterns' window. Carefully, she took it off the hanger and slipped it over her head. The fit felt perfect. The length was ideal. It was as if Patty made the dress especially for her. She knew she was beautiful. Seeing the final effect would have to wait until she presented herself to her husband. The bathroom mirror was too small, and still fogged up anyway.

Mandy wiped the mirror with a towel. The little preview it provided told her she was on the right track. As usual, she applied very little makeup. Stuart always told her she didn't need it and beyond covering little blemishes, she really had no idea how to use it right anyway. At least Stuart would never be kept waiting on her for too long. She slipped on her new shoes, low heels with blue rhinestones, and went out into the main room.

Mandy peeked out the doorway and saw Stuart futzing with his tie. She waited for him to get the knot he wanted and then said, "Yoo-hoo."

When Stuart turned, Mandy heard his sharp intake of air and she knew she was everything she wanted to be for him. "Angel," he said. "You look...beyond incredible."

Denny poked his head around the corner. "Wowie wow! Thannnnnnk you."

She looked the two of them over. "You two are looking good yourselves."

"Except I don't got a tie after all," Denny said. "Uncle Stuey won't let me wear the one I got."

"Kid, I told you twice already. You're no criminal mastermind. You picked up an adult's tie, and a tall man size to boot. If we put that on you, you'd be tripping over it."

"But I wanna look good too. Why can't we just wrap it around a few times till the ends are the right size?"

Stuart snapped his fingers. "Now there's an idea," he said slowly. "We could wrap it around...tighter and tighter...and tighter and..."

"I've got an idea," Mandy said. She went into her makeup case and got her cuticle scissors. With a little work and patience, she shortened the tie from over-tall man to under-short boy. "The end's a little ragged, but nobody should be able to see that." She knelt in front of Denny and put the tie on him. "There. Two good looking escorts for this lovely lady."

Stuart took Mandy's arm. "Ready?"

Mandy linked her other arm around Denny's. "The Mason family is ready to see the town in style."

She felt funny using the name Mason when Mandy spent most of her life dreaming of being Mrs. Stuart Masamoli, but the change in name was a small price to pay for the family they'd become. She paid careful attention to the town of Penobscot as they drove. It was a nice little town, after all, and everyone here had been so friendly. She could see her, Stuart, and Denny settling down here and beginning the life they all deserved. Even the little voice was losing steam as she took in the town.

The restaurant looked particularly inviting with a blazing late afternoon sun behind the brick building. In front, red spotlights highlighted the bricks, giving the whole place a glowing, welcoming feel. Stuart remembered to open Mandy's car door for her, which made her glow as well, and a crimson-uniformed doorman ushered them inside. The lush maroon carpeting felt like heaven.

A well-dressed man approached them, his crimson carnation and pocket handkerchief seemingly coordinated with the tablecloths and napkins. "Welcome to The Embers," he said. "I'm Gerard and it will be my pleasure to be your host. Your name?"

"Stuart," Stuart said.

The man looked at a sheet of paper. "I'm sorry. I don't have a Stuart party listed. Do you have a reservation?"

"Lady over by the hotel said—"

"Ah, you must be the Masons. Mrs. Welkin at the Blue Waters told us to expect you. Right this way."

"Thank you," said Denny.

"You're quite welcome, young man."

Once they were seated and Gerard was gone, Stuart said, "No pushy table show-er and rude people staring at us tonight, Angel. This is heaps better than that place in Wisconsin."

"Everything here is better than Wisconsin." Mandy mentally hushed the voice in her head once and for all, she hoped. "Stuey, I've been doing some thinking."

"So have I, Angel. And I think we might be thinking the same thing." He picked up his menu. "We'll talk about it tonight. The three of us."

After a few moments, a young woman probably no older than Mandy appeared at their table. "Good evening and Welcome to The Embers." She didn't sound like she cared if they felt welcome or not. "My name is Julie and I'll be your waitress this evening. May I start you folks off with something from the bar?" Though the waitress addressed everyone, she never took her gaze off Stuart.

Mandy cleared her throat. "I'll have a Coke, thank you." The ice in her tone could have chilled all the drinks in the room.

"Can I have a Coke too, Aunt Mandy?"

Mandy used her left hand to brush a stray blond strand from Denny's forehead. She made sure to linger long enough for the waitress to see her wedding and engagement rings. "Sure, Dennis."

Julie never so much as glanced in her direction. "And is there anything I can get for you...sir?"

"I'd like a beer."

"We have several on tap. Do you have a preference?"

"Surprise me," Stuart said.

"Oh, I'm good with surprises. Let's see what I can do. I'll be back in a moment with the drinks and to take your order." She headed toward the bar, her hips swaying generously.

"Looks like she's got a wire loose in the caboose," Mandy said.

"Flirting for tips, Angel. Nothing else."

"Best not be."

"I bet she stuffs," Denny said.

Mandy nearly spat out the water she just sipped. "What?"

"You know, her chests." Denny cupped his hands in front of his chest. "To make them look bigger. One of my sisters used to wait tables at the Cow and Cluck and Mama told her to stick some tissues down there and she'd get bigger tips. So she did. Worked too."

Stuart laughed and, not knowing what else to do, Mandy joined in. Their laughter was just dying down when Julie appeared with their drinks. "Two Cokes." She put the sodas in front of Mandy and Denny with just enough force to jostle a bit of liquid out of each. "And a mug of Milwaukee's finest for the gentleman." She lay a coaster on the table and gently placed Stuart's beer upon it. "Are you ready to give me your order, sir?"

Stuart never looked up from the menu. "I'd like the house sirloin, with a baked potato and a bowl of chicken noodle soup."

"How would you like your meat done?" Julie asked with a small giggle.

"I like mine well done," Stuart said, still without making eye contact.

Julie's eyes never left Stuart. "And for the lady and the young gentleman?"

Denny looked from Julie to Mandy and back to Julie. "Me. Over here. I'll have fried chicken and mashed potatoes."

Mandy smiled across the table at him. "Lake trout and rice."

The waitress made notes on her pad, then said, "Will there be anything else, sir?"

After a slight pause, Mandy said, "Nope. You've done all you can do for us. Thanks, sweetie." She wished for a moment she hadn't left the little gun locked up in the trunk.

The waitress swayed away again. "Stuey," Mandy said, "maybe now is a good time to talk."

"About what?"

"Our future."

Stuart took her hand in his. "Is this the where?"

Mandy nodded. "I like everything we've seen and everyone we've met, with one exception, and I can handle her."

"They ain't real," Denny said.

"Seems like there's a few factories over by the lake. I should be able to find a decent job, I bet."

"Factory owner would be a fool if he didn't hire you."

"A guy can tell," Denny said.

"Hell, Angel, I'll be a foreman in a year."

"I know you will, Stuey."

"They just ain't right," Denny said.

"Didn't that lady at the diner say her brother does house rentals?"

"Oh, Stuey, we could have our own house in a couple days."

"I woulda known anyways cause they're kinda lopsided," Denny said.

Stuart rubbed his forehead then looked at the boy. "Kid, what the hell are you yammering about?"

"Our waitress' chests. They aren't all her."

"How would you know?"

"Simple. The tops are bouncy like they're supposed to be, but the bottoms just kinda sit there." Denny took a sip of his soda. "They're supposed to bobble." He looked pleased with his manly knowledge of the world.

Mandy noticed Julie heading their way with a tray and, sure enough, there was far more movement at the cleavage than down below. Smart kid to notice that, but she didn't plan on praising him for noticing.

"Your dinner, sir," Julie said as she laid a massive plate in front of Stuart. "I think it'll be just the way you like it." She plopped Denny's chicken in front of Mandy and Mandy's fish in front of Denny. "Let me know if you need anything else."

"Ketchup," said Stuart.

Julie left and was back in a flash, ketchup bottle in hand. She handed it to Stuart, winked, and went away again. Stuart uncapped the bottle and shook it vigorously. Nothing came out, so he smacked the bottom. A glob of ketchup flew out onto Mandy's arm. "Uh, sorry, Angel. Guess I'm stronger than I look." He offered her his napkin.

"Don't worry," she said, standing. "I'll just go wash it off. Be right back."

She headed off to an alcove where she thought the restrooms would be, but instead found herself at a doorway leading to an alley. She started to turn around when she heard voices.

"I've got to get a new job." Mandy recognized Julie's nasally, whiny voice. "This place doesn't get decent tippers. Nothing but old farts that tip a bright, shiny dime or farmers who give even less."

"I noticed you giving that young guy at table twelve a lot of attention."

Julie laughed. "Only got three sets of customers left and he's the only one under a hundred and forty. I don't think he's worth much for a tip, but I'm pissing off the bitch he's with, so that's fun at least. And, if I get the guy thinking he's got a chance at getting in my pants, he'll tip more. Like that bozo would have a shot at getting anything from me."

"I've seen worse," the other girl said.

"Not much."

"Give me a drag off your cig. Mine's gone and I've still got old Mrs. Polskawicz to deal with."

"Here. I'm telling you, Eve. I gotta get outta here."

"Well, yeah, you got that cute new convertible. I'd wanna be out cruising too, I was you."

"Instead I got bozo, bitch, and the boy to finish up and the other couple of tables. Can you imagine how young she started putting out to have that kid already? Anyways, once I'm done with those three tables, my ass is out the door. See ya inside."

Mandy quickly got out of the hallway and headed for a different alcove where the bathrooms actually were. How dare that bimbo call her Stuart a bozo! He was a respectable family man and Julie was clearly some little tramp who slept with customers, one who helped her buy a convertible. Probably the convertible was as used as she was. And calling her a bitch, why? She knew nothing about Mandy. Was the waitress looking in a mirror? Stuart would be pissed when Mandy told him about the comments. And she was definitely going to tell him. She'd make sure that he didn't so much as contribute gas money to the little whore.

After quickly washing her arm, she headed back to the table, where she filled Stuart in on what she overheard. During each of Julie's many appearances to check up on him, Stuart kept his eyes strictly down, barely acknowledging her. The one time he did look up, he waited for her to be gone and said, "The kid's def right. Stuffed." To Mandy's great delight, he kept Julie running—more water, a second napkin, a round of Cokes all around, a dessert menu, a doggy bag. When they were just about finished eating, he said to the others, "Just go with whatever I say, okay?"

When Julie showed up again to clear their dessert plates, she presented Stuart with a leather folder. "I hope you found everything to your liking, sir. Here's your check."

Stuart sat back. "Oh, not tonight. This is a special occasion. My wife is treating me to a night to remember. So the bill goes to her, not me."

Mandy felt her smile broaden as Julie's collapsed into a frown. She recovered pretty fast, though, and said, "As you wish, sir." She handed the check to Mandy.

"Thank you," Mandy said. She made a show of checking over each item and then counted out cash from her purse, handing bill and money to the waitress. "Keep the change."

The trio got up and left the restaurant. As soon as they were outside, Stuart said, "Angel, you let her keep the change?"

"Sure. Her service was worth four cents, wasn't it?"

Walking back to the car, Stuart stopped short. "Didn't you say the flat-chested wonder had a new convertible?"

"Yeah."

"And it's parked in the front lot?"

"Yeah, so what?"

"Nothing." He pointed. "Just we're parked right next to her. It's the only convertible out here."

"Oh."

Mandy pulled her hotel key out of her purse. She wasn't usually destructive, but when someone really made her angry, they needed to know it. Back in Bascombe, Alice Benowski made a play for Stuart and Mandy let it slide, but when it happened a second time, that was too many and Alice came out of school to find a nice long scratch in her beat-up old

Studebaker. Nobody got away with being nasty about Stuart. She sent Denny around to get in on Stuart's side of the car and, as she walked to the passenger door, she left a trailing scratch in the shiny silver paintjob. Mandy got in the car, slipped the key back in her pocketbook, and didn't say a word to Stuart about what she did.

Once everyone was in, Stuart backed the Olds out of the parking spot and shifted. He pulled forward and there was a sudden squeal of metal on metal. "Shit," Stuart said. "Clipped that convertible." He in no way sounded contrite. "We best get the hell out of here." He backed up, straightened the wheel, and they left the lot. As they went by, Mandy noticed a satisfying accordion crunch on the little car's bumper.

Back on the road to the hotel, Mandy asked, "How do you suppose a waitress can afford a fancy car like that?"

"Special tippers."

"Dang," Denny said. "I'd be a waiter in a flash for tips like that. Maybe you should be one, Uncle Stuey."

"Don't think so, kid. I ain't made that way."

"What's that mean?"

"It means shut your yap. I'll explain it when you're old enough to handle it."

They pulled into the motel and Stuart snagged the closest parking spot to their room. "Man, oh, man," he said. "After that supper, I'm for sitting on my ass and loafing for a while. That food was great."

"Can I go in the pool?" Denny asked.

Mandy checked her watch. "It's eight forty-five. Why don't you wait until, say, nine fifteen? Let your food settle a little so you don't get cramps."

"Aw, I've swum lots of times after eating and I—"

"How about nine thirty?" Stuart asked.

"Nine fifteen works. Maybe I can find a ballgame to listen to till then."

They went in their room and all three stretched out on their beds, Denny with his transistor. Mandy and Stuart cuddled together, not saying a word. They just relaxed, the deserved end of a beautiful day.

Mandy had no idea when she drifted into a nap, but she awoke to her shoulder being shaken and Denny saying, "It's nine fifteen, Aunt Mandy. Wake up." She opened her eyes and found herself face-to-stomach with Denny's belly button. The boy was definitely ready to go.

She sat up. "Tell you what. You go on out and me and Uncle Stuey will be there in just a few minutes. Stay in the shallow end until we get there."

Denny ran out the door and Mandy turned to wake Stuart, which turned out to be unnecessary. He was just emerging from the bathroom in his swim trunks. She sent him on his way and went to the bathroom for her hopefully dry swimsuit.

She found the guys splashing and wrestling in the pool and decided to sit on the sidelines and watch for a while. The night was clear and warm and the lounge chairs were awfully inviting. Except for one man reading a newspaper a couple of chairs over, they had the entire pool area to themselves. It was a perfect night for daydreaming.

Mandy let her mind drift to the next day. It looked like she and Stuart and Denny were going to stay here in Penobscot to start their new lives, so the first order of business would be to look up that real estate guy and see about renting a house. Or maybe getting Stuart a job should come first. Either way, she didn't want to stay at the motel too long. It was a nice place, but she wanted a home. She'd spend her first days fixing it up, then it would be time to enroll Denny in school and then homework and whatever else came next.

"Are you with them?"

The voice of the newspaper reader startled Mandy. "Umm...what?"

"I'm sorry. I didn't mean to intrude on your thoughts. I was just wondering if you were with those two young men." He indicated the pool with a wave of his hand.

"Oh. Oh, yeah, my husband and my nephew. We're looking for a place to settle down." Mandy launched into the now-familiar story of their marriage, Denny's mother's death, and how they made the decision to restart their lives anew.

The man was an attentive listener and Mandy was eager to see how the whole story put together would sound to a stranger who had no reason to listen other than polite conversation. The guy seemed to accept everything, no sweat, and Mandy knew in her heart that everything was as it should be.

A commotion from the water distracted Mandy from her conversation. She looked up and saw Denny sputtering and spitting water and Stuart clapping him on the back and wiping snot from the boy's face. "Stuey, what's wrong?"

"Hell if I know."

Stuart lifted Denny, still coughing and hacking, and sat him on the side of the pool. Mandy moved over by them to see if she could help. After a moment, the spew slowed to a trickle. "Denny, are you okay?" Mandy asked.

A noise that reminded Mandy of her father's post-closing time beer belch came out of Denny. Despite their concern, Mandy and Stuart laughed. "I'm okay," he said in a boy growl.

"So...what happened?" Mandy asked again.

"Nothing."

"Stuey?"

Stuart shrugged. "No idea. We were floating and talking and he suddenly went under."

"Denny?"

"I just slipped." He looked away when he said it.

"You just slipped? From the top of the water? Kid, what were you doing?"

Denny took a sudden interest in his feet dangling below the surface. "I was just curious is all."

"Curious about what?"

Denny's gaze never left the water. "Nothing important."

"Angel, this ought to be a doozy knowing this screwball. Spill, kid."

"Do I have to?"

"Wanna see tomorrow?"

"Aunt Mandy?"

"We won't laugh." Mandy hoped she wouldn't anyway.

"Just spill it, kid. You're gonna have to eventually."

"I...I farted in the water."

"You little pig," Stuart said. "Was it such a strong fart it pulled your skinny butt under?"

"Uncle Stuey..."

"Stuey," Mandy said. "It happens. Remember that time you—"

"So what happened, kid?" Stuart said quickly.

Denny still hadn't made eye contact with any of them. "I...I wondered if it smelled underwater."

She didn't want to, but the laugh was out before she could stop it. Stuart didn't hold back either. "You...you tried to sniff underwater?" Stuart was practically giggling like a little boy.

"Yeah." Denny sniffled. "I wasn't thinking."

Stuart suddenly turned serious. "Well?"

"Well what?"

"Could you smell it?"

For the first time, Denny looked up. He seemed lost somewhere between ready to cry and completely baffled. Then he started to laugh, making Mandy and Stuart crack up again. When the boy managed to stammer out "no," the adults laughed even harder, which made Denny follow suit, his embarrassment clearly forgotten.

Stuart jumped out of the pool and sat next to Denny. He put his arm around the boy. "We good?"

"Good," Denny answered.

"Feel better?"

"Yeah."

"Okay then." Stuart pushed Denny back into the water and slid in after him. In moments, they were back to their goofing off. Mandy glanced over at the loungers, but the salesman was gone, so she eased into the water herself.

After a few minutes of roughhousing, the guys floated much more leisurely, their conversation punctuated by Denny's giggles. Once in a while, one would splash water on the other and there would be a little tussle, but they'd settle back down quickly. It was so relaxing, so peaceful, so much what a family should be, that she let it go on longer than she probably should have. She didn't want to bring their good time to an end, but they all needed their sleep for what would be a very full Tuesday.

Surprisingly, she encountered no resistance when she said it was time to pack it in and get ready for bed. She knew why Stuart didn't resist. He wanted her tonight and she'd willingly oblige. Denny was the shocker, until she saw him let out with a huge yawn. Her boy was simply tired.

Getting Denny and themselves to bed proved to be easy. Mandy was spot-on with Stuart's desires and fulfilled them with her own. As they drifted off to sleep, Mandy's thoughts meandered to the dream house they'd find soon.

Tuesday

At breakfast Tuesday morning, each member of the family had a different idea of how they should spend their first full day in Penobscot. Denny wanted the pool or the lake, reasoning that they were on vacation and they should enjoy themselves. Mandy, who secretly wanted the lake as well, made the case for finding a place to live. A family needed a home, after all. Stuart hoped to start his job search, figuring it would be easier to rent a house once he knew what they could afford. The discussion went back and forth over stacks of French toast and sausage until Em gave them the solution.

"Such fussing, you three. Land sakes, this isn't so hard to figure out. Give everybody everything they want." She took a pad from her apron pocket and wrote something on it. "After you're through here, go to this address. That's Penobscot Real Estate, my brother Stone's office. It's just around the corner. I'll give him a call, tell him you're coming and what you'll be needing. When you're done, Stuart takes you two to the beach, he goes and fills out job applications, then he joins you. I know most of the personnel managers in town, so I can let them know you're coming and that you're working with Stone on finding a place to live. House, job, beach. Check, check, and check. Now how does that sound?"

Mandy swore she saw that twinkle in Em's eye again. "That sounds perfect. And now we don't have to spend all morning arguing."

"My pleasure, kids," Em said. "Sometimes it just takes an outsider to get you moving." She topped off Denny's water and went on her way.

"Guess we know now why everybody calls her Ma," Mandy said.

A few tables away, she noticed the man she spoke with at the pool the night before. He had an open briefcase on his table and he ate with one hand while writing something with the other. Mandy felt sorry for him, away from home and, she assumed, his family, not having enough time to eat his breakfast before work called. He caught her eye and saluted her with his fork. She smiled back at him. She wanted her Stuart to be successful, of course, but not like that. Family first, then business, was how she thought it should be.

As they finished their breakfasts, Em returned to the table and handed Stuart a sheet of paper. "That's a list of six personnel managers who know to expect you to be in today about finding work. Stone's about your height, so he's going to loan you a jacket. It'll be too big around, but it'll do. I bet you'll have a job by Friday."

Denny cocked his head. "How come you're so nice?"

"Because you're nice people." She took the money Stuart held and went for his change.

Nice people. That's something Mandy and Stuart were never called back in Bascombe. So who was right? The people in Bascombe or the people here? She thought about how she used to feel every day back in Wisconsin and how she felt right now and knew the answer. They were nice people, no matter how they got there.

Bill paid, the trio walked to the offices of Penobscot Real Estate, which was only a block from the Shamrock. Everything here was orange and brown and very, very male. Still, she liked it. It felt very homey to her, and it just made sense that a place that found people homes should feel like home.

There was no doubt Stone was brother to Em and Sapphire. He had a broad, friendly face, salt liberally sprinkled in a full head of pepper, and an incredibly friendly way about him. When he shook Mandy's hand, it was like she'd known him all her life. Her little voice chimed in again, trying to tell her something, but she ignored it.

"So, are you thinking of renting or buying?" the real estate agent asked once he had them all settle in his office.

"Renting. For now," Stuart said.

"Smart move. No point in buying when you're so new in town. Two bedrooms, or—" He looked at Mandy. "Do you anticipate a need for a third anytime soon?"

Mandy felt herself blush. "Two. For now," she said, but in her heart, she was thinking three.

"Sounds good. I have several nice houses available. Near the schools and shopping. Good landlords. Everything you could want. I have one in mind that I think will fit you to a T. Perfect home for the family just starting out. Would you like to see it? I have the keys right here." He reached in his desk drawer and pulled out a ring, which he dangled in front of them.

"I suppose we got time to look before I hit them personnel offices," Stuart said.

"Perfect. It's just about a mile from here. Now, if I know my sister, she said you could just leave your car at the Shamrock. Am I right?"

Mandy and Stuart both nodded.

"That's her way. In that case, rather than you walking back there, I'll give you a lift, we'll take a look at the house, then I'll drop you back at the Shamrock. Unless, of course, we come back here to sign the paperwork," he added with a laugh.

The agent led them to a Ford and they all piled in. As they drove, Mandy made note of everything they passed. If this trip was leading to her new neighborhood, she wanted to be sure she knew where everything was. They went by a shopping plaza with a market and a drug store and other things and Mandy pictured herself buying groceries and doing all the things a wife and mother did. Beyond it was a playground with a ballfield for Denny.

Two blocks after passing the junior high school, a building that brought a groan from Denny, they turned into the driveway of a small, neat bungalow type of house. Just looking at it, Mandy felt something she couldn't identify wash over her. This little house was blue with white trim and a large picture window in what was sure to be the living room. She could see herself watching out that window for Denny to come home from school and, later in the day, Stuart from work.

Mandy followed the others inside, still planning her future despite the emptiness of the house. The sofa would face the fireplace, with two easy chairs on either side of the window. When they bought a television one day, some rearranging would be necessary, but for now, her plans were perfect.

"As you can see, the home is unfurnished," Stone was saying when she tuned back in. Mandy wanted to disagree with him. She had it completely furnished in her mind. This would be home.

The agent led them through the rest of the house. It wasn't large, but it was clean and in good shape. No cracked windows to freeze her in winter. No peeling paint or chipped plaster. The wood floors and the linoleum gleamed. She wanted this house. She looked at Stuart.

He nodded. "When can we move in?" he asked.

Stone smiled wide. "As your new landlord, I say send the lady shopping as soon as the papers are signed."

There were hugs and handshakes all around before the foursome returned to Stone's Ford. "Soon as we get the paperwork out of the way, the house is yours," he said. "I think we should start with a six-month lease. By then you'll know if you can afford better or, maybe, need more space for any additions that may come along."

Mandy patted her stomach. It was possible, she supposed, that Stuey Junior was already a bun in her oven. Part of her hoped so, part hoped not. The three of them were a good team right now. Once Denny was a teenager and started to break away, then it would be easier to start thinking about adding to the family. They'd be settled in and Mandy would have some time on her hands.

"Here we are," Stone said as he pulled the Ford up to the curb in front of his office. "Let's go finish the deal."

When they entered Penobscot Real Estate, there was a man sitting in the lobby. Mandy was surprised to see it was the same salesman yet again. "A busy man's work is never done," he said by way of greeting.

"May I help you with something?" Stone asked him.

"Your girl has me comfortably settled, thanks. I didn't make an appointment. I hope it's not an inconvenience for you."

"No, no, not at all. I'll be all finished with these folks in just a few minutes and then my time is your time." He led Stuart and Denny into his office.

Mandy stopped when the guy said, "Nice looking family you have, Miss."

"Thanks," Mandy said, marveling over the word nice once more.

"It looks like they're waiting for you in there. I'll be in town for a while yet. I'm sure we'll bump into each other again," the guy said.

Mandy went into the office without replying. Something in the guy's manner made her uncomfortable, like he wanted more than he said. She forgot all about him, though, when the paperwork began. It felt like she and Stuart were signing their lives away in that office, but it was worth it. So very worth it.

A half hour later, Mandy, Stuart, and Denny emerged from the office of Penobscot Realty with keys to their first home and a six-month lease in hand. As they walked back to the Shamrock Café, Stuart took Mandy's hand. "I promised you back in Bascombe we was gonna make it and less than a week later, here we are. A home. A family. Real soon, a job. We're on our way."

"Are we gonna sleep in our house tonight?" Denny asked.

"There's no furniture, goofball."

"Stuey? Could we? We could buy some pillows and blankets and sleep on the floor. Get some food at the grocery store and make it a real campout."

"Can we, Uncle Stuey? Please?"

"Well, if you wanna do the shopping while I'm job applying, it's okay with me." He paused. "No, that won't work. You'd be stuck at the store waiting for me. Besides, we already paid for our hotel room." He pulled his keys from his pocket. "Tell you what. Since we already got the room, why don't we just take the bed stuff from there and bring it back tomorrow. That way, you guys can still go to the lake and the only place we have to hit is the grocery store."

"Good thinking, Uncle Stuey."

"Natch. Good thinking is what I'm best at."

They got in the Olds and Stuart drove them back to the Blue Waters. Mandy and Denny stripped the beds and loaded the pillows and blankets into the car while Stuart changed into his good clothes and borrowed jacket and took off. Mandy and Denny took turns in the bathroom putting their swimsuits on and headed to the sand and water adjacent to the hotel. As they did the day before, Mandy spread the blanket out and she and Denny weighed it down with towels and shoes. They moved quickly, both eager to get to the water. Mandy wanted to ask Denny if the lake called to him like it did to her, but she didn't think he'd understand.

Instead, she talked with Denny about junior high and his fears of being the smallest boy in his class. He brightened some when she told him Stuart was among the smaller boys and he turned out fine. She learned from Denny that he was a pretty typical boy. His grades were okay, about what Gil Tattinger predicted for him on his faked report cards, but he would rather spend his day anywhere but there. He mostly stayed out of trouble because, as he put it, "anything that made the school call home was a very bad thing." Mandy assured him he'd never have to feel that way again.

Denny floated past her and Mandy decided to take advantage of the quiet moment. "Denny, why did you decide to stay with us?"

"Because I could tell you guys are nice."

Nice. Again. Mandy could get used to this. But there were still questions she wondered about. "You don't have to tell if you don't want to, but what was it like in your family?"

Denny closed his eyes. "Nothing special."

"Everybody thinks that about their families."

The boy stopped floating and stood; the water up to his neck. "You've seen part of it," he said, then turned around as if to make sure she got the message.

"What's the rest?"

"Mama told the police I died rather than trying to find me." He said this without turning back. "It's...it's better this way."

Mandy heard a hitch in his voice and decided to drop the subject for now. Instead, she turned the conversation around to his room in the new house. "When we move into our house, do you want your room painted any special color?"

"Cubs red and blue," he said without hesitation.

"Hey, there's a good idea. We can do your whole room in baseball stuff if you want."

"Cool!"

She'd at least gotten his enthusiasm back. "Your uncle Stuey loves baseball. He even played it in school. For a little while." Until Coach

Fratiello kicked him off the team for smoking, telling him to come back the next year after he kicked the habit. Stuart stopped, but the next year never came, thanks to Old Poppin-Snot."

"Aunt Mandy, you think that school's got a baseball team?"

"I wouldn't be surprised. If they don't, we'll find you one somewhere."

"I'm not a great player, but I like—"

Denny's words were cut off when the boy suddenly disappeared beneath the water. A moment later, he resurfaced, sputtering and, beyond him, Stuart roared with laughter. "Gotta watch out for lake sharks, you little sea monster." He dunked Denny again.

"Stuey, how'd you get done so fast?"

"Fast? You guys have been here for over three hours."

"Really?"

"Yep, and I don't know about you two, but I'm starved. Job applying is hard work."

Denny splashed a handful of water in Stuart's face. "I could eat."

Mandy started to protest, but shut her yap. She lived here now. This beach, the lake, they were hers. They'd be here tomorrow and the next day and the next. And so would she. She followed Stuart and Denny out of the water and the three gathered up their things. Together, they headed to the Olds.

"Did you notice any grocery stores near the house, Angel?" Stuart asked once the car was loaded and they were out on the street.

"There was an A&P right before we got to the turn," Mandy said. "On the left." She paused. "But we got no cookware."

"Shit. That's right. Sack of burgers it is," Stuart said. "Looks like we start buying house stuff tomorrow."

As planned, they went to the house to unload the car. "We can put this stuff inside and go to the hotel to swim for a while before coming back here for supper."

"Can we get a snack?" Denny asked. "We never had lunch."

"If the feeding frenzy in the backseat doesn't mind, I think we should get the burgers now, get some chips and stuff at the A&P, and have an early lunch/supper, and then have a game party at the house tonight."

"I like that better," Stuart said.

"Me too," said Denny.

They pulled up in their driveway and a huge surge of pride swelled up in Mandy. A week ago, none of this would have been possible. And then Stuart said marry me and suddenly everything was more than just possible. She'd done some things she wasn't proud of, but who couldn't say that? And who did she hurt really? There were no innocent victims. Just nasty people who needed to be taught a lesson. Still, once Stuart had a job, everything would be in place and she'd convince him to get rid of the guns. Her little keying adventure and Stuart's not-so-accidental accident were their last antics, as Poppin-Snot would have called them. Going forward, they'd make it on their own; maybe even find a way to pay back the money once Stuart was successful.

Stuart's face was suddenly in her window, mere inches from her. "Angel? We're home. Kid's already got most of the stuff in the house."

"Sorry," she said as she got out of the car. "My mind was wandering."

"It's okay. He can do the work. Gives him a reason for being."

"Denny's reason for being, Mr. Mason, is to make our family complete," Mandy said, a little more harshly than she meant to. "And don't you forget it."

Stuart kissed her on the forehead. "Yes, ma'am."

Denny came up to them. "Aunt Mandy, Uncle Stuey, we got a problem."

"Yeah, but Aunt Mandy says we gotta keep you since you followed us home."

"Very funny."

Mandy asked, "What's wrong?"

Denny shrugged. "No lights. Guess Beef Stuey didn't pay the bill."

"Electric just hasn't been turned on yet, Wilfred. But that does sort of mess up our plans. Hard to play games in the dark." He leered at Mandy and whispered, "At least with a kid."

"Gross," said Denny.

"Muttface has the hearing of a dog, too," Stuart muttered.

"No problem," Mandy said. "There are stores by the A&P. We'll get candles and matches. Be even more like a campout."

"Cool." Denny smiled at her. "I brung everything in."

Stuart opened her door. "We best check and see where he put stuff."

Mandy got out of the Olds and they went into the house. Denny had the board games stacked neatly against the living room wall. "Suitcase is in the front closet," he said. "Everybody's clean clothes are in their rooms. Dirty clothes are in the bathroom."

"I'm impressed," Stuart said. "Maybe you'll grow up into...something."

Denny bowed. "Thank you," he said in his sweetest voice.

Mandy left the guys to their jostling and headed into the bedroom. When she walked in, all of her doubts about anything they did to get here vanished. She knew Stuey loved her now and always, of course, and now she knew for sure Denny did too. In the window, stuck into the frame, were all the postcards she collected along the way. Blue sat on the windowsill, with Denny's bear laying with its head in Blue's lap. Between his paws was a piece of paper with a heart drawn on it. In the middle were two words: *Thank you.*

Back out in the living room, Mandy gave Denny a wink and a smile, which he returned before breaking out into a full-blown beam. She mouthed him a thank you, figuring he would be embarrassed if she told him how sweet he was, especially in front of Stuart.

"So, do we want to relax a while or should we get chow now?" Stuart asked.

"Now," Denny said. His tone left no room for argument.

"But we should stop at the grocery store first so our supper won't get cold while we're shopping," Mandy said. "Maybe we should make a list of what we need."

"Oh, man," Denny whined.

"Chips, pretzels, soda, beer, candles," Stuart said. "Let's go."

"Stuey, how are we gonna keep soda and beer cold?"

"In the fri—oh."

Mandy sat against the wall. "Denny, get me paper and a pencil."

He ran off and Stuart sat beside his wife. "Angel," he said, "you're turning into a real mother." He paused. "The good kind, I mean."

A pad of paper and a pencil fell into Mandy's lap and Denny plopped down at her side. "Okay, chips, pretzels, soda and beer," she wrote under the header *Grocery Store*. "Ice, cooler, candles, matches," she added. These went under *Find a Store*. "Anything else?"

"Candy and a battery," Denny said. "My radio needs a new one."

Mandy added these items to their list. "We should maybe get a flashlight or two, too. In case we need them in the middle of the night."

"More batteries," Stuart said. "For the lights."

She wrote these and asked for more. "Bottle opener," Denny said.

"Good thought, kid."

"Thank you. Can we eat now?"

"No, we can shop now," Mandy said.

Denny sighed and sat up. "Then let's get going. I'm starting to starve."

The trip to the A&P was quick, given the family was limited to foods that didn't need cooking or refrigeration. Potato chips, pretzels, cookies and soda were quickly bagged and in the trunk of the Olds. Their second stop was at an S.S. Kresge store in the same shopping center. This stop wasn't so quick. The written part of their list was easy enough, but there were so many other things to look at, to think about. It took some talking before the three agreed to stick to the list and make plans later to come back when they were more settled.

Mandy and Denny were at the massive candy counter debating how best to spend the quarter she limited him to when she heard a familiar whiny voice. "That's the tight ass bastard who smashed into my car." Julie, the waitress from The Embers. How did she know Stuart did it? "Daddy is pissed about it." A moment later, two male voices were going at it, with Julie's whine interjecting comments.

Mandy told Denny to stay put and she went off in search of the angry voices—Stuart's, Julie's, and some guy. Probably the sucker Julie sexed the convertible out of, Mandy figured.

"I don't know what the hell you're talking about," Stuart was saying when Mandy showed up behind the other two.

Julie moved in on him. "I got cigarettes out of my car last night and it was fine. You and that bitch of yours were the only people who left between then and me going out for my scarf. Had to be you."

"And now I lost my job when my boss saw the dents," the guy said. "And you're going to pay for it, assface."

"How do you know somebody didn't drive in and do it?"

"Don't be a spaz. There ain't that many heaps in and out of that place."

Stuart backed away a little "My car is out the lot right now. You can go look at it and see it don't have no dents or scratches."

The john, Mandy decided that's what he had to be, clenched his fists. "Julie says it was you, it was you." His hands looked like hams at the ends of muscled tree trunk arms.

When Julie's sucker moved toward Stuart, Mandy glanced around and saw a rack of cast iron skillets. Feeling like a suspicious housewife in a bad comedy, Mandy grabbed one and swung it at the john's head. There was a satisfying thud of dull metal against duller cement and the guy went down. Julie startled at the sound and the suddenness of it all and turned just in time for the backswing to catch her full in the face. She, too, went down.

The look of total shock on Stuart's face was fast replaced with admiration. He stepped over the unconscious threats and went to his wife. "Holy crap, Angel," he said as he took the pan from her and replaced it on the shelf. "Holy crap."

"You would've done the same for me," Mandy said. "Let's get our boy and get out of here."

Denny was still at the candy counter, clearly oblivious to what just transpired two aisles over. "Hey, Aunt Mandy, Uncle Stuart. I'm all set to go." He held up a bag. "We just need to pay."

Mandy gave the girl a quarter and the three rushed to the front of the store. While they were in line to check out a policeman raced by, heading toward the housewares department. "There's our cue to get out of here, Angel. Take the kid and go wait in the car. I'll finish up here."

She didn't have to be told twice. She grabbed Denny's arm and practically dragged him out of the store and into the Olds. "What the heck was that all about, Aunt Mandy?"

That, she thought, was stupid. Stupid with a capital S. What she did was stupid, but she had to defend her husband. No, she chastised herself.

What was stupid was keying the waitress' car. That was her mistake, and that mistake lead to Stuey's crunching the little convertible's bumper and then to the scene in the Kresge's. Time to grow up and be Joan Amanda Mason, not the Mandy Heinemann she was back in Bascombe.

"Aunt Mandy?"

Shit. How did she explain all of this to Denny? "Well, there was a little problem in the store," she started. "That waitress from last night said some stuff to Uncle Stuey and her boyfriend said some stuff and, well, it was better to just get out of there and not create a scene."

"Maybe the police are there because she's bad news. Girls who stuff and guys who like them always are," Denny said. "My sister sure was."

Despite her fears for Stuart, Mandy managed a smile. "That's probably it."

A moment later she spotted Stuart strolling casually out of the Kresge store. Once he was away from the doors and in the parking lot, he picked up his pace and got to the Olds. When he arrived, he threw the bundles in the back seat and jumped up front. "We got to agitate the gravel before we get caught up in that mess." He started the car, gunned the engine, and they sped off to their third stop, the Shamrock Café.

Though the restaurant wasn't as busy as during the breakfast rush, business was still fairly brisk and Em was still on duty. She saw them, grabbed menus, and said, "This way." This was the first time Mandy didn't see that twinkle in Em's green eyes or hear it in her voice. She wondered how many hours a day the older woman worked. At least twelve, Mandy figured. No wonder the sparkle was gone. Em must have been exhausted.

"We aren't staying," Stuart explained. "We just came in to get a sack of burgers and fries. We're celebrating our new house that your brother helped us find."

"Thank you," Denny said.

Em smiled weakly at him and tousled his hair. "Was a pleasure." She pointed to a padded bench by the door. "Wait over there. I'll get your food together." She walked away.

They did as instructed. "Miss Em seems wrong," Denny said. "You think she's sick?"

"Nah, just tired," answered Stuart. "Before my old lady took a powder and disappeared, she was a waitress and by the end of the day her feet were so sore she was nothing but cranky."

Denny looked up at him, curious. "What do you mean, she took a powder and disappeared?"

"What I said, kid. We come home from school one day when I was about your age. No Mom, no Dad. We knew Dad was at Blansky's, drinking up his unemployment relief, but Mom was usually done by then unless she got extra hours."

"Okay, so what happened?"

To Mandy's surprise, Stuart didn't tell Denny to shut his yap. Instead, in a soft voice only she and Denny could hear, he launched into the story. "Me and Ralph, that's my older brother, went out and played like we always done, and came in when the streetlights went on, just like we were supposed to. No Mom. No Dad. Me and Ralph found some crackers, called them supper, played a while, and went to bed. Next morning, and every day after that, no mom."

Denny looked crestfallen. "And she never came home?"

"No. Never seen her since. Don't miss her none neither."

Denny sat there for a moment, then glanced up at Stuart. "Yeah," he said.

Though she was female, Mandy knew what that "yeah" meant in boy-speak. Denny knew how it felt to suddenly one day be dropped out of a mother's life. He knew the pain of that loss, even if the mother in question wasn't particularly warm and loving. Stuart never talked about his mother after that day when she left an eleven and a thirteen-year old alone with their miserable excuse for a father. Until now. With their boy.

Tramp was the word her own miserable parents called Mrs. Masamoli after she went away. Axel Gilroy left his wife and kids behind that same day and everybody knew Mr. Gilroy was a regular at the Speedy Dash Hash House, where Stuart's mom worked six days a week. When Mr. Gilroy returned home two years later, armed with candy and flowers and toys and apologies, his kids let it be known their dad was gone on post-war related secret government business they couldn't tell anybody about. Mandy never believed that. She doubted anyone really thought a small-town brewery worker had any skills the government could use, but nobody ever called the kids on it. The day Stuart heard Mr. Gilroy came home, he ran out after school without waiting for Mandy. For a week, he raced out of the building and, she learned later from Ralph, headed for home. Then things went back to the way they were and Stuart continued to act as if he never had a mom.

"Sack of burgers and fries." Em thrust a greasy paper bag at Stuart, giving him the check as well. She handed Denny a little bag. "There's an apple and a carrot in there for you, young man. Growing boys need fruits and vegetables at every meal." She tousled his hair again. "Promise me you'll remember that."

"Thank you," Denny said.

"You're welcome." She kissed his forehead. "Goodbye, youngster. Enjoy the food." She trudged off.

"Must be having a really long day," Stuart said as they headed for the car.

"Looks like it," Mandy answered.

Maybe once they were settled and Denny was in school during the day, Mandy would offer to work for Em part time, help her out and earn a little money for herself.

"Burgers smells great," Denny said, interrupting her thoughts. "Heavy sack, too. Miss Em must have loaded us up."

"Don't be opening it up and letting the hot out," Stuart said. "Ain't like we can reheat anything."

"One French fry?"

"One knuckle sandwich?"

"We'll eat soon," Mandy promised. "One more stop then home for game night."

"What stop now?" Denny asked, his irritation obvious.

"Liquor store. We need ice," Stuart told him.

"Where we gonna put it?"

Stuart looked to Mandy. "I bought a big bowl at Kresge's," she said. "We'll put the ice in the bowl and put it in the freezer. It won't melt so fast that way, even if the freezer isn't working yet."

"That's pretty smart, Aunt Mandy. Can we get ice fast so we can eat?"

"Shut your yap. Only be a couple more minutes."

The liquor store was close to the house and Stuart was in and out quickly, returning with a bag of ice and a paper bag. "Grown up treat," he told Mandy with a wink. "Christen the new place."

"New home," Mandy corrected.

"Yeah."

There was yeah again, but this one was completely different. It said Stuart understood what she was thinking, what she was feeling, because he was thinking and feeling the same. He said it all in one word. Incredible.

Back home, they brought in the groceries and other purchases and Mandy set about putting out the food while Stuart filled the ice bowl. Denny stood by, watching while he munched on an apple. "You know," Mandy said, "we didn't think about plates and cups."

"We don't need plates," Denny said. "And we can drink the Cokes right out of the bottles."

"They're still warm, dopey. They've only been on ice for a few minutes."

"So? Warm Coke is better than no Coke."

"Good attitude, kid. Still, we'll keep them on ice till Aunt Mandy says it's chow time."

"It's chow time," Mandy said.

"Cool," Stuart said. "Cokes should be nice and cold now."

The threesome laughed and carried their food into the empty dining room, where Mandy had the beach blanket spread on the floor. Stuart went back into the kitchen. Mandy heard Coke bottles being opened shortly after. Denny raced off toward the bedrooms. Mandy had no idea what he was up to.

Both came back to the dining room at the same time. Stuart had three bottles of soda and passed them around. Denny had his transistor radio. He made a show of pulling out the earphone plug and turned the radio on. "Supper music," he said.

"That's a great idea," Mandy said.

Stuart, who was still standing, bowed deeply. "Thank you."

Denny put the radio on the windowsill and sat at a corner of what Stuart called their "floor table." He popped a handful of fries in his mouth.

"I didn't know you had a brother, Uncle Stuey," he said between chews.

"Yeah," Stuart said around a huge bite of burger. "Ralph. Couple years older than me. Knocked up—"

"Stuart!"

Denny laughed. "Aunt Mandy, I know what knocked up means. I got two sisters who both had babies."

"Oh. Well, go on, Stuey."

"Right. Ralph got his girl pregnant and they had to get married. A year later, they have a screaming brat and hate each other. Why you got to be set in life first, like me and Aunt Mandy are doing. Learn from us, kid."

"How 'bout you, Aunt Mandy?"

Mandy took a drink from her bottle. "I've got an older sister and a little brother."

The last thing she wanted to do was talk about her former family or anything to do with Bascombe, but the boy had a right to know about their lives. "Linda's a year older and Craig's four years younger."

"I got a mess of brothers and sisters," Denny said. "I'm the youngest. You don't wanna be the youngest in a mess. You don't get nothing new or your own bed or nothing. All you get is picked on."

"How many is a mess?" Stuart asked.

"Eleven. And I don't miss none of them." Denny's voice was surprisingly strong when he said this.

At that moment, the radio disk jockey announced the next song would be "Earth Angel." Stuart scooted over by Denny and, when the record began, Mandy's two men serenaded her. She put down the French fry she was about to eat and just watched them. Whatever love Stuart lost when his mother disappeared or his father beat him, whatever love Denny salvaged from an eleven-way split, she had all that much and way, way more for them. She made a decision while the boys sang on. Tonight, they'd talk about whatever came up from their lives and, starting the next day, never mention them again. The past would truly be past.

When Mandy was little, a revival evangelist came to Bascombe and her grandmother forced her and her siblings to go. All she remembered of that night was the guy shouting about being reborn and her wishing she could be. Now, she and Stuart and Denny would be.

When the song ended, both guys fell backwards, their laughter bouncing from the ceiling. "Kid," Stuart said, "please tell me you ain't in choir."

Denny, whose voice cracked a couple of times during the performance, said, "You ain't exactly Perry Como."

"I thought both of you were great," Mandy said. "Finish eating so we can get to the games."

"I'm done," Stuart said.

"Me too. For now."

After Mandy led the cleanup, the group moved into the living room. By piling up the pillows and using the now-empty suitcase as a table for their candles, they created a cozy little area for games. They started with Denny's choice, Sorry, to finish up the World Series they started back in Valhalla.

The first games passed quickly and they were all tied up at three wins a piece. The next game would decide the winner. "What's the prize for the winner?" Denny asked.

Stuart pursed his lips. "Dunno. Didn't know we needed one."

"Heck, yeah. There ought to be a prize."

"Well, we been talking about what we want for the house," Mandy said. "What say the winner gets to pick one special thing?"

"Sounds good," Stuart said.

"Deal," said Denny.

"Then we're set. Let's play."

They reset the board quickly and the game was on. It didn't go well for Mandy, who couldn't draw the necessary one or two card to get one of her yellow markers on the board. She didn't care though. She didn't know what she wanted that she didn't already have.

It was different for the guys. They both had three men home and the fourth headed that way before Mandy even had her third on the board. Each turn of the cards was met by groans by the two. Finally, Denny drew the three he needed and, after Stuart threw a fake fit and insisted the deck was stacked against him, the boy was declared the winner. "So, you lucky little cheater, what's your special thing?" Stuart asked.

Denny didn't hesitate. "A dog."

"Why? We ain't looking to replace you."

"Stuey, be nice."

"Well, I'm mad. The kid stole my idea."

"Really?" Denny grinned.

"Man. Boy. Dog. It's a natural."

"I agree," Mandy said. "Once we're set up, we'll get a dog."

"Yep. What's one more funny smelling beast in the house?" Stuart said.

"Yeah, we already got you."

"Kid...I warned you."

Stuart lunged at Denny, holding him down with one hand and tickling him with the other. Denny's laughter filled the room.

Mandy took advantage of the ruckus to sneak into the kitchen for a second round of Cokes and the snacks. In the kitchen, she felt herself smiling. A dog. Of course Denny would want a dog. She'd never been allowed to have one and neither had Stuart. If Denny had one back in Legion, the poor thing would have had eleven kids wearing it out. Their dog, when they got it, would be the most spoiled pet in the history of animals.

When she returned to the living room, Mandy saw the tickling had evolved into a full-fledged wrestling match. She put the snacks and drinks in the corner and moved the candles a safe distance away. Mandy looked out the picture window at their new street. It was dark now and, with the streetlight being a little way down the block, the cars in the driveways and in the street, the trees, the bushes, everything looked black, but somehow safe. There were lights on in some of the other houses and she wondered who lived in them. Were there boys around Denny's age for him to play with? Maybe in one of those houses was the girl he'd grow up to love the same way she and Stuart grew up and into love together on the same street. Was there a best friend out there for her and a buddy for Stuart? People to go out with and grow old with? Not that they would be old anytime soon.

"Aunt Mandy? It's your turn to pick a game."

"Huh?"

"I thought Uncle Stuey picked next."

Stuart shoved Denny over. "I picked tickle the crap out of the kid.

So it's your turn."

Mandy shook her head and laughed. "I'll decide in a minute. Cokes and popcorn are over there. I need to go to the bathroom."

She grabbed a flashlight and made her way down the hall. Carefully, she placed the light on the sink, bulb pointing toward the wall, illuminating quite a bit of the small room. She gazed longingly at the bathtub. A hot bath in her own tub sounded like heaven. Mandy undid her jeans and was just about to sit and do her business when a thought hit her. She reached over to the sink, turned the closest knob, and...nothing.

She pulled up her jeans and returned to the living room. "Guys," she said. "We got another problem. No water."

"So? No water, no bath," Denny said.

"And no toilet, goofus," Stuart countered.

Denny's expression was equal parts horror and fear. "How are we supposed to...you know?"

"Backyard is full of trees," Stuart said.

"But what if we have to do more than stand?"

"Grab the roll, a flashlight, and a comic book, go out back, and squat."

"Are you kidding?"

Stuart shook his head. "No other choice, kid."

"And let's make a deal," Mandy said. "If there's a girl out back, no guys. And if there's a guy, no girls."

"Deal," Stuart said.

"Double deal," Denny said. "For sure."

"You two stay in here," Mandy said. "I'll be right back."

Mandy headed out the backdoor. She was so focused on the inside of the house when they had their tour that she paid very little attention to the yard. She wasn't sure now where the trees even were. She shone the light around until she picked the most likely spot. As she prepared, again, to do her business, she kept turning her head, making sure she couldn't be seen from any neighboring windows. She wanted to meet people, but jeans down wasn't how she wanted to do it. Tomorrow, she decided, their first two tasks would be to have the water and electric turned on. Then, of course, shopping and the lake.

A few minutes later, she was back in the house. Stuart and Denny were playing cards. "Is this a two-man game or can a girl get in?" she asked.

Stuart shoved a handful of chips in his mouth and crunched loudly. "You can get in the next hand. We're playing poker. Kid's an easy mark. Gonna owe me a year's allowance by the end of the night. You could even beat him."

"No thanks," Mandy said. "I never did get that game."

"Me neither," said Denny. "But Uncle Stuey's a good teacher."

Mandy left the boys to their game and went into the bedroom for another of the romance novels she bought back in Valhalla. She picked one, went back to the guys, and stretched out on her pillow. She was soon lost in her story and the magical world of love. The author kept the hero and heroine apart, which was typical but frustrating. Being apart from Stuart would kill her.

"Aunt Mandy?"

Just as she was getting to the good part. "Yes sir?"

"Uncle Stuey fell asleep. You wanna play something with me?"

"What time is it?"

"About eleven-thirty."

"About bedtime then. Why don't you go brush—wait, no, you can't. We'll have to skip tooth brushing tonight." She yawned. "Why don't you go on out back and I'll get your blankets and stuff set up?"

Denny looked at her as if she sprouted a third arm. "Go out back? Alone?"

"There's nothing out there but grass and trees."

"I can hold it."

"In the morning, it'll be daylight and people will be able to see."

"Oh. How far back do I gotta go?"

"Wherever you feel comfortable."

Stuart stirred from his spot. "Why's it so dark?" he asked.

"It's night," Denny said.

"Funny kid." Stuart stood up and stretched. "I need to take a leak. Where's the flashlight?"

"It's on the kitchen counter. Take Denny with you."

"I don't need help with this."

She shot him a look. "Just take him."

"C'mon, kid. Let's go flood the backyard."

The two went out and Mandy grabbed a pillow and went into Denny's room. She decided he'd lay with his head under the window so the sun wouldn't wake him too early. In her room, she arranged the bedding so she and Stuart would be very close all night. Having had a week of sharing a bed with him, she discovered how much she liked the closeness.

The backdoor slammed and, within seconds, the guys were in the room. "This kid," Stuart said, "is no Davy Crockett."

"What?"

"'Uncle Stuey,'" Stuart said in a mocking voice. "'I can't poop out here.'" Mandy tried not to laugh when Denny blushed a deep scarlet. "So, I had to check out the house next door. Nobody home, door unlocked, so I quick hauled his skinny butt in there." He turned to Denny. "Don't expect me to do that again."

"No, sir."

"Uh...Stuey?"

"Yeah, Angel?"

"You think maybe they still ain't home?"

Stuart exhaled loudly. "Oh, for Christ's sake, come on." He reached out his hand for her and they went off. They quickly scooted from backdoor to backyard to backdoor and into the neighbors' house. Mandy did her business by moonlight, fearing someone might see the light when no one was expected to be home. She didn't dawdle and was soon finished. The flush sounded like a monsoon in the empty house and she raced out of the room to Stuart.

"From what I can see, this looks like a nice place," he said. "They got a television, so we might—"

The beam of car headlights sweeping across the room cut his sentence off. Wordlessly, Stuart yanked Mandy through the house and out. As they snuck to their yard, they could hear the neighbors out front. Angry voices, ugly words. They'd clearly been drinking and there was some flirting going on wherever they'd been. "Angel, we ain't ever gonna end up like that," Stuart whispered.

"Nope. Let's get back in to Denny. He should be in bed by now. It's getting late."

Hand-in-hand, they went back through their own door, which Mandy closed softly, and went to Denny's room. The boy was already undressed and snuggled into his blankets, the orange bear peeking out discreetly from beneath the pillow.

Mandy and Stuart sat on the floor on either side of Denny. Together, the threesome made a list of plans for the next day—turning on lights and water, furniture shopping, housewares buying. "Aunt Mandy knows how to use a skillet like nobody's business," Stuart said with a laugh.

"Shut up," Mandy said, though she didn't mean it. She defended her husband. No crime in that.

"What else we got to do tomorrow?" Stuart asked.

"The lake," Mandy and Denny answered simultaneously. Inwardly, Mandy smiled. Denny did feel it. Her boy got it.

"Well, natch," Stuart answered. "Natch."

"If we're gonna do all that and have time to enjoy the water, we need to get some sleep," Mandy said. She fished in her jeans pocket and pulled out the earphone she picked up off the dining room windowsill.

Denny sat up and gave Stuart a hug. "Goodnight, Uncle Stuart. Love you."

"Love you too, kid."

He switched over to Mandy's side and gave her a long hug and a kiss. "Goodnight, Aunt Mandy. Love you."

Mandy kissed him back. "Love you, too. Now and always." She squeezed him tight. "More than you'll ever know."

Denny snuggled into the blankets and Stuart blew out the candle. He gave the boy another quick man hug and stood. Mandy followed suit, only her hug for the boy lingered a little longer before she stood. They went to their own room after another whispered goodnight.

Once their door clicked shut, Stuart drew Mandy to him and they kissed, long and deep, the way Mandy figured a movie kiss was after *The End* flashed on the screen. They weren't high schoolers making out in the corner booth of the soda fountain or dropouts doing it behind a loading dock. They were husband and wife and this was passion and need, desire and greed.

Mandy allowed Stuart to undress her. A few days ago, she was still a little shy about being completely naked in front of him. To her, it felt like they were kids those first few nights, out on an adventure that was destined to end. But this, this was so right. They were grownups and this was lovemaking. This was two becoming one, which Mandy was pretty sure the judge said when he performed their ceremony.

Then, suddenly, Stuart pulled away. He took her face in his hands. "Angel, you get yourself all comfortable and I'll be right back." He slipped out of the room, leaving the door open behind him.

She did as he requested, snuggling into the layered blankets, and waited for him to return. In less than a minute, he was back, a bottle and two glasses in his hands. "What's that?" she asked.

Stuart set the glasses and bottle down on his side of the hotel comforter. "Champagne, Angel," he said. "Told the guy I wanted to celebrate our new house and to give me the best they had." He unscrewed the top and poured them each a glass.

Mandy took hers. "Where did you get these?"

"Filched 'em from the house next door when I was there with the kid. One day, we'll give them back."

Stuart started to take a sip, but Mandy stopped him. "I think we're supposed to say something first."

"You mean like, over the tonsils and down to the gullet..."

"Kinda, but romantic."

Stuart kissed her lightly. "Okay." He paused, a bit longer than Mandy would have liked, but he found his words. "To my angel, the woman I love, and our new life," he said. "I love you."

"I love you too."

They clinked their glasses and drank. The first taste hit and Mandy wanted to spit it out, but she managed to swallow. It reminded her of the time when she was a little girl and she and her friend Carol Gardenhire decided to open a lemonade stand, only they had no lemons. They combined whatever they could find, including a few things from the Gardenhire liquor cabinet. That didn't end so pretty. Still, she'd finish the champagne for Stuart.

He looked none-too-eager to down more than a sip himself. When he put his glass down, unfinished, so did she. She rolled into his embrace. "Tomorrow, Angel, will be the best day of our lives," Stuart said. "House, kid, maybe a job. Everything's coming together and tomorrow is when we move forward."

Mandy spread her arms to him. "I don't think you'll have any complaints tonight, either, Mr. Mason." She welcomed him inside her and enjoyed their first night in their new home.

Wednesday

Mandy peeked into the oven for the umpteenth time. The roast beef looked perfect, simmering in its own juices like the cookbook said. By suppertime, it would be just right. The potatoes and carrots would be cooked through but not mushy. She had everything ready to toss the salad, and the dessert; chocolate cake, Stuey's fav, was frosted and waited under its cover.

Denny was in his room, drawing and listening to the radio. He was none-too-happy about having not only to come inside early, but take a pre-supper shower as well. Still, he understood this was a special night and he was being cooperative, even though it meant dressing up.

The kitchen smelled fantastic. The table was all laid out and set. Stuart would be home soon, so she adjusted her new apron; a pink and frilly one from the Kresge's, checked the roast one more time, and sat down at the table to wait.

The neighbors, Letty and Hank and their kids, were coming over for the first time and Mandy was sure they'd be impressed with the meal and the house. Their son, Donovan, was about a month older than Denny and would be starting junior high with him in the fall. Denny and Donny were a matched set in a lot of ways, so a friendship was already forming. Trudy was two years younger and clearly had a crush on her brother's new buddy, though Denny was still young enough to be oblivious. Everything was working out perfectly.

The sunburst clock showed she still had a bit of time until Stuart got home from the factory, so Mandy allowed herself a few minutes to sit and daydream about the future. Denny, grown up, out of college, and all set up in the business world, and Trudy, a beautiful bride, ready to be walked down the aisle in the two families' combined backyards. Stuart was everywhere that day, making sure everything was perfect, as he always did. Of all of her dreams, this one was her absolute favorite.

"Aunt Mandy! Uncle Stuey! Wake up!" Denny's insistent voice echoed in the nearly-empty room.

Mandy roused herself as best she could without losing the blanket covering her and opened her eyes. "Denny, what's going on? What time is it?"

"I don't know, but there's a buncha cars outside our house."

It took Mandy a minute to get her bearings. Their house. Bedroom floor. Denny, wearing only his shorts, insisting they wake up. "What time is it?" she asked again.

"I don't know. I got up to find something to eat and there's all these cars outside—"

Stuart swatted at him with a pillow. "Kid, it's a neighborhood. People live here. Go back to sleep."

"Uncle Stuey!" Denny's voice squeaked, near-hysterical. "These ain't neighborhood cars. They're all black. And all of them got guys in suits in them."

Stuart bolted upright. "Get dressed." His voice was a raspy growl that didn't sound just like early morning sleepiness. "Now. Both of you." He stood up, not caring he was stark naked. "Move!"

Denny raced from the room and Mandy tried to untangle herself from the bedding. "Stuey, what's happening?"

"Don't know, Angel," he said. He slipped on a t-shirt and boxers and opened the closet door. From inside, he said, "But it won't hurt to be ready." He emerged a second later, gun in hand.

"Stuey! No!"

"Just being careful, Angel. Not gonna use it. Finish getting dressed."

Though she did as Stuart instructed, Mandy's eyes never left the gun. Back when they were leaving the bank, Stuart told her guys got caught because they did something stupid. Mandy prayed Stuart wouldn't get killed doing just that.

She just finished doing up her jeans when there was a pounding at the door. A gruff voice hollered something, with all the echoing, Mandy wasn't sure what it was, and a split-second later, the door frame shattered open. Three men with three guns burst into the living room. Mandy saw more men with more guns at the windows. Done for. They were done for.

The dream was over.

One look at Stuart and Mandy knew he knew it too. His shoulders slumped and his head was down. When one of the men in suits moved for Stuart's gun, he didn't stop him. He didn't do the stupid thing. Even in defeat, her Stuart was smart.

She stole a glance at Denny, who was a trembling, wide-eyed bunny hunched in the corner. Beside a large policeman or whatever the hell he was, the boy looked even smaller than he was. She wanted to hold him, to shield him from seeing all this, but another guy in a suit—the salesman she first talked to at the Blue Waters pool, she realized—held her tight. When Denny caught her eye, he smiled, just a little. She smiled back, the only encouragement she could offer. She knew it wasn't enough.

When she returned her attention to Stuart, he was in handcuffs and being searched, which she thought looked ridiculous given that he was only clad in t-shirt and shorts. He looked at her and shook his head. "I love you," he said. "Don't never forget. I love you, Angel." Still just in his underwear, he was led out of the house.

A severe-looking woman in a severe-looking suit entered the house and made a beeline for Mandy. She smacked Mandy's wrists into handcuffs and searched her roughly, not caring whether or not her huge hands hurt her or touched her private parts a little too privately. From the corner of her eye, she saw Denny trying to squirm past his guard. She gave him the slightest of head shakes and he stopped. No point getting him hurt too.

Once the search was over, the guy she thought was a salesman stood directly in front of her. "Mrs. Masamoli," he said, "I'm Agent Creighton of the Milwaukee Office of the Federal Bureau of Investigation. You're under arrest for the robbery of the First National Bank of Cloverdale and for the kidnapping of a minor child and transporting him across state lines. Other charges can and will be proffered by various state and local agencies."

Mandy nodded. It was all the acknowledgment she intended to give him. Instead, she glanced sidelong at Denny. "I'll always love you, kiddlywink. Always and forever."

The boy was openly crying now. "I love you, too. Now and for always," he said before she was led to the door. "Mom," she thought she heard him say before she was taken outside.

Agent Creighton brought her to one of the black sedans parked on the street in front of the house. He was surprisingly gentle as he helped her into the Ford and even closed the door as mildly as he could rather than slamming it at her. He walked around to the driver's side and got in. Once seated, he said something using codes and jargon that ended with "in custody" into the radio. They pulled away from the curb and Mandy wondered which of the other sedans Stuart was in, if he wasn't gone already, and which one would steal Denny away.

"Mrs. Masamoli?"

"Yeah?"

"Would you like me to open my window and get some air in here?"

"Sure."

The agent rolled down the window and a blast of hot air filled the Ford's overheated interior. It offered no relief, but at least it moved the stagnant air around a bit.

As they drove past the Blue Waters, Mandy wondered where she and Stuart made their mistake. Who recognized them? Who turned them in to the Feds? Who stole their happiness?

About a block past the Shamrock, Agent Creighton signaled for a left turn. "Where are we going?" Mandy asked.

The Fed made his turn then looked at Mandy via the rearview mirror. "For now, the Penobscot Police Department. There you'll get your phone call and we'll straighten out the booking. With the bank robbery and the kidnapping of Dennis Under—"

"Denny," Mandy corrected him.

"The kidnapping of Denny Underwood, the Federal Government has priority in your case." That the agent listened to her and called Denny by the name he preferred comforted Mandy a little, though she wasn't quite sure why.

"What about—"

"Mr. Masamoli will be there, too, though you won't be allowed to speak to him. I doubt you'll even see him unless someone doesn't do their job right."

That hurt. "And Denny?"

"Good question. Tonight, he'll stay at the county home for boys. As a guest, not a detainee," the agent added quickly. "After that, it's up to the courts. Don't worry, Mrs. Masamoli. They'll take care of him and make sure he isn't hurt."

Agent Creighton's gentle manner took Mandy by surprise. In the movies, Federal agents were always cold and impersonal. But this guy seemed to be going out of his way to reassure her. She wondered if it was a trick. If it was, this guy was a very good actor.

"One thing I can guarantee won't happen to Dennis—Denny," he said. "If it will ease your mind any."

"What's that?"

Even from where she sat, she could see the agent tense up. "He won't be going back to that so-called mother of his in Legion, or to any member of that disgusting family."

Mandy upgraded her earlier opinion. If Agent Creighton was acting, he was the best actor ever to walk the earth. No matter what her fate and Stuart's were, Mandy felt sure Denny would be protected. Thank the good Lord for small blessings, her grandmother used to say. Mandy finally had a clue what that actually meant.

Only when her car door opened and she saw Agent Creighton beckoning her out did Mandy realize they'd arrived at the Penobscot Police station. As she got out, she had a quick glimpse of Stuart being led inside and her heart pounded a protest. This was real. This was really happening. No matter how nice her FBI agent was, he was an FBI agent and she and Stuart were under arrest and would still be going to jail. They'd be apart for who knew how long.

Mandy felt a little tug at her arm. "Mrs. Masamoli? We need to go in now."

"Sorry," she said and let herself be led inside.

At the door, Mandy and Agent Creighton were met by a wide, motherly-looking woman in a uniform. She identified herself as Louella Clontz and said she was a matron at the county jail, which was attached to the station. She had a cigarette dangling from her lips, with burnt ash at least an inch long at the end of it. Mandy wondered how it didn't fall off when she moved. She told the agent she'd get Mrs. Masamoli processed and dressed and have her waiting in the interrogation room just as fast as she could. He nodded, smiled at Mandy, and left.

Mrs. Clontz led Mandy down a green-tiled hallway. "Saw your husband," she said around her cigarette. "Not a bad looking boy. I don't know why they'd call him nondescript."

"No," Mandy said. "They know what he looks like now."

They arrived at a door marked *County Jail—Woman's Division*. Mrs. Clontz spoke into an intercom, informing the wall that she was with Amanda Joan Masamoli. A buzzer sounded from somewhere and Mrs. Clontz unlocked the door. They crossed over the threshold and when the door closed, the matron pushed another button. Again, a buzzer sounded and a second door opened. Mrs. Clontz led Mandy through this one and the door slammed shut behind them, air whooshing at Mandy's back.

"So, the FBI man tells me you've been a naughty girl," Mrs. Clontz said through a cloud of smoke. The dangling ash was still there and didn't seem to have grown or shrunk.

"That's what they tell me," Mandy answered.

The matron laughed. "Thatta girl. Great answer, honey. Don't admit nothing to nobody. Make 'em work for it. Bugs the shit out of the boys when they can't scare a girl, 'specially a pretty blonde like you. They ain't got nothing but scaring people to work with. Stick to your guns."

What? Mandy thought. Was the matron actually encouraging her to be defiant, as her teachers and old Poppin'-Snot used to call it? Or was this an act? Were there cops or agents or whatever who didn't think she was the worthless white trash her parents always told her she was?

Mrs. Clontz opened a metal cabinet, looked Mandy up and down from head to toe, and pulled out a black and white striped pile of cloth. "Standard prison gear," she explained. "Not very attractive." She threw the clothes on the table and said, "Go on and change." She added a dingy gray bra and panties to the pile.

Mandy looked around. Table, cabinet, matron. Nothing else. "Here?"

"Honey, I seen naked women from nineteen to ninety and I still go home to Mr. Clontz every night, so you ain't got nothing to worry about. There ain't no blemish, bump, sag, rash, wrinkle, birthmark, bruise, tattoo, cut, scrape, freckle, or crevice that can shock me. I've even seen a couple of man parts on what was arrested as ladies. So, get changed so's we can get this show on the road. Just leave what you're wearing now there on the table and I'll see it all goes with you and is waiting when you get out."

Mandy wasn't sure if Mrs. Clontz was just having fun with her or was mocking her. Either way, she tuned her out while she changed into the prison garb. Even though she knew Stuart was probably wearing something similar, only with pants and shirt instead of a jumper, she was glad he couldn't see her like this. She always wanted to look her best for him.

The matron stood and flicked her cigarette in the general direction of the ashtray and returned it to the end of her mouth. Somehow, it still had an inch of burnt ash on the end. "Let's go."

Mrs. Clontz brought Mandy back through the double set of doors to a small, windowless room where Agent Creighton and a uniformed police officer sat waiting. "Be careful, honey," the matron warned in a whisper while they were still out of earshot. "They got to prove you guilty, remember, not the other way around. This ain't Communist Russia. Don't never forget that." She helped Mandy to a chair across from the two men and left.

"Welcome back, Mrs. Masamoli," the FBI agent said. "This is Sergeant Nicholas Poole of the Penobscot Police Department. He's here to represent the town's interests in your case and act as a proxy for the other local jurisdictions. All I'm interested in are the Federal cases. The states and cities are on their own. Is that clear?"

His words swam around in Mandy's head, searching for a place to stop for interpretation. Finding none, she said, "No."

The FBI agent smiled and the policeman scowled and Mandy instantly decided which one she liked better. "What all that means, Mrs. Masamoli, is my interest is strictly the bank robbery in Cloverdale and the kidnapping of Denny Underwood. Anything else you may or may not have done doesn't mean a hill of beans to me."

Sergeant Poole leaned in at her and leered. "All of the rest of the beans in the pot are mine to stir up and question you about. For as long as it takes." His smile was all crooked, tobacco-stained teeth, but she wouldn't let herself pull back. Stuart would want her to hang tough.

The look that passed between Creighton and Poole was sheer annoyance on both parts. "Mrs. Masamoli, you're entitled to your phone call before we begin," the agent said. He glared at the policeman. "In private."

Poole stood. "Local call only. I'll be back in ten minutes." He screeched his chair on the tile to push it back in place.

"Mrs. Masamoli, take the time you need. And if you need to make a long-distance call, the Bureau will reimburse the police department. Ask the operator for help if you need a phone number." He reached around Poole for the doorknob. "Would you like a glass of water before we go?" There was a slight but definite emphasis on the word 'we'.

"Yes," she said. "Thank you."

The simple act of saying thank you conjured up an image of Denny bowing at Stuart, and Mandy had to force back the tears. Never mind how she messed up her own life. What had she done to that boy's?

With the agents gone, Mandy forced herself to push the thought of Denny's future aside and concentrated on her one phone call. No way she could call her parents or Stuart's. They wouldn't care. Who else did she have?

Then it hit her. She picked up the phone and asked to be connected to Valhalla, Illinois. Clara Tattinger came on the line and when her tone brightened at hearing Mandy's voice, she knew she made the right choice. She explained the situation and Clara turned the conversation over to Gil, saying he knew far more people who could help than she did.

"Say nothing to nobody," Gil said by way of greeting. "I don't care how nice they are or what they promise or even what they threaten. I got a friend near there owes me a favor. You'll have a lawyer there within an hour, two tops."

Mandy sighed, though she wasn't sure if it was relief or frustration that she knew nothing of these things herself. She probably would have told Agent Creighton and Sergeant Poole anything they wanted to know. Well, the FBI agent anyway. The policeman was a crumb. "Thank y— thanks," she said.

"And I'll make sure someone is there for Stuart, too," Gil said. "And you need anything—anything—or if they treat you bad, you tell your lawyer. Just keep reminding yourself that if they ask you a question, it means they aren't completely sure of the answer, even if they say they are."

"I'll remember."

"Is there anything else I can see to for you right now?"

Mandy didn't hesitate. "Can you find out what they're gonna do with Denny?"

"My little buddy? Don't you worry about him. His Uncle Gil will make sure he's treated right. Don't you worry about that. Anybody ain't looking out for him, I'll come to Indiana and kick some ass personal."

"Thanks. I appreciate it."

"What family's for, girl. You keep your chin up and don't take any crap from them. Go mute until the shyster gets there and then let him do the talking." He paused for a second and Mandy could hear Clara saying something in the background, though she couldn't make out what. "Listen, little girl, I know you can't hang on the line much longer and Clara's got something to say, so I'll let you go for now. Love you, girl. Know people out here care about you three."

Clara was on the line with a breathless "Mandy, listen to Gil," before Mandy could even reply to her husband. "He knows his way around such things."

"I know I can trust you both," Mandy said.

"Watch out for family first, that's my rule. Love you, little sister. You take care of yourself and we'll take care of you."

"Love you, too," Mandy said. It startled her to realize just how much she meant it.

Mandy hung up the phone and sat back. Family is a strange thing, she thought. Mandy, Stuart and Denny all hated theirs. Gil didn't even have one to hate or to love. Clara lost hers, at least she lost her brother. Yet somehow, they all found each other and made a new family, one they could like. One they could love. It was a very different thing for her, liking her family. Loving them. But she did. In the span of a few days, she did what she couldn't find a way to do in her first twenty years of life. The whole thing was just overwhelming.

The door swung open and Agent Creighton and Sergeant Poole were back in the room. Mandy sat up straight. "Mrs. Masamoli, did your phone call go okay?" Creighton asked.

"Just fine," Mandy said. She looked straight at Poole. "My friends in Illinois say I'll have a lawyer here in an hour or so."

Poole exhaled forcibly. "Illinois? Why in the hell did the switchboard—"

"My orders," Creighton said without looking in the sergeant's direction. "The Bureau's nickel. Don't sweat it."

"It ain't just the money," Poole protested. "It's coddling criminals that I don't like."

Creighton ignored him and faced Mandy. "So, Mrs. Masamoli, care to tell us what happened that led us all here today?"

"Bad upbringing," Poole muttered.

"I've been told I should wait for my lawyer before saying anything," Mandy said.

"Why?" Poole demanded. "You can get this over and done with and be in a nice, comfortable cell if you just talk to us now."

"Sergeant Poole, the Sixth Amendment of the Constitution of the United States of America guarantees a detained suspect the right to have an attorney present during all questioning," Creighton said, his voice the model of school teacher patience. "At the Federal Bureau of Investigation, we follow the Constitution. If Mrs. Masamoli has counsel coming, our questions will just have to wait. Simple as that. I'll stay here with Mrs. Masamoli while you go and get the matron to escort the suspect to her holding cell to await the arrival of her attorney."

"But—"

"Sergeant Poole, please summon the matron. I'll assume complete responsibility for the suspect. The Federal Bureau of Investigation thanks you for your cooperation." Though she didn't want to, Mandy admired Creighton's mix of cool professionalism and sarcasm.

From chair to door and out, Poole muttered under his breath. Agent Creighton looked as if he wanted to laugh but knew he shouldn't. Mandy wasn't sorry to see the sergeant go.

"Mrs. Masamoli, whoever told you to wait for your attorney gave you very sound advice. Mr. Hoover insists we agents follow legal protocol at all times, but sometimes these small-town police departments make up their own rules on the fly."

Though the FBI agent spoke like he really cared about her, Mandy decided she just couldn't trust him. She remembered how friendly he was by the pool and in the real estate office and realized she just might have been wrong earlier. Maybe he was just that good an actor. "Why didn't you just arrest us at the pool and get it over with?" she asked him.

"Well, I'm supposed to ask questions and not answer them, but I'll make an exception. It was watching the three of you. I was sure I was working on a bum steer, seeing how well the three of you fit together. It was as if Denny was part of your lives since he was born, rather than just for a few days. I wasn't sure when I spotted you back in Brownstalk, but even there you three seemed like a family."

Mandy remembered the man who glanced at her in the restaurant and realized it was indeed Agent Creighton. "So how did you know it was us then?"

"That I can't tell you." He sounded regretful about it. Actor or not, Mandy appreciated this.

A knock at the door followed by the appearance of Louella Clontz brought an end to her discussion with Agent Creighton. He excused himself and left the room. As before, the matron took Mandy's arm and escorted her out.

Again, Mandy was led down the green tiled hallway with the two-toned green walls. Somewhere, somebody made a lot of money off this ugly combination of mismatched greens, she thought. All ten and a portion of her years in school were spent in buildings with the exact same color scheme. When you came right down to it, she supposed, how different were school and jail, really?

"We ain't putting you in with the general population," Mrs. Clontz told her as they walked, her ever-present cigarette with its one-inch of ash bobbling as she spoke. "The Feds decide where to keep you, not us. So, you'll be a guest in one of our holding cells for now. It ain't the most comfortable," she added, almost apologetically.

They arrived in a back area and Mandy had her first ever look at a jail cell. The matron was right. It sure didn't look comfortable. A bench, a blanket, a pillow, a toilet, and a sink. This would be all she had until the lawyer got there.

Until he did show up, Mandy decided, she would stretch out on the bench. She was too nervous to sleep, but she hoped lying down would help calm her. The metal bench was even harder than she expected it to be, so she arranged the scratchy wool blanket on it to serve as a pointless makeshift mattress. The pillow wasn't much softer than the bench and it was even thinner than the one on her bed in Bascombe. She sighed. This was all worse than she ever imagined.

Mandy lay down and turned to face the wall. For the first time all day, she allowed herself to cry. Whose fault was all this? Hers? Stuart's? Their parents? Bascombe's? She'd never been a bad girl, not really, just a little fun-loving and adventurous. Yet now she was about to be answering questions regarding two Federal crimes. This was serious shit and she and Stuart were in it up to their necks.

Stuart. He was somewhere in this building. What had they put him through so far? Did he have a decent FBI agent like Creighton talking to him, or was his more like nasty Sergeant Poole? Did he know he had an attorney coming? Did they even have to tell him? Who did he call with his one phone call? She wondered if her lawyer would know.

And poor Denny; stuck for the night, and maybe longer, in some horrible home for boys. He was so small. Would the other boys pick on him? Was he scared? Did they let him take his orange bear with him? He didn't deserve to be punished for anything she and Stuart did. He was just trying to escape a terrible life, just like her and Stuart. Was that really so bad?

The tears, eventually, were done, and Mandy's thoughts were on to trying to hold on to the good times of the last week. Mrs. Clontz appeared and unlocked the cell door. As always, smoke enshrouded every word she said. "Lawyer's here, honey," she told Mandy. "And somebody's looking out for you and your husband good. Couple lawyers come all the way from Gary for you two. Sergeant Poole's beside himself with piss and vinegar."

Mandy thought about asking who Gary was, but she remembered

Gil's advice to keep quiet.

For the fourth time that day, Mrs. Clontz took Mandy by the arm and led her along the green tile. She was brought to the same room as before. This time, an expensive-looking man in an expensive-looking suit sat at the table, with Creighton and Poole lurking just behind him. The guy stood and extended his hand. "A. Winston Bush, Braxton, Bush and Plunkett. A friend engaged our firm to represent you as counsel of record." He pulled out the chair Mandy used earlier. "Please, sit, and try to relax. I'm on your side here."

Mrs. Clontz put a hand on Mandy's shoulder. "I'll be waiting for you just outside, honey," she said before she left the room with Agent Creighton behind her.

When the attorney resumed his seat, Sergeant Poole took the chair next to him. No one spoke for a full minute. Finally, Poole broke the silence. "We gonna get started or what?"

Bush yawned. "Yes, *we* are," he said, "as soon as you're out of the room. This is attorney-client privileged conversation."

Poole stood. "Fine. Your excellency." He bowed, scraped his chair noisily across the tile, and slammed out of the room.

Once the sergeant was gone, Mandy felt herself relax. A little. Her lawyer already proved he was working for her, and that helped. She started to thank him, but he shushed her. "Give me a minute."

He placed his briefcase on the table and flipped the latches. "First things first." Bush pulled out a large rolled up piece of paper and some cellophane tape. In response to Mandy's unasked question, he whispered, "I guarantee you Sergeant Poole or one of his cronies is on the other side of that mirror, watching us. This will stop that."

The attorney moved to the mirror and unrolled the paper. On it were the words *Nothing to See Here*. He blew a kiss at the window and taped his banner across it. The side facing Mandy said *You Have Rights Too*. "Step one done," he said so softly Mandy barely heard him.

Back at his briefcase, Bush pulled out a portable radio. He switched it on and soon the small room was filled with loud choir music. "Those little boys in Vienna will screech the shit out of any microphone they have in here. Scoot over and we'll be able to hear each other and they'll listen to nothing but high-pitched underdeveloped love of God."

The last thing Mandy expected to do in this place was laugh, but she couldn't help herself. A. Winston Bush was definitely on her side. She offered up a silent thanks to Gil Tattinger for sending him. She hoped Stuart's lawyer was as good. Mandy was about to ask about this when Bush quieted her again. "Step three first, then we talk."

The attorney reached into his case one more time, pulling out two bottles of grape soda and an opener. "I don't know about you, but I'm thirsty." He opened a bottle and handed it to her. "May as well enjoy it. I'm sure you won't get anything but water in here."

Grape wasn't her favorite, but Mandy was too thirsty to care. She brought the bottle up to her lips. The lawyer stopped her just before she could drink. He held up his own bottle and clinked it against hers. "To helping you and your husband as much as we possibly can."

They both took a long swig from their bottles before the lawyer turned serious. "Again, remember, I'm on your side, even when I'm asking questions you may not like. You have to tell me the absolute truth if I'm going to be able to defend you. We have a lot to talk about and not too much time, I'm afraid. Rest assured, though, you'll have the best defense. Our firm is committed to cases like yours."

Whatever that meant. "What about Stuey? Stuart, I mean. My husband."

"Sinclair Braxton is speaking with him right now. Braxton is our most experienced partner. He knows criminal justice—and injustice—inside and out. Really, you have no need to worry, Amanda."

"Mandy."

"You have no need to worry, Mandy. The firm of Braxton, Bush and Plunkett may sound fancy, but we really are here for the underdogs, the people society wants to lock up and forget about. Our plan is for us to talk to you and your husband this afternoon, get your side of the story, and then for my partner and I to get together and figure out the best strategy to pursue. I won't lie to you, Mandy. You will definitely be going to jail. Short of a miracle, there's no way we can prevent it. Our goal is to minimize how much time you and your husband are there."

Mandy took a long, slow drink of her soda. It couldn't be a good sign that her lawyer thought she had to go to jail. The whole thing was hopeless before it even began. Why was she even bothering? Why was he?

"Before we get down to your situation, our friend in Valhalla had us put an associate on a very special case. The preliminary report is that Denny is just fine. With what he's told the police about his home life, he won't be going back to his family in Legion."

"Where will he go?"

"I wish I could tell you, but it has to be determined. Right now, he's a ward of the court back in Illinois. You will, through me, receive regular reports about him, don't you worry about that. From what my associate said, it's obvious that boy loves you and Stuart. That's going to be in our favor in your case, if we play it right."

"He won't be in court, will he?" Mandy longed to see Denny again, but not there.

Bush shrugged. "I can't say for sure one way or another right now. I wish I could be more definite, but we don't even know what strategy we're going to pursue yet. That depends on our conversation today and what I can learn from the other side."

The other side. The so-called good people. The ones against her and Stuart. The ones who were always against her and Stuart. "I see."

"We should get started." Bush consulted some papers in front of him. "It looks like you and your husband have been pretty busy for the past week." He put up his hands before she could answer. "I'm not judging you. I'm sure you have good reasons, which we'll get to. But you need to understand just how complicated your cases are. First, you have three potential Federal charges against you—bank robbery, kidnapping, and..."

"We didn't kidnap..."

"I know. I heard the story Denny told, but the law sees it differently. The Feds are going to take top priority on this one."

Something the attorney said hit her. "Three charges? The FBI guy said two."

Bush shrugged and a hint of a smile crossed his lips. "Maybe he doesn't know about the credit account you opened in Fountain Grove at Horvath's Discount City. That little act was a form of bank fraud. Federal crime. The amount of money involved is so small they may not even bother with it. We'll find out. I know I won't bring it up."

"I guess that's good."

"Next in line in terms of seriousness is a Federal charge just against Stuart. They're sure to charge him with violating the Mann Act."

"It's against the law to be a man?"

A sad look crossed Bush's face and for a moment he reminded her of one of many teachers at Bascombe High. "The Mann Act. M-A-N-N. Basically, it's a law that prohibits a man from bringing a woman across state lines for immoral purposes. It's usually used when a spouse is cheating."

"We're married!"

Bush nodded. "But the law covers immoral purposes, so committing other crimes can fit it too. They're sure to try it. Since you're legally married, we'll try to get the judge to throw it out." He looked at the papers again. "Next in priority is probably Penobscot, Indiana. They have two counts of assault with a deadly weapon against you."

"A frying pan is a deadly weapon?"

"Sure is, when you use it as you allegedly did. They also have the two of you for vandalism and leaving the scene of an accident."

Mandy sat back and sighed. "Yeah, we did them things."

The attorney waggled a finger at her. "No, you didn't, unless it's to your advantage to say you did. Don't admit to anything, unless you're talking to me. Penobscot also has theft from an innkeeper on their list."

"What's that?"

"Pillows and blankets from the Blue Waters Motel were found in the house you rented."

"We only borrowed them for the night. We were gonna bring them back."

"Doesn't matter. Trust me, any little thing Poole and his chief can conjure up, they will. Poole wants the two of you badly." He ran a finger down the top sheet of paper. "Devlin's Crossing, Wisconsin, has just as serious a charge with Grand Theft Auto, as does Bascombe. Then there's theft in Brownstalk, Illinois, using forged identification in both Illinois and Indiana, shoplifting, and a whole bunch of other things."

Mandy looked down at the table. "So what do we do?"

Bush steepled his fingers and inhaled and exhaled slowly before answering. "If we can convince them to drop the little stuff and you plead guilty to the two big Federal ones, I think we can get the sentence down to somewhere between ten and fifteen years. The biggest local felonies are the grand theft auto and the assaults. The car and the truck are easy enough. The owners got them back. There was no damage. You two took care of them, and that can be thrown in the bargain bag. It might help."

"So we did good, right?"

"In a sense." Bush consulted his notes. "In my conversation with Agent Creighton, he told me you and Stuart made one mistake."

Mandy remembered Stuart saying most guys do stupid shit and that's what tripped them up. They didn't get into any fights or make themselves stand out in a crowd. "What was that?"

"The waitress at The Embers. Julie. Hitting her car and then hitting her and her boyfriend with the frying pan were your mistakes. Agent Creighton was pretty well convinced he was trailing the wrong people until those two incidents."

"Why?"

"Because Julie's last name is Poole. Her father is Sergeant Nicholas Poole of the Penobscot Police Department. He pushed hard when he found out you and Stuart were persons of interest in the bank robbery cases. Insisted the FBI step in."

Her jealousy and temper. Stuart would have never touched her convertible if Mandy hadn't said anything. This was all her fault. "Agent Creighton would have let us go?"

"He said he wasn't convinced that he had the right people. That the three of you seemed to be the nice young couple and their nephew that you said you were."

Nice. Mandy would never get enough of hearing that word.

Bush gave her a pat on the hand. Mandy wasn't sure if this was for reassurance or to bring her attention back, so she took it as both. "As for the assault," he said, "that could be our ace in the hole."

"Huh? How could that be?" This was all so confusing.

"Well, there's a piece of information I picked up that could get some of this business dropped as part of a deal. You've been talking with

Sergeant Nicholas Poole, right?"

Mandy shook her head. "I haven't told him nothing."

"Sergeant Poole was in the room with you when you were interrogated, right?"

"Yeah, but I haven't told him nothing."

"But he was here. He's been in the room with Stuart too, and that's the thing that will possibly help us."

"That guy wouldn't help us."

"No, he's a jackass, but he shouldn't have been in the room. Since the waitress you allegedly hit with the alleged frying pan is his daughter, he shouldn't be involved in the investigation at all. Agent Creighton was not happy to learn that Poole has a direct interest in the case."

"Cool if it could help," Mandy said. Her thoughts traveled out of the room to the jail cell. Ten years? Fifteen? She and Stuart would be thirty-five in fifteen years. Thirty-five when they got out. Denny would be twenty-seven. He'd probably forget almost everything about his aunt and uncle. "What if I don't say I'm guilty? What then?"

"Then your friend foots a much larger bill and you face Federal trials, a state trial, and numerous local trials, and spend the rest of your life going from Federal to state penitentiaries. I hate saying it this harshly, but that's the reality of your situation."

Mandy let the sobs out then and J. Winston Bush made no move to stop her or to comfort her. She wished she could talk to Stuart, find out what he was thinking. She knew that was impossible. She wanted Denny. That was impossible too.

The lawyer prattled on some more about different possibilities and deals and such, but Mandy barely listened. She just couldn't take any more of this. To shut him up, she said, "Go for the ten to fifteen years. Better than my whole life."

"Done."

They sat in silence for a moment, until there was a knock at the door. A moment later, Agent Creighton poked his head in. "About finished?" he asked. "I've got an ugly, overweight police chief breathing down my neck out here."

Wordlessly, Bush put his papers in his fancy leather briefcase, turned off his radio, took down his banner, and moved toward the door. "We're done, for now. Please see to it that no one on the staff here harasses, bothers, annoys, coerces, or offends this young woman in any way," he said to Creighton. "And see that you don't yourself. Also, since I arrived here at lunchtime, I'm sure she hasn't been fed, so make sure she eats and eats well. Neglect isn't a charge you or the police department want to face, I'm sure. After I consult with my colleague on Mr. Masamoli's case, the three of us will have to have a discussion. You may want to inform your Special Agent in Charge that you'll be needed here for a few days. I'm staying at the Blue Waters Motel, room 104. Give me a call to determine the where and when of tonight's meeting." A. Winston Bush was out of the room before Agent Creighton could answer.

"That is one fast-talking, fast-moving lawyer," Mrs. Clontz said from behind Agent Creighton. Mandy didn't even know she was there, though the cigarette cloud encircling the agent's head should have been a clue.

"Fast and formidable," Creighton said. "I'm sure I don't want to be questioned by him in court." He turned away and headed off to freedom.

"You ready to go back?" the matron asked, not that Mandy had any choice.

Once more, Mandy was led down the green tile. She was sick of green tile and wanted nothing more than to rip it all out of the ground. Instead, she just walked, a model prisoner. She was tired and hungry and angry and sad and scared all at the same time. There was way too much for her to understand. She wasn't in any condition to try.

At the cell, Mrs. Clontz opened the door and Mandy entered, unsuccessfully willing the clang of its closing not to be too loud. A mattress, a very thin one, had been added to the bench, and a tray of food waited for her. She started to cross the cell when Mrs. Clontz said, "Mandy?"

"Yes, Mrs. Clontz?" It felt good to have somebody other than the attorney address her by her first name.

"I'm going off-duty now and I have no idea if I'll see you again, but you seem like a nice girl, no matter what you done."

Nice. There it was again, and just when she needed it. "Thank you."

"There's an extra apple and piece of bread on your tray. It's not much, but it was the best I could do. There's also a newspaper and some magazines under the tray. Don't bother to hide them. You're allowed to have them. There's no matron on night duty, so you should be left alone until morning." She gave her a sad smile. "Good night, Mandy, and good luck."

Mandy wanted to reach through the bars and hug the older woman, but she knew she'd never be allowed to. Truth was, she wanted the woman to stay. Mandy knew that once Mrs. Clontz was gone, she'd be all alone and alone was something she was never supposed to be again. So, Mandy summoned what strength she had left and simply thanked her and watched her disappear. Mandy's energy disappeared with her.

She sat on the bench and looked at her...lunch? Dinner? Mandy realized she had no idea what time it was and wondered if it even mattered. The meal, chunks of something in grayish-tan gravy over noodles, plus two apples, and bread, reminded her of mealtime in the Heinemann house or in the school cafeteria. The food held no appeal, but she ate it anyway. Stuart would want her to stay strong and eating was part of that. Besides, it gave her something to do.

After a while, there was nothing left on the tray and Mandy was bored. Restless. Scared. She started to pace as best as she could in her cramped quarters. She tried to keep her thoughts happy, but a terrifying question seized control of her mind.

What if A. Winston Bush was wrong? What if she did end up in prison for the rest of her life? What if she never saw Stuart or Denny again?

Then she'd be back to the world of alone forever. A body among strangers, just as she was in Bascombe, in school, and in her family home. Stuart was the only person who saw Mandy for who she knew she was, and now she faced never seeing him again. She didn't know how she'd survive that. She wasn't sure she'd even want to.

Somewhere, someone turned off the light in the hall outside her cell door, leaving just a bare bulb way above her head. She had no idea what time it was. Without windows, Mandy didn't even know if it was still daytime or not.

Mandy curled up on the bench and pulled the ratty blanket over her shoulders. She wanted Blue to hold onto. She wanted to hear Denny's deep, even breathing while he slept. Most of all, she wanted Stuart spooned beside her, his reassuring arm wrapped snuggly around her. She didn't want to be alone again.

One Month Later

My Opinion
By Reuben J. Penobscot, Principal, Bascombe High School
Special to the Bascombe Bugle

The cases of Stuart Masamoli and his wife, Amanda Masamoli (nee Heinemann) are now closed, but is that the end of the story? The odds are against it. Why? Because theirs was a miscarriage of justice that will come back to haunt our entire community. Just thirteen years in prison for Masamoli and ten for his wife? A litany of crimes, from kidnapping a defenseless boy and dragging him across state lines, to bank robbery, theft, assault and who knows what they got away with that is yet to be discovered. Combining their sentences into twenty-three years each wouldn't be enough for these criminals. Decent citizens of Bascombe, of Wisconsin, of Illinois and Indiana, of the United States, have good reason to be concerned.

Already in the hallways of our high school, I've heard boys and girls talk about how 'cool' the Masamolis were for committing their heinous acts against society. Make no mistake, it's not just from the lower-class strata that these children are praising our now-infamous criminals. The misplaced admiration comes, surprisingly, from children from all levels of

Bascombe society. It is our job, as parents, as educators, and as law-abiding, God-fearing citizens, to reeducate these children with a lesson they should already know. Admiration of American ideals should be their lives' goals, not blind allegiance to criminality and subversive thinking. Lawlessness leads to Godlessness leads to Communism, and this cannot be allowed to take root in Bascombe, especially amongst our youngest citizens.

In short, Stuart Masamoli and Amanda Heinemann Masamoli were undesirables in their youth, they are undesirables now, and they will be undesirables in 1965 and 1968, when they are released, still young and still more than certain to return to their criminal ways. And what will their next crime be? Murder? Be assured, this travesty of justice will come back to haunt us in the 1960's, the 1970's, and beyond, if justice is not avenged.

Mandy threw the newspaper on the table. "Old Poppin'-Snot still hates us? Jesus. I haven't even seen the old bastard since he kicked us out of school four years ago. Murder? Communists? What's he even talking about?"

"Mandy, calm down." Bryce Strattlemeyer removed his feet from the table and sat up straight in his chair. "Reuben J. Penobscot's opinion doesn't mean shit or shinola. The deal is done, and all his whining in some shit town newspaper isn't going to change a damn thing."

"So why did you bring it to me?"

Bryce shrugged. "I thought you'd want to hear from the folks back home." He put his feet up again and rubbed the bristles of hair on the back of his head. "In all seriousness, I showed you this not to rub your nose in the opinion of some outdated old fogey who thinks there's a Commie around every corner and under every bed. I brought it to you to show you that you and Stuart have support out there, people who believe in you."

"High school kids," Mandy said. "Who cares about high school kids?"

"High school kids who'll be voters when you two come up for parole," Bryce corrected. "And voters put the people in office who pick the parole boards. You could be out long before you're thirty."

Mandy sat down. "Stuey too?"

"Can't promise, but I don't see why not. You two are famous, darling. There was an article about you in one of the Chicago papers. *Their Lust for Crime was Only Exceeded by Their Lust for Each Other* was the headline. Tawdry, but it promised one thing and delivered quite another. The writer showed you two as human beings willing to take a desperate chance. That strikes a chord with lots of people out there."

Mandy laughed for the first time in a month. "Why didn't you bring that article instead of Poppin-Snot's?"

Bryce glanced left and right. When he spoke, his voice was a whisper. "The fascist keepers wouldn't allow such Communistic propaganda over the threshold," he explained in an exaggerated Russian accent.

"Are you kiddin' me?"

"Of course I am, doll. I just forgot it. I'll send it to you in...in your new place."

New place wasn't something she wanted to think about, but she was grateful to Bryce for being here for her. "I'm so glad Stuey thought to call you. You're helping to make this a little easier."

Bryce doffed an imaginary hat. "As the future newest member of the law firm of Braxton, Bush, and Plunkett, subversive agitating attorneys extraordinaire, it's been my pleasure. Relax. We will be there to help with parole, probation, or whatever needs doing. Mr. Bush intends to use your cases to help push for reforms in education. Eliminate the Poppin-Snots."

While Bryce continued to talk about things she didn't understand, Mandy turned her mind to the questions she had for the law student before his visiting time was up. She knew, however, that he wouldn't answer anything until he yammered whatever he had to yammer. She waited as long as she could, but her patience was gone.

"Bryce, how's Stuey?" she blurted. "I haven't seen him since court and we couldn't talk then."

"In surprisingly good spirits. When the two of you earn mail privileges, you'll be able to get in touch."

"Stuey's not much of a writer. I guess I'm not either."

"You'll learn to be," Bryce said. "I saw Stuart yesterday, you know. I talked to him for a few minutes before they sent him off to Terre Haute."

Stuart at least got to stay in Indiana. She had to go far away. It didn't seem fair. "Why can't I go there?"

"It's a men's prison. There are a ton more prisons for men than there are for women."

Mandy sunk in her chair. "But West Virginia? So far from Stuey and Denny?" She felt the tears welling and didn't bother to stop them. Bryce would understand.

Bryce snapped his fingers. "That reminds me. I do have good news."

Good news. Those two words were like a ray of hope. "What is it?"

Bryce handed her his handkerchief. "Denny. With his mother declared unfit and facing charges of her own and his father unknown and his adult siblings not wanting him, young Dennis Wilfred Underwood has been remanded into the custody of Gilbert and Clara Tattinger. It seems there were documents provided to prove he is a blood relation to them." Bryce grinned. "I could learn a lot from that man," he said, admiration clear in his voice.

"How long will he be there?"

"Until he's an adult. Gil Tattinger says he's personally going to bring Denny to West Virginia before school starts." Mandy's heart skipped a beat at this news. She didn't want Denny to see her in prison, but if the choice was that or not seeing him at all, it would have to do. "And I have something for you," Bryce said. He pulled an envelope out of a folder, handed it to Mandy and stood. "And now, it's time for me to take my leave. Just know the Tattingers have promised to bring Denny to West Virginia as often as they can. Hell, knowing that guy, he probably has a private plane on call. You'll see your boy, don't sweat that. And who knows? Maybe me and Troy will make it out there someday too."

Bryce motioned for Mandy to stand. "God knows I don't have much experience at this with women, but I have to do it. We both need it, I think." Bryce wrapped Mandy in a massive hug and held her tight.

"Thanks," she said.

"Amanda Joan Masamoli, know one more thing," he said softly. "You have plenty of people out here who care about you. Even way out in West Virginia, you'll never be truly alone." He released her, gave her a smile and a kiss, and left.

Mandy sat at the table again and opened the envelope the law student left, expecting something official and serious and confusing. Instead, she took out a sheet of paper torn from a tablet. On the page was a letter written in a boyish hand.

> *Dear Aunt Mandy,*
> *I don't know where you are but don't be scared ok? We had fun for a few days like I never got to before. I'll never forget that or you and Uncle Stewy. When you're out I'll be there. I promise. I love you.*
> *Love*
> *Denny*

Beneath the words were two drawings. On the first were three bears and a little note. *Sorry I only had black ink.* The other drawing was water, with the words *Lake Michigan* underneath and a smiling sun above, pouring rays down onto the water. He did get it. Her boy shared her connection to her lake.

She held Denny's note in her right hand and held out her left in front of her. She didn't have her wedding or engagement rings on. She wouldn't have them again until she was out of prison. But there was still a mark where the band had been and, in her mind, she could see that ring Stuart bought her. Her husband's ring. Her boy's words. Symbols of her family. Of their love for her and of hers for them. She had more than she could ever hope for.

A month ago, Mandy Heinemann had nothing. Now, Mandy Masamoli had a real family and a week of pure, unbridled happiness. Being branded a criminal, being thrown in jail, none of it could take that away from her. It was all worth it. For one week, she was the happiest woman in the world. She wouldn't trade that for anything.

About the Author

Michael Giorgio lives in Waukesha, Wisconsin, with his wife, writer Kathie Giorgio, and his daughter, Olivia. He is the author of the novels *Justice Comes Home* and *The Memory Swindlers*, as well as short fiction appearing in *The Strand, The Mammoth Book of Tales from the Road* and many other magazines and anthologies. He is creative writing instructor for AllWriters' Workplace and Workshop, both in their Waukesha studio and online.

FOR THE FULL INVENTORY
OF QUALITY BOOKS:
http://www.roguephoenixpress.com

Rogue Phoenix Press
Representing Excellence in Publishing

Quality trade paperbacks and downloads
in multiple formats,
in genres ranging from historical to contemporary romance, mystery
and science fiction.
Visit the website then bookmark it.
We add new titles each month!